THE MAD
MONTECASSINO

Lorn Macintyre

To write is to think and to live – even to pray.'
Thomas Merton (1915-1968)

For my friend Kenneth Fraser,
who helped so much with this book.

*Typeset in St Andrews by Print & Design,
University of St Andrews.
(Special thanks to Mrs Margaret Smith of
Print & Design for her expertise and patience.)*

Chapter One

When Cavaliere Ernesto Grillo requested that Angela Boni meet him in his office at Glasgow University that morning in June 1938, she feared that he was going to ask her out, because of the way the professor had focussed on her in his theatrical lectures. He sat behind his desk, clean shaven, with a pronounced Roman nose, high cheekbones and penetrating eyes, immaculately turned out in a dark suit and wing collar, as if he had copied the arrogant pose of John Singer Sargent's 1906 self-portrait, which Grillo would have admired in the Uffizi Gallery in Florence when he was Director of the Anglo-American Institute in that city. The insignia in enamel on the professor's cufflinks was that of a Knight Officer of the Crown of Italy.

'Your first class Honours in Italian and Latin was to be expected, of course. In fact, I've never had the privilege of correcting such a distinguished set of papers. You have such a profound understanding of Dante, and your written Italian is flawless,' Grillo complimented his student. 'Of course you're a native speaker.'

'But not raised in Italy,' she corrected him.

'What does it matter? Your parents gave you the precious gift of the language of Dante,' he reminded her with a flourish of his hand. 'Your answer on *Inferno* was brilliantly insightful.' He wanted to ask: *How is it that a beautiful young woman, worthy of the brush of Pietro Scoppetta, should have such understanding of Hell?* 'It's obvious what you do next: you study under me for a doctorate in Dante, and then you join my department as a lecturer. To help you acquire research skills in preparation for your doctorate I suggest that you spend a year in Italy. I know from conversations with your parents that you have an uncle and aunt in the Cassino region. I've a friend who has an estate near Cassino. He wrote to inform me that he's in the process of having his family papers catalogued. I've written to recommend that he gives you employment.'

'It's very kind of you, professor, but I'll need to discuss it with my parents.'

'Of course.'

Angela walked down University Avenue in the sunlight to the family café. Heads turned as the twenty year old student passed in her white dress, satchel of Italian texts swinging at her shoulder. A man repairing a chimney started to hum 'A Pretty Girl is Like a Melody' from the film *The Great Ziegfeld* which he had seen four times. The young woman on the road below was the double of Luise Rainer, one of the stars of the musical drama.

On Byres Road a black-faced man at the reins of a horse and cart laden with sacks of coal saw the female in the white dress as a vision in the grimy city, and as a tram squealed to a stop an alighting passenger, holding on to the steel pole, removed his soft hat and made a sweeping bow with it to the passing beauty, who acknowledged the greeting with a wave.

Angela's flawless skin didn't require face powder, or

her mouth lipstick, vain embellishments which her mother wouldn't allow, but which other students at the university used, standing outside between lectures, stylish compacts open on their palms as they fitted their features into the mirrors to apply the powder puffs, then screwing one of the new Elizabeth Arden colours from tubes to paint their lips. One of Angela's fellow students in the Italian class, a blonde, had been sent blue false eyelashes from a pen pal in America, and Cavaliere Grillo couldn't take his fascinated eyes off her as he enthused over *The Divine Comedy*. Angela's eyes were deep blue, and would never have a mascara pencil near them.

Students from Whitecraigs and other affluent suburbs went weekly to fashionable salons to have their hair set in permanent waves, their heads linked up to many heated curlers hanging from a crown-like contraption on a stand. But the Bonis didn't have the money, or the beliefs in such indulgences. Angela sat on a chair in the kitchen of their flat while her mother used the technique of finger waving on her daughter's head, pinching the wet hair between her fingers, combing it in alternating directions into S shaped curved undulations whose beauty turned the envious heads of other females in the streets.

A female student, wearing a white pullover with white wool slacks in spring and early summer, went out to her sports car as soon as the Italian lecture was over. Her golf clubs were in the back, and she drove out to Hilton Park for a round with friends. Other students wore costumes with padded shoulders, and one even had a fox fur, but Angela's wardrobe consisted of skirts and cardigans, and simple sleeved dresses of floral patterns for summer which Rosa ran up for her on a Singer machine, humming Italian songs as she worked the treadle. She would teach her children modesty and economy.

Joseph and Rosa Boni had arrived, newly married, in Glasgow the May before the outbreak of the Great War, with missals, rosaries, and a crucifix in their cardboard suitcases, and with no knowledge of English. But they had the determination to work as many hours as God was pleased to allocate to them. Joseph had become a waiter in a restaurant, and Rosa washed the dishes he brought through, kissing her neck as he piled them by the sink. The proprietor of the restaurant exploited them, never leaving them idle for a moment. Rosa scoured pots until her fingers were raw, going home at midnight to a room in a condemned tenement of bold cockroaches, with the only ornament their crucifix on the wall above the bed to which they knelt in devotion morning and night. The money Joseph made from tips, and the residue of their earnings after minimum living expenses, went into a bank account.

In their love life they followed the safe period according to the teachings of the Catholic Church, but their calculations were out, when Angela was born in July 1917. Rosa stopped work to look after her infant, and Joseph took on heavy labour in a warehouse when he wasn't serving in the restaurant. On Sundays after Mass he took a bus into the countryside in the autumn to gather mushrooms at a secret place which he had discovered in a wood. He sold the ceps to the restaurant for pennies, but it was money. The remainder of the ceps he dried and preserved for his family to eat.

By 1922 they were able to pay a month's rent in advance for a small café, which they bought five years later, then sold to move to bigger premises on Byres Road in the west end of Glasgow, close to the university. They rented the flat above the café in which priests were always assured of free food and beverages. They had two boys and a second daughter.

Angela went between the marble-topped tables and across the black and white chequerboard tiled floor to the kitchen, taking down an apron from a hook. As she had done since she was ten years old, she helped out in the café when she wasn't studying or attending lectures, attracting customers whose ices melted in their fluted dishes as they followed her graceful movement between the tables, admiring her smile which seemed solely for them. Many Glaswegians despised Italians as an inferior race, but the Bonis were popular.

Over a cup of coffee after the café had closed for the evening she told her parents about Professor Grillo's plan for her. As always, the conversation within the family was in Italian.

'Certainly your aunt and uncle at Cassino will be pleased to see you in your free time,' Rosa said.

But her daughter could hear the uncertainty in her mother's voice.

'It's not your safety, because God will protect you; it's the cost of your travel to Italy,' Rosa confessed.

'But that's going to be taken care of,' Angela revealed.

'By whom?' her father wanted to know.

'By Cavaliere Grillo.'

'Out of his own pocket?' her mother queried with surprise.

'He says he has access to funds.'

'What funds?' her father pursued the topic.

'I don't know. Is there a problem?' his bewildered daughter asked.

'There could be, if the money for your fare is coming from the Opera Nazionale Balilla.'

Angela had to ask what that was.

'It's an organization sponsored by the Fascists to brainwash the young.' The café owner turned to his wife. 'Remember that boy who came in here a couple of years ago with his parents, the Pasquales? He'd just come back from Italy, from a camp run by the ONB.'

'I remember,' Rosa acknowledged the recent memory. 'He was wearing a black shirt and a fez. I thought he looked silly, as if he was going to a fancy dress party.'

'It's a uniform inspired by the Fascists,' her husband explained to their daughter. 'The boy, who was very arrogant, boasted that he had exercised with scaled-down versions of the service rifle of the Italian army. He said he wanted to join it when he was of the age, and his parents were delighted.' He turned to Angela again. 'I wouldn't want any child of mine involved with the ONB.'

'Professor Grillo never mentioned that name,' Angela reassured her father. 'He said that he'd arranged with this friend of his for me to go and work in his archive to gain experience.' She was smiling as she added: 'I don't expect to be drilling with a rifle and giving the Fascist salute. If you want me to, I'll ask the professor where the money for my fare to Italy is coming from.'

'You're making too much of this, Joe,' his wife cautioned him gently. 'Angela knows how much we despise Fascism and Mussolini - how much it terrifies us, in fact. I'm so glad that we got out to raise our family in a free country, which Italy certainly isn't. My sister at Cassino is frightened to put her feelings into letters, in case they're opened by a censor. It will give Angela experience to go to Italy, and it will give pleasure to my sister and her husband. Don't embarrass Professor Grillo by asking who's paying her fare.'

Angela's parents encouraged her to take up Scottish country dancing as recreation from her studies and her work in the café. The previous Christmas she had gone with several university friends to a dance in St Andrews Halls. Her parents bought her a long dress, and she had tinsel in her hair. She was asked up for an eightsome reel by a tall, fair-haired handsome young man in kilt and black velvet doublet with silver buttons engraved with thistles, and with lace at his throat. He was an accomplished dancer, and when he turned her with both hands in the reel he looked into her eyes and didn't release his hold until the last moment. After their exertions he brought them both lemonade and introduced himself as Christopher Murchison.

After they had exchanged names his next question was: 'What's your subject?

'Italian.'

'You look Italian.'

'My parents are both from Italy. What are you studying?'

'I graduated in medicine last year. I'm a houseman in the Western Infirmary.'

He had felt an instantaneous attraction to this beautiful young woman as they danced together, but he had noticed the small gold cross at her throat, and deduced that she was a Catholic. Now this was awkward. Christopher Murchison's father George hated Catholics. He had been a prominent lawyer, but had had to give up his practice on becoming a Sheriff. An elder of his local church, he was a leading member of a Masonic Lodge.

As a young lawyer in the city returning from a football match, wearing a Rangers scarf, George Murchison had been attacked with a razor by an irate Celtic fan of Irish descent, livid that his team had been beaten. The assault had left the victim with a permanent razor scar on his face and hatred in his heart.

Thousands of Irish had crossed to Glasgow in the latter part of the nineteenth century because of the famine in their own country caused by the failure of the potato crop and oppressive landlords. They had disembarked on the Clyde with prayer books and fiddles in their trunks. George Murchison maintained that these immigrants had turned parts of the city into slums from which disease had spread to other areas. Any Catholic offender who appeared before Sheriff Murchison was most likely to be sent to prison in cases where a Protestant might have escaped with a fine.

Christopher had been educated at Kelvinside Academy. His father assumed that his son would follow him into the law, but Christopher, gifted at science, wanted to be a doctor. His parents were going to set him up in an exclusive private practice in the west end, with a secretary to make the appointments on the telephone.

Christopher was sitting out the strathspey *Monymusk* in the St Andrews Halls so that he could talk to Angela, who was telling him above the seductive music that her family owned the café at the bottom of University Avenue and that they lived above it.

'Where do you live?' she asked.

'At Park Circus.'

'That's very posh.'

His parents' large house had a full-length stained glass window, commissioned by his father, featuring the patriot William Wallace, a massive sword raised in his fist. The residence took three servants to run, not including the chauffeur who conveyed George Murchison in the Daimler to the sheriff court and to Masonic meetings.

Having danced the final dance of the evening, the reel *The Duke of Perth*, Christopher asked her if he could run her home, since his car was parked in the street outside.

'That's kind of you, but I'm going home in a taxi my father arranged.'

'Can I see you again soon?'

'Not over Christmas, because the café gets very busy and I have to help.'

'What about when university begins again next month? Will you come to lunch with me?'

'I go down to the café for lunch and then help out until it's time to go back up to the university.'

'Will your parents not even give you an hour off?'

'They don't force me to work in the café. I want to, because they're so good to myself and my sister and brothers. Why don't you come to the café?'

'Can I come tomorrow morning?' he asked eagerly.

'You're very welcome. I'll find time to have a chat.'

When he went into the café the following morning at ten Angela, an apron round her hips, was serving coffee. She came over to his table and asked if he would like one.

'Black or with milk?'

He took the woman serving behind the counter to be her mother because of the similarity of facial beauty and elegance of carriage. He saw that like her daughter she wore a cross at her throat. He knew that the Italians of Glasgow were devout Catholics, because his father disparaged them for being 'in the power of priests.' After dancing with the young woman who placed his coffee in front of him with a smile, he hadn't been able to sleep for thinking about her. He had sat at his bedroom window, looking down into Kelvingrove Park, pondering the problem that he was a Protestant and Angela a Catholic. He couldn't become a Catholic because of his bigoted father's attitude, and an Italian Catholic wouldn't give up her faith. But that didn't mean that he and Angela couldn't meet as friends.

It was the unforgettable summer of the Empire Exhibition. Both Angela and Christopher were in a Scottish country dance demonstration team performing in this enchanting art nouveau city in Bellahouston Park, with its cascading fountains and flags of the dominions, its 300 feet high tower. Wearing a straw hat adorned with a ribbon, she went with Christopher on one of the sky rides, clutching him on the dizzy descent. He treated her to tea in a pavilion, and when they passed a sinister looking tank on display he protested: 'Why is such a thing in a place like this?'

Chapter Two

Angela informed Cavaliere Grillo that she had permission from her parents to take up his generous offer of a sojourn in Italy.

'That's excellent. I'll arrange a berth for you on a liner leaving next month, if that suits.'

'This is so generous of you, professor.'

'For my most brilliant pupil who appreciates the beauty and profundity of all things Italian, nothing is too generous. You have been blessed with parents who cared for their Italian heritage and spoke their native language to their children; and your mother even taught you to write it. Many parents who emigrated to here don't speak Italian to their children because they want to be accepted as Scots.'

He leaned over his desk and looked at the book in Angela's hand.

'You're reading Silone's *Fontamara*?' he said with dismay.

'It's a very interesting story.'

'It's an attack by a Communist on Fascism, which has done so much good for Italy, a backward country full of strife and superstitions until the arrival of Mussolini. Far better for you to read D'Annunzio, Miss Boni. He's not only Italy's greatest novelist; he was instrumental in bringing Italy into the Great War, and so helping to secure the Allies' victory. And he's also been an inspiration to Il Duce.' Grillo pointed to a signed photograph on the wall, showing a group of men in uniforms and peaked hats marching at the head of troops. 'D'Annunzio gave me that at Fiume in 1919. No one who was there will ever forget his stirring speeches.'

'Fiume?' Angela queried.

'In the second year of the war Italy made a pact with the Allies in which Italy was promised all the Austrian Littoral, but not the city of Fiume. After the war, at the Paris Peace Conference, this distribution of territory was confirmed. But Fiume was joined with adjacent Croatian territories in the kingdom of Serbs, Croats and Slovenes. This enraged D'Annunzio, and so in September 1919 he led over 2,000 troops from the Royal Italian Army, Nationalists and Irredentists, to seize Fiume. His speeches fired the imaginations of all Italians, and he was hailed as another Garibaldi. Mussolini learned a great deal from him.

'The fatal error which scholars make is in considering both the political and literary history of modern Italy apart from that of ancient Rome and medieval Italy. There's perfect continuity, and many of the Fascist ideals are a sacred inheritance handed down by our great forefathers. Il Duce's strength lies in the fact that he's the representative of the will of the whole of the Italian nation. His power rests solely on the mass of public opinion. The nation believes that at last they have a man who feels for Italy alone, and not for his party's fortune, or his pocket, or his titles. When I think of Il Duce these lines from Canto 11 of *Inferno* on Aeneas come to mind:

> *'ch'ei fu dell'alma Roma e di suo impero*

nell' empireo ciel per padre eletto.'

(for in the empyreal heaven, he was chosen to be
the father of generous Rome, and of her Empire).

'What about his invasion of Abyssinia?' Angela asked.

The Italian professor's hand dismissed the question as spurious. 'There were no doctors, no medicines, and no hygiene in Abyssinia. It was a fertile land, yet hardly 100,000 acres were cultivated. Italy made many treaties with that country, but had always been disappointed because Abyssinia, during the past half century, had never fulfilled her obligations.'

He went to his extensive bookshelves and brought back a volume which he laid in front of his visitor. It was the novel *Le Vergini delle rocce* (*The Maidens of the Rocks*) by D'Annunzio.

'This should be required reading for every young woman,' her Italian teacher told her enigmatically. 'Forget the untruthful discord of *Fontamara*, an insult to Italy.'

Christopher Murchison couldn't get Angela out of his mind despite the religious division. Friendship wasn't going to suffice for him. One morning in June he went down to St Peter's Church in Partick to watch Angela praying on her knees in her delicate lacework mantilla, then going up to the altar to have the priest put the wafer on her tongue. He slipped out without her seeing him. But instead of driving to the Infirmary for his day's work, he strolled along the street, to make it look as if their meeting was unintentional.

'I'm having a walk before work,' he told her. 'And you?'

'I've just come from Mass. As I told you, I go every morning. I'm going to miss St Peter's. I'm leaving for Italy next month.'

'For a holiday?'

'I'm going out for a year to learn to be an archivist before I begin a doctorate under my professor here.'

His sadness showed in his face.

'Will you write to me?'

'Of course.'

'Regularly?'

'If you'll do the same.'

'At least let me take you to dinner before you leave.'

'My parents don't like me going out at night – unless it's to the Scottish country dancing class. I'm working in the café, usually until it shuts at ten.'

'Can't you take time off, even for a walk in the Botanic Gardens?'

'I can probably manage an hour on Monday afternoon.'

He delayed his lunch hour, and they met at the gates of the Gardens, busy in the sunshine, with the benches crowded. They walked a deserted perfumed path.

'I'm in love with you,' he blurted out.

'But you hardly know me,' she responded with surprise.

'I know you enough to be sure of my feelings. We have to get engaged before you go out to Italy, that's all there is to it.'

'I can't, Christopher,' she told him, utterly taken aback by his insistence.

'Why not?'

'My parents wouldn't allow it.'

'But you're a woman now. Why do you have to consult your parents?'

'Because they love me and they've always supported me, emotionally and financially. Besides, I'm going away for a year.'

'Anything can happen in a year, Angela.'

'I can convert,' he said desperately.

'I don't understand.'

'Become a Catholic.'

'What do you know about my religion?'

'I've been to Mass at St Peter's.'

'When was that?' she asked, intrigued.

'Recently, to see you.'

'You go to the Catholic Church to be close to God, not to be close to people. You can't convert because of any love you feel for me; it has to be for the love of God. I couldn't live with a person who had used the church for his own convenience.'

'Can I have a kiss before we part?' he asked plaintively.

She offered him her cheek.

He walked her back to the café before going on disconsolately to the Infirmary.

Cavaliere Ernesto Grillo had called into the café.

'You realize that you have a brilliant daughter, Mr Boni?'

'We're very proud of how she's doing, Professor.'

'I've never had a better student. She'll benefit greatly from her stay in Italy.'

'It's very kind of you to make the arrangements.'

'I've chosen a sailing from London to Naples – a comfortable cabin.'

As he had promised his wife, Joe didn't ask who was paying the fare. Angela's twenty-first birthday party in the café on 5 July was also to wish her Godspeed on her journey. Her parents gave her a gold bangle, engraved on the inside with her name and a blessing in Italian for a long life. The gift from her two brothers and sister was a St Christopher medal. Her father had made the cake and piped on the greeting: *Buon Compleanno Bella Figlia* (Happy Birthday Beautiful Daughter). Father O'Brien, the family's priest, drank coffee with froth on top made on the new machine. As he was giving the blessing at the end of the celebrations Angela's face bent to her hands reminded him of the serene lovely face in Fra Fillipo Lippi's painting *La Vergine in Adorazione* which had enthralled him so much on a visit to Florence that he had sank to his knees in front of the revered image.

The following day Grillo wrote to the Marchese Battagliero, and received a reply on handmade paper embossed with his coat of arms, informing him that he was looking forward to the arrival of his assistant archivist.

Christopher was in St Peter's the morning before Angela

was due to depart for Italy, and this time he waited for her, handing her a little black box.

'Open it, please,' he urged.

She looked at the box, thinking with dismay that it contained an engagement ring. He took it back and lifted out of it a gold locket on a chain.

'It's very beautiful, but you shouldn't have gone to the expense.'

It was a modest purchase out of the generous allowance he received from his father, who had given him an imported Mercedes touring car when he graduated.

'There's something inside.'

When she opened it she saw two small photographs inset in the two halves, one of her which he had taken at the St Andrews Halls ball, the other of him.

'I regard this as good as an engagement ring,' he told her.

She knew that she couldn't wear it in front of her parents without them asking about it, and, if she told them the truth, which she had been brought up to do, they would say that it wasn't appropriate to accept such a gift. But she couldn't give it back to Christopher without offending him.

'I'll keep it very safe,' she promised.

'This is the address to write to me at,' he told her, handing her a piece of paper.

'The Cardiology Unit, the Western Infirmary, marked Personal?' she queried.

'It means that I get your letters in the morning, instead of having to wait until I get home in the evening.'

He was making this arrangement, so as not to arouse the suspicions of his parents when letters for him started arriving from Italy.

Joe closed the café for an hour on Friday 15 July so that he could join his family to wave Angela off at the railway station. Angela was tearful, clinging to her parents and siblings because this was the first time that she had been separated from them. She leaned out of the train window, waving to their diminishing figures before taking her seat – first class, courtesy of Cavaliere Grillo - for the journey to London. She stayed overnight with Italian friends of her parents, and on the following day she boarded the Australia-bound liner *Otranto* which called at Naples. Having gone out on deck to watch the coast of England disappearing, fragmented in the heat haze, she went into dinner. But Grillo didn't want his star pupil, a future Dante authority and colleague, dining alone. He had written a personal note to the Captain, and Angela was ushered to his table on that first evening. Two couples, one from Glasgow, the other from Aberdeen, were also guests. The Glaswegian male was an elderly shipowner in an evening suit, his bejewelled wife in an ankle-length gown.

'Where in Italy are you bound for, Miss Boni?' the shipowner enquired.

She explained to the attentive table that she was going to get experience as an archivist near Cassino.

'We know Cassino,' the wife of the Aberdonian, a

veterinary surgeon, entered the conversation. 'We've visited the beautiful monastery there. But you're going to a castle, you said?'

'It's an interesting time to be going to work in Italy,' the shipowner estimated. 'Mussolini has certainly got the country well organized. That's what we need in Scotland, a disciplined workforce. There are far too many agitators, some of them Communists, in the Clyde shipyards.'

Three days into the crossing Angela was interrupted in her reading in the tourist class saloon by a young man, heir to a vast New South Wales sheep farm, travelling in Europe with his parents, though neither the dome of St Paul's Cathedral in London nor the beguiling Mona Lisa in Paris had moved him. He had become fixated on the solitary female passenger who sat reading for most of the day, until two whiskies gave him the courage to stop by her wicker chair and observe: 'Your story must be very interesting, the way you're absorbed in it.'

Angela raised her head to inform him that it was a novel by the Italian writer D'Annunzio.

'Is it good?' was the only question the Australian traveller could think of, because he wasn't a reader, except of farming journals.

'It's very interesting.'

It became obvious to the interrogator that she didn't want to answer further questions, so he moved away to watch a game of deck quoits. That evening at the dinner table the young sheep farmer's mother asked why he wasn't eating the succulent beef, the blood running as he liked it.

'I'm not hungry.'

'But everyone gets hungry at sea, Anthony,' she said, perplexed. 'Do you require to see the doctor?'

He couldn't tell his parents that he was lusting after the passenger sitting by herself five tables away, who had refused wine from the steward's carafe in favour of mineral water. The last desperate bid by the young man for her attention was to watch for her going to the toilet before he laid on her book a note: Will you dance with me tonight? When she returned he spied from behind a newspaper at a nearby table, but she crumpled the note and continued to read D'Annunzio's *The Maidens of the Rocks*. She soon discovered that the protagonist spends the greater part of the novel searching for a superior vessel in which to plant his super seed in order to father a messianic child, with the woman subservient to his needs. The story repelled Angela, and she decided to abandon it.

She was going to be away from Glasgow for a year, and in that time there could be big changes. When Hitler had annexed Austria, Cavaliere Grillo had told his class that it was 'historically inevitable and just.' No one dared to argue with him. He was a Fascist supporter, but he was also an inspired teacher, particularly of Dante. When he read *Paradiso* to the class, she saw the Throne surrounded by the angelic host.

Chapter Three

Angela had decided to keep a Journal of her year in Italy, and had bought a handsome blue leather book with a lock before leaving Glasgow. The first entry in her Journal was on Sunday 24 July 1938, written with the Waterman fountain pen which Cavaliere Grillo had given her on her graduation.

I arrived in Naples today after a wonderful voyage, and boarded the Rome-bound train. The woman sitting beside me was travelling with a cantankerous hen in a wicker basket. She talked to the hen for the journey and completely ignored me. When I alighted at Cassino a very muscular and tanned man, wearing a ragged straw hat and dungarees, was holding up a piece of card with LA BELLA ANGELA written on it. I knew immediately that I was going to love my Uncle Benigno De Santis, though his hug almost squeezed the breath from me. As soon as we moved out into the sunlight the intense heat hit me, as if it had solidified into a wall, making me feel soporific. Mama told me that as soon as I arrived at Cassino I was to raise my eyes to see one of the wonders of the world, the monastery of Montecassino on the mountain. It looks like one of the white ice cream confections that Papa sometimes makes for customers for birthdays and celebrations. 'Don't worry, we don't have to walk up there,' Uncle said. 'There's a cable car, thank God.'

We went to a cafe to drink coffee before ascending to the heights. Uncle explained that Cassino is a typical market town of central Italy. 'We aren't short of churches,' he said, holding up four fingers. 'For those who don't keep to the Commandments, there's a prison.' There are orchards and vineyards. I loved sitting watching the town go by; motor cars with impatient horns, but the mules pay no attention, plodding on their way with their panniers. A very stout man who looked like a sultan, with a towel wrapped round his head, and in a flowing robe, passed, sweating as if he was about to collapse on the pavement. Uncle said that he was a Fascist businessman who had just come from the thermal baths, 'but hasn't managed to sweat Mussolini out of his system.' A nun passing with a basket over her arm bowed to us.

The cable car operates from Cassino to a pylon just outside the monastery, and from my elevated seat I could see the countryside around. 'That's Monte Cairo there,' Uncle pointed. He explained that the Monastery is built on the south-eastern spur of Monte Cairo. 'And there's the Liri Valley which leads to Rome.'

When we arrived at the monastery we walked for about a quarter of a mile down a sloping track to Uncle's smallholding. Aunt Beatrice is small and rather stout, with such a warm heart. As soon as I stepped inside their home I loved it. Despite the fierce heat outside, the kitchen is so cool. The floor is worn flagstones, and the table is rough wood. Around it are half a dozen stools. Aunt Beatrice saw me looking at the hoops of wood hanging from the rafters, and explained that they were to save mice getting at the small sacks of flour. 'The mice are like the poor, always with us,' she said. As if it had heard her, a kitten called Annabelle, meaning beautiful and graceful in Italian, rubbed against my leg. I feel we are going to be great friends.

The fireplace in the kitchen is whitewashed and has flowers on the mantelpiece, with a large wooden crucifix above, making it look like an altar. Off the kitchen is a small room, with a board resting on the bare earth, supporting two copper pails, since there is no running water in the house. The well is two hundred yards away, and I will take my turn fetching the water when I am here.

There are two rooms upstairs. Uncle and Aunt have one room, and I have been given the other one. Aunt Beatrice had prepared a big pot of polenta, and Uncle Benigno placed a flagon of wine on the table. After we had eaten (delicious food), Uncle said to me: 'You must meet my four boys.' I was bewildered, since they have no children - to their sorrow, Mama told me. Uncle led me a hundred yards down through an olive grove, to a small field where four mules lifted their heads from grazing. 'Gionata and Luca,' he introduced the two chocolate-coloured ones. 'They're brothers. And these are Paolo and Samuele.' He stroked the two light-coloured coats. 'They're also brothers, but they sometimes nip each other if they're annoyed.' They are adorable, with such expressive, intelligent eyes. Uncle Benigno says that they're very wise and alert, and very good with people. He's a mountain guide, and he uses the mules to carry children and elderly people who want to get close up to Monte Cairo, some to see the view from the summit. 'And this is Bongo,' he told her, introducing the large dog which accompanies him everywhere. 'He sleeps a lot because of the heat, but when he's out with me he runs like the wind, *retrieving the hares I shoot.'*

The house doesn't have electricity, and when it began to get dark Aunt lifted the globe to light the oil lamp in the kitchen. When it was time for bed she handed me a candle which cast a yellow circle like a spell round my zupei, the noisy wooden shoes they both wear. Aunt has given me a pair of hers.

When I told them that I hadn't been to Mass because of travelling all day, Uncle said: 'We must do something about that,' so after supper we walked up the slope to the monastery for Compline. The basilica is massive, and so beautiful that I can't find words to do it justice. After the chanting there is the Greater Silence when the monks retreat to their cells. From my bedroom window I can see the monastery in the moonlight as I write this. God has given us such a beautiful world. I have Christopher's locket with me, but haven't yet worn it. Can I wear it with my cross?

Angela was taught how to milk the cow and the goats. At first her efforts missed the pail and squirted over her *zupei*, to her jovial uncle's amusement. Beatrice made the goats' milk cheeses which Benigno took down on the cable car to Cassino to sell. When the monastery Angelus bell sounded three times a day her uncle and aunt stopped their labours, whatever they were doing. Benigno removed his straw hat and both bent their heads, as in Millet's evocative painting, a copy of which hung in the Boni home in Glasgow. The painting showed a steeple in the distance, but in the small field the monastery towered above, casting a broad shadow as the sun declined. Angela also observed the Angelus, her arms round the necks of two of the mules, which seemed to understand that the bell required them also to be still as she said the prayer of the Annunciation. She became used to the bell and waited with pleasure for its pealing early in the morning, at noon and in the early evening.

The rhythm of the day didn't depend on the clock which ticked unobtrusively on the kitchen mantelpiece, beside the vase of flowers, but on a silent, more subtle measurement which came from the growth of the crops, the monastic bell, the mules cropping the grass around the olive trees, the movement of shadows with the sun. The mountainsides around were covered with oak, fir, acacia, with the yellow fire of ginestra spreading up the slope. The landscape was beautiful, but poor soil to scrape a living from.

Benigno took his niece to a small wood to collect fungi. He showed her the traditional art of preparing them, holding the mushrooms upside down on the fire-tongs and pouring a little olive oil over them, then sprinkling on salt or chopped parsley or onion, before roasting them over the embers, 'a gift from the *Napaeae*, the nymphs of the dell,' her uncle called them, because he believed in the old rural superstitions which Mussolini in his Rome palazzo was determined to stamp out.

Benigno was obsessed with a game called *morra*, and three friends had dropped in to play with him during Angela's stay. Two of them sat on opposite sides of the table. One man from each side raised his right hand and together they banged their hands on the table in rapid succession. For each bang they held out a different number of fingers and shouted a number. The one who called the correct number of fingers of both hands added together won a point. He marked the score by holding out a finger on his left hand. Then he played with his two opponents alternately until he lost. Fifteen points won the game.

'It looks simple, but you have to be smart,' Benigno explained with the pride of an expert to his niece. 'Your hand must be on the table at the same moment as the man's you're playing against. If you're before him he'll count your fingers and call the right number, and you'll be at a disadvantage if you put out your fingers before the last moment. Did you notice how his eyes never left my hand? And I had to watch his hand, otherwise he'll cheat.'

'I hope you're not trying to involve Angela in *morra*,' Beatrice scolded him. 'It's a silly game for men who have nothing better to do. Your friends never bring us any wine, though they empty our flagon.'

On Sunday mornings the De Santis's put on their best clothes and went up to the monastery for Mass. Angela stopped to speak to the tame raven perched on St Benedict's statue. The bird was sacred to the monks because a raven had stopped the Saint from eating poisoned bread. The raven answered to its name Nico and was rewarded with the piece of polenta from Angela's pocket. When she was seated in the magnificent basilica she looked up and saw angels sitting on the cornices, as if they had been resting and were about to take off at any moment to wing round the heads of the worshippers. She heard the chanting of the Benedictine monks in their elaborate carved stalls while several of the Brothers assisted at the altar in the celebration of Mass.

At the end of Mass a tall grey haired figure in the long black vestment of the Benedictines was waiting on the broad steps of the basilica. Dom Pietro Contadino was Angela's uncle, Beatrice's brother, his surname derived from the family's traditional occupation as farmers. As a child he had played within sight of the monastery, and with his parents walked three miles each way to worship in it every Sunday. The monks had heard of his precocious intelligence and piety at the village school, where his classmates, who would become small farmers and housewives, preferred playing games to reading and prayer. Instead of lamenting the waste of talent the monks offered Pietro a place in the monastery's boys' school, where men who could have been professors in Italian universities taught because they loved God, and in their spare time in the peace and pious atmosphere of Montecassino they could use its priceless library to advance their own studies.

Pietro Contadino proved himself an exceptional pupil, and was writing perceptive essays on Dante at the age of twelve. Though he wouldn't dare to challenge his teacher's interpretation, he doubted that Hell was a place of intolerable fires, but was convinced that the dead were indeed judged, and that those who didn't believe that their earthly actions were sins had to live in a grey region until they were ready to repent. Pietro could have studied almost any subject at a university almost anywhere in Europe, and was particularly gifted in writing, but decided to become a monk at the monastery, having a great desire to serve God, as well as having no problem with celibacy.

'Welcome to Montecassino,' Dom Pietro greeted Angela with a hug.

'I don't know what to call you,' his niece confessed in the hot sunlight.

'Call me *Zio Pietro* (Uncle Peter). Do you like Italy?'

'I love it.'

'Well, there are Benedictine convents down in the town, if you feel attracted to the monastic life,' he said with a smile.

Her uncle and aunt held a gathering to welcome their Scottish niece. Beatrice made plenty of polenta, and there was a flagon of wine, as well as a jug of their own olive oil on the table, and warm bread with herbs. Friends brought their families, and gifts of cheeses and dried goat meat. One of the men had a concertina with mother-of-pearl buttons and bellows which expanded to reveal the face of Cecilia, patron saint of musicians. He played sitting on a stool, his black waistcoat opened while Benigno danced with slightly bent knees, his chin in the air, making his niece laugh as his absurd constricted shadow travelled across the white wall.

Like thousands of other Italians, Benigno's brother Bartolo had been working in America and told the company about the deafening din and the stink of flowing blood of the Chicago stockyards where he helped to slaughter cattle so that the Americans who hadn't been affected by the Wall Street crash could still have their outsized steaks. Bartolo had been taught the tango by a South American whore in Chicago and tried to teach it to Angela, steering her around the floor while the others clapped.

Bartolo sang for the company, leaning against the fireplace which Benigno had whitewashed for his niece's arrival.

> '*O cari giovanotti*
> *Domani dobbiamo partire;*
> *A costa di morire,*
> *In America voglio andar.*
> *Quando sarò in America,*
> *Quando sarò in America…*'

> ('Oh, dear boys and girls,
> Tomorrow we must part,
> Rather than starve here,
> I must go to America.
> When I am in America,
> When I am in America…')

'Tell us about the place you come from,' a young woman with a shawl round her head, her face aged by anxiety at feeding five children, asked Angela as they sat round the table, talking between mouthfuls of polenta.

'It's a city called Glasgow,' she explained.

'Is it big?' the questioner continued.

'Very big.'

'Bigger than Rome?' the woman asked in wonder, though she had never been to the holy city, except in her dreams, an excursion inspired by an engraving of St Peter's Basilica above her bed.

Angela appealed to her uncle.

'I wouldn't think it's bigger than Rome,' he pronounced, though he had never visited Glasgow. 'Very few places are bigger than Rome, I'm told. I went there once, and I was amazed by the size of the buildings, and the marble figures on the Trevi Fountain. I began to think that giants must have lived in Italy in times past.'

'Is this Glasgow warm?' the woman with the shawl persisted.

'It can get very cold,' Angela told her. 'Last winter the pond in one of the parks froze over and people were skating on it.'

'And do you have the mosquito in Scotland?' another of the guests wanted to know.

'We don't have any mosquitoes, but we have a tiny insect called a midge. When we go into the country for the day we're surrounded by them.'

'Do they carry malaria?' Angela was asked.

'No, they don't carry malaria, or any other disease. But a girl in my school had red hair and a sensitive skin. When she was bitten by a midge her skin came up in a lump, and the itch drove her mad.'

'No malaria,' one of the men said with a sigh, shaking his head, as if he couldn't believe there was a country where people were free of the scourge.

'You have the bagpipes in Scotland,' another man observed, moving his fingers as if he were playing an imaginary chanter. 'Do you play them?'

'No I don't,' Angela said with a smile. 'I sing and do Scottish country dancing.'

'Please sing for us.'

Angela sang a selection of Scottish songs, including 'The Bonnie Banks o' Loch Lomond' while the guests tapped their *zupei* on the flagstones and hummed the refrain.

In this house, as in so many others in rural Italy, there was no photograph of Il Duce, because he belonged in another world, that of Rome, and because he was perceived to have done nothing for the workers in the fields, allowing corrupt landowners in collusion with Fascist officials to exploit them.

Chapter Four

A month after arriving in Italy Angela went down into Cassino to be taken to the place of employment as an archivist arranged by Cavaliere Grillo.

'That's the castle,' the chauffeur announced through the speaking tube after ten miles of travel through narrow country roads, including a halt while leisurely white and steel grey coloured cattle of the ancient gentle Chianina breed, their praises sang by Virgil, crossed. One of the most notable medieval fortifications in Italy was approached through an avenue of poplar trees. Its massive tower was for family security in time of war, since trebuchets and other siege engines could never have penetrated its four feet thick walls.

Angela looked up at the notched merlons along the walls as the limousine rumbled over the functioning drawbridge and into a cobbled courtyard. One footman in scarlet livery took charge of her suitcase while another led her through corridors into a long room where a silver haired man in a white suit made for him in London was standing smoking a cigarette in a black ebony holder. Angela estimated that he was in his fifties as he approached to welcome her to his ancestral home with a formal handshake. The urbane Marchese Battagliero's surname, warlike in Italian, described the bellicose origins of his lineage and their social and political ascent through the battle-axe and ruthlessness. He was an international traveller to the principal cities of Europe, and in Paris had had the privilege of being introduced to Marcel Proust in the Ritz, when the reclusive writer had risen from his sickbed to check with a countess friend the colour of the dress which she had worn to a ball years before and in which he wished to clothe one of his characters in his massive work in progress, *À la recherche du temps perdu.* Angela had the impression that her fluency in Italian was being tested by her new employer, but he seemed satisfied as he led her down another corridor to the library where the archivist was sitting at a long table.

'This is Dr Murino,' the Marchese introduced him. 'He's trying to put some order into our family history. There are documents going back eight hundred years, to when the castle was built. I'll leave you in his capable hands.'

Angela took an immediate liking to this untidy looking elderly man in pince-nez whose white hair trailed over his collar, and whose waistcoat was stained by the generous meals of his employer. He showed the enormity of the task he was facing by spreading his arms wide, to take in the piles of dusty documents occupying the entire twenty feet long table.

'You may find reading the old script tricky at first, but you'll soon get used to it,' Murino reassured Angela. 'It's fascinating material, because the Battaglieros were prominent in the Crusades, and one of them was a Cardinal. I suspect that there's a good deal of bloodshed and intrigue in these documents, but that's the way families like this established and maintained their power. A person, perhaps even a relative, can be dying of starvation in chains in the dungeon while the Marchese – it's a very old title – is sitting to have his portrait painted by Bronzino, with a hooded falcon quiescent on his gauntlet, his face serene.'

'The Marchesa Battagliero,' the footman announced on an afternoon in October 1938.

Benito Mussolini was sitting in a black uniform behind his desk in his office in the Palazzo Venezia in Rome, a former papal residence built in the fifteenth century of massive stones looted from the Colosseum in the vandalism which also characterized his rule. The Sala del Mappamondo had been chosen by the dictator because of the dimensions of this gallery, sixty feet long by forty feet high. Two mosaics had been laid on the floor. In one Mussolini the keep-fit fanatic was saving the Princess Europa from the bull of Bolshevism; and in the other, the dictator was the sea god Triton embracing a sea nymph, symbolic of the Mediterranean.

The cavernous apartment was devoid of furniture, apart from two armchairs, a reading stand with an atlas to satisfy his constant pangs of territorial hunger, and the thirteen feet long desk. It wasn't covered in state papers, but small piles of loose change, which he handed out to petitioners, the price of a *gelato*. He also kept a pistol in the event of an unwelcome caller.

The distant door opened to admit his visitor. From his psychologically advantageous sedentary position which intimidated male visitors he watched the Marchesa advancing, a fox fur round her shoulders, its eyes replaced with glass. Her hair was a black helmet surmounted by a white feather in her sloping blue hat the size of a saucer. But Mussolini wasn't interested in the appealing features which had already been preserved on canvas by one of Italy's leading portrait painters. The man behind the desk was watching the swaying hips in the tight black costume approaching.

Many women had fallen in love with the diminutive but well-built dictator, sending him photographs and adoring letters, and, having made his selection, he invited them to visit. Some of them were intellectuals who followed keenly events in Italy and Germany, and who realized that Stalin was a menace to the west. Others were society women who only read fashion magazines or the novels of D'Annunzio, and who had affairs out of boredom.

The visitor's high heels clicked towards the desk, and she bowed. Mussolini had five children by his loyal wife Rachele, and his current mistress was Clara Petacci, who waited for him in a feathered silk gown in her aromatic chintz and satin bedroom suite.

The dictator was rising from his desk.

'This is a great pleasure,' he told his visitor.

'The pleasure is mine, Excellency.'

But the dictator didn't lead his visitor to one of the two armchairs to discuss his ambitions for Italy. Instead he took her by the hand to the mosaic in which he was depicted as a bull, and while she was admiring it he was opening his breeches. He unzipped her skirt, dropping it to her shoes while she stood there, either petrified or honoured. He cursed the suspenders and instead of undoing them from the silk stockings, broke the black tethers in his powerful fists and ripped off the skimpy panties.

The caller was taken without words, without foreplay, naked from the waist down, the fox fur with the unseeing eyes still round her neck. She was taken, brutally, her buttocks bouncing on the mosaic, but he had no intention of withdrawing. One woman who had come to sketch him had left, not with a portfolio of drawings, but with child.

The audience was finished, the Marchesa, unsteady in her high shoes, was trying to fix the wreckage of her suspender belt, her ruined panties stuffed into her handbag, his teeth marks like a vampire's on her neck, his semen battling to her womb. He didn't escort her to the door and thank her for the pleasure, but returned to his desk, to read a report on the mosquito menace in the north, and how his 'visionary scheme' was eradicating the insect with the pernicious bite. He threw aside the document and meditated on the future. The Fascist revolution needed to be given new impetus throughout Italy, including the most backward rural areas. Fascism had failed to achieve the intellectual rigour that the socialism of his fiery younger days had reached. And there was the problem of the King, who lacked the heroic nature that would have enhanced Fascism. Mussolini disliked Hitler and the Axis, the Rome-Berlin alliance of 1936. Victor Emmanuel had told him that when Hitler was his guest at the Quirinale, the German dictator had asked for a woman, which had thrown the royal household into confusion. Since no whore from a *bordello* would do, a society woman would have to have the honour. But it wasn't sex that Hitler had been after: evidently the Führer, a mother's boy, was unable to sleep until a female had turned down his bed.

When Angela visited her uncle and aunt for the weekend, they held a gathering of the same neighbours as they had done on her arrival in Italy.

'Angela's working for the Marchese Battagliero,' Benigno informed the company.

'For that family of Fascists?' a voice called out.

The speaker was a young man, Augusto Faccenda, a part-time mountain guide who helped his grandmother run their small farm. His father had been killed in the Great War when Augusto was an infant, and his mother had died in the influenza pandemic in 1919. Angela, sitting on the floor and playing with the kitten, had taken notice of his presence already, sitting cross-legged on the flagstones, his spine to the wall, black hat, favoured by females as well as males, pushed to the back of his head, sipping wine and listening.

'Do you think there's going to be a war involving Italy?' the accordionist asked, leaning over his instrument to hear the opinion of the young man he respected.

'It's clear to me that Mussolini invaded Ethiopia because he wants to show that he's as powerful a leader as Hitler and capable of making war,' Augusto answered him. 'Did you see Hitler's picture in the paper last week, with those staring eyes? He's a madman, as is Mussolini. The Nazis will be allowed to annex the Sudetenland, part of Czechoslovakia, with the connivance of Italy, Britain and France. But Stalin will take care of Hitler and Mussolini in his own time,' he added vengefully.

'For God's sake don't say that outside these four walls,' Benigno cautioned. 'You know how Mussolini hates Communists. Your leader Gramsci is dead, and most of the Central Committee is in prison, so your cause is more or less lost.'

'It's the only system that will give the common man fairness and dignity,' Augusto replied with the assurance of one who had read deeply and pondered the subjects in the books he had borrowed from Cassino's public library. Like most Italians he had left school at fourteen, but had carried on educating himself as best he could. He thought he would have liked to have gone to university in a society more equal than Italy's; but in any case, the universities were now run by Fascists.

'What about the treaty that Italy and Germany signed in Berlin two years ago?' another voice queried. 'What does that commit us to in the event of Hitler going to war?'

'I tell you this, if war comes, you won't find me with a gun in my hands – at least, not fighting for Mussolini,' Augusto said heatedly.

'You won't have any choice. They'll come and take you by force,' Benigno warned.

'We'll see.' Augusto drank more wine, then asked provocatively: 'Have you ever considered what a crazy nation we've become?'

'Explain yourself,' Benigno requested.

'D'Annunzio started it by talking about war as if it was to be desired, and Mussolini followed him. At Fiume that rabble-rouser and fanatic D'Annunzio raved on and on about the blood sacrifice of the youth of Italy. He wasn't interested in the benefits that war could bring, such as new territory; he craved violence on the grand scale. Mussolini's the same. It's a sickness of the mind, and it comes from our history, dating far back beyond Garibaldi to classical times and the emperors of Rome. That's why Mussolini will lead us into a war which will be a disaster for Italy. Remember what he said: "War is to a man what motherhood is to a woman."'

'That's madness,' Angela entered the conversation. 'No, not madness, wickedness.'

'So do you regret coming to this wicked country?' Augusto addressed her.

'No I don't. I love it here. We should all pray that there won't be a war.'

'I don't believe in prayer,' Augusto said.

'But you were raised a Catholic,' Beatrice reminded him.

'I lost my faith in religion at the same time as I lost my faith in Italy.'

'I find that sad,' Angela told the aggressive young man.

'Why sad?'

'Because being a Catholic is a great comfort and support.'

'I've never found that,' he answered with a dismissive gesture. 'The world I'm in is enough for me.'

At two in the morning Beatrice told the company that it was time to go home, and they went out into the warm summer night, the path going through groves where birds slept undisturbed, used to their laughter and song. The furthest house was only half a mile away, and the moon was their lantern.

From Angela's Journal for Friday 12 August 1938:

> I didn't require a candle to see my way up to bed tonight. The moon is illuminating the windows of the monastery, as though the monks are studying scripture late in their cells. As I undress I'm thinking about Augusto, the fiery young mountain guide. How strong his convictions are! I don't agree with him about Communism because it's a godless philosophy. I shall say a prayer for him before I lie down on my oh so fragrant mattress of hay. The latest letter from Christopher is beside my bed.

Chapter Five

'I have to take a party to Monte Cairo,' Benigno informed Angela during a visit she was making in October. 'Do you want to come with me? We need to put on stout footwear. See if your aunt's shoes will fit you.'

Benigno saddled two of his mules, and put panniers on the other two before he and Angela led them up to the monastery. Half an hour later two Fiats driven by chauffeurs arrived with the six people making the day's excursion to Monte Cairo. The food and wine they had brought with them were loaded into the panniers on the mules. The countryside between the monastery and the mountain was undulating.

Look at them,' her uncle whispered to Angela. 'The women think they're in a fashion parade with these breeches, and the men's boots are so new, they'll be hurting before long. But I have to keep my mouth shut, I'm told. They're friends of Herr Hitler's and have been staying with him in that house he built for himself in the mountains in Bavaria. Since we don't speak their harsh language we won't have to listen to their German claptrap about what a great man Hitler is.'

The mules' hard hooves were secure on the mountain paths as they plodded upward at a safe steady pace through beech groves, lost, it seemed, in their own ruminations. Angela had strong calf muscles through Scottish country dancing, but after an hour's ascent the German women complained that their legs were aching, and the men took silver flasks from their jackets and drank schnapps after their exertions.

'What did I tell you?' Benigno whispered to Angela as they led the mules to a mountain stream. 'This is the great German race, yet they haven't the stamina for the climb. You see that man over there, mopping his brow with his handkerchief, as if he's reached the summit already? He's a General in the German army, one of Hitler's favourites - so the interpreter who's with them told me. These people aren't fit enough to fight a war. They would have been better staying on the terrace of their hotel in Cassino, sitting with their magazines and their drinks with ice in them. Schnapps? Now isn't that a very ugly word for a drink. It sticks in your throat, whereas vino -' he took a small flask from his pocket and winked at Angela as he swallowed, then shouted in Italian to the interpreter: 'Tell your party that it's time to get going, if they want to go higher!'

The mules' hard skin meant that they weren't affected by a day in the fierce sun, or downpours of rain. As they climbed it became hotter and hotter, and after an hour two of the women sat down beside the track, moaning that they couldn't possibly go on.

'I've got a reception to go to in Munich next week, to meet the Führer,' one of them announced, to make the other females in the party mad with jealousy at this revelation, for many society women had crushes on the moustached dictator with the blue eyes who handed round tempting plates of cakes with compliments with the panache of an aristocrat in the Carlton Tea Rooms in Munich. 'If I go on like this my feet will be so swollen that I won't be able to get into my new gold shoes,' the female climber complained, turning to the interpreter. 'Would you tell our guide that we'll wait here until the party comes down?'

The men started complaining about the steepness of the ascent, the dust, the heat, and the persistent insects. One of them sank down by the wayside and pulled off a boot to show Benigno his blistered foot.

'I can't go another step,' he moaned. 'I've got military manoeuvres next week.'

'Have you been to Herr Hitler's residence in the mountains of Bavaria?' Benigno asked the interpreter as they walked down with the mules, two of the women riding with the rest of the footsore party following, complaining with each step. 'They say it has magnificent views.'

'I wouldn't go near him.'

'But you're a German,' the mountain guide said in astonishment.

'I'm also an undercover socialist,' the young man disclosed, making sure that the women on the mules couldn't hear him. 'These tourists I'm taking round don't know it. If they did, they'd turn me over to the Gestapo. That's why I'm not going back to Germany. I'm making for France. I want to start a new life in a country where Socialists aren't in danger.'

'It's a long way to France,' Benigno observed.

'I'll reach it safely,' the young German assured him. 'I'll slip away from the party later today.'

'But if you're caught the Italian police will return you to Germany,' Benigno warned him.

'I won't get caught. I'll get to France,' the young man assured his guide.

'Good luck,' Benigno said, gripping his hand.

Her mother read Angela's letters to the family at the supper table in the flat above the café. Her three siblings looked envious as their sister described the castle she was working in, and her idyllic weekends with their uncle and aunt, the four mules, the goats and the kitten. She sent cartoon sketches of their uncle and aunt standing outside the farmhouse, Beatrice with a hen under her arm, Benigno stroking the head of a goat. She also sent a sketch of the mules, ears protruding through the straw hats on their heads, and one of their Uncle Peter the monk, with the tame raven perched on his shoulder. Her siblings waited eagerly for the next set of cartoons and asked if they too could go to Italy.

Rosa chatted with a customer who was in the habit of walking down from the university to take his morning coffee in the café.

'Have you been away on holiday?' Rosa asked Professor Henderson.

'I've been in London, talking to people.'

'That sounds very secret,' Rosa said with a smile as she put the strong dark brew in front of him.

'We were discussing the war.'

'What war?' Rosa queried.

'The war that's going to break out between Germany and Britain.'

'But I thought that there wasn't going to be a war,' Rosa said, leaning over the back of the chair opposite the professor. 'Mr. Chamberlain got Hitler to sign a paper promising peace, didn't he?'

'That paper wasn't worth anything,' Professor Henderson revealed. 'Anyway, it's history now. The German-Polish Non-Aggression Pact, signed in 1934, gave Hitler time to rearm. He has Poland in his sights.'

'Our daughter Angela's in Italy,' Rosa told him. 'It won't become involved, if there's a war, will it?'

'It's not thought in London that Italy will join Germany in a war, so your daughter is safe in that sunny country.'

In a state because Il Duce was coming to stay for a night, the Marchesa Battagliero left unfinished cigarettes smoking in ashtrays in the castle as she went about, haranguing the servants. She picked up a fork wrought by Benvenuto Cellini, the great Italian goldsmith, thrusting it at the butler as if intending to wound him, yelling that 'one of the most important men in the world is coming to dine here. Look at the prongs of this fork; they're filthy!' She descended to the kitchen and interrogated the cook about the menu, then climbed three staircases to inspect Il Duce's suite and the bed, enclosed in brocade curtains, which had accommodated centuries of births, deaths and violations. With the cellarman she went over the list of wines which were to be served with the various courses for the grand banquet, and authorized the uncorking of a port which had been laid down when Garibaldi was still active.

Now it was the turn of the head gardener. He showed the Marchesa the flowers he would cut and hand in a basket to the housekeeper to arrange in a vase in the bedroom of the most powerful man in Italy. She wanted red roses because he was a full-blooded man who knew how to satisfy a woman as well as a nation.

But the Marchesa wasn't finished, and there was a consultation with her maid about the selection of garments she would wear for the visitation. They had been fitted to her in the haute couture houses of Rome and Paris. While she was standing in her silk underwear, admiring herself in the pier glass, the pig that would provide one of the dishes for the guest was being slaughtered with much anguish at the home farm, its blood spurting into a basin.

'This is the one I'll wear to the banquet,' the Marchesa announced finally to her patient maid, indicating a gown by Elsa Schiaparelli, the simple white silk evening garment with a crimson waistband featuring a large lobster painted by Salvador Dalí on the skirt. It had been chosen after she had unlocked her crocodile skin diaries to check that she hadn't worn the Lobster Dress in the presence of Il Duce at a reception and ball in Rome.

'Now, shoes.'

The floor of a wardrobe which ran the entire length of the thirty feet room was devoted to her footwear, from Rome,

Paris, London, all made on her personal lasts. It took her twenty minutes, matching the selection to the Lobster Dress, to decide on crimson evening shoes handcrafted by Salvatore Ferragamo.

The maid was now unlocking the wall safe and bringing out the two feet long jewel box. It took half an hour of her holding silver, gold and platinum in various designs at her mistress's neck in the mirror before the Marchesa selected a halter of diamonds which had been in her husband's family for centuries, and was believed to have been the property of Lucrezia Borgia.

The Marchese had been dining in the Residenz-Casino in Berlin in 1928 when he noticed an attractive woman at a table across the restaurant. She was a dancer in a nightclub in the same city, her pudenda shielded by ostrich feathers. The Resi had private telephones fixed to the tables, so that diners could contact other tables or flirt anonymously with guests. But the Marchese didn't avail himself of this service. Instead he consulted the menu, not for food, but for one of the one hundred plus gift items. He selected a necklace and had it sent to the desired dancer via the pneumatic tube system suspended above the tables. He danced with her among 1,000 others under the hundred mirrored globes opening and closing to the rhythm of the orchestra. That night he was in her bed. A week later she returned to Italy as his wife-to-be, and on the train he concocted for her a Bavarian pedigree to satisfy his aristocratic circle, none of whom would check the *Almanach de Gotha*.

There was one final task for the chatelaine of the castle, the most delicate of all. One of the maids had a pronounced nose. The Marchesa had demanded her birth certificate before employing her, and had satisfied herself that she wasn't Jewish, but in case Il Duce would be offended, since he had told her that Jews were 'reptiles,' she praised the servant for her hard work and gave her the weekend off, with her train fare to Rome, along with a modest amount of spending money.

Meantime the Marchese was stocking the cigar humidor and checking the selection of whiskies in the library. There was no point in putting books beside Il Duce's bed because he was a man of action, not a reader. And though he was known to be virile, it would be too risky to provide him with a woman. The Marchese wondered if he should ask the archivist and his assistant to remove the documents piled on the long table, but decided that they should be left to show the Leader that his host's family was an old and distinguished one in Italian history.

'This is an important occasion in the castle and your family's annals, Excellency,' the archivist remarked as the Marchese smoked a dangerous cigar near the piles of inflammable history on the table.

'It is indeed. I'll dictate an account of it so that you can put it in the archives,' the Marchese promised.

As he was speaking he was looking at Angela, her head bent to the old charter she was deciphering. He hadn't appreciated before how beautiful she was, with the light from the leaded window falling across the table to illuminate her face. It occurred to him that the scene would make an evocative painting, though he himself had no skills with the palette.

'Have your researches reached Garibaldi's visit to the castle?' he asked the archivist, to prolong his stay in the library so that he could admire his assistant archivist from Scotland.

'Ah, we're a long way from that, Excellency. Your family has been distinguished for centuries, since long before the Medicis. I'm very excited because I say to myself: the next bundle whose tape I'll undo is bound to contain a communication from the great Leonardo, and maybe even Michelangelo himself.'

'I recall my grandfather saying that we had been offered a painting by da Vinci, but had declined it. However, we do have the exquisite Madonna by Raphael.'

All the time he was reminiscing the Marchese's eyes were on Angela. He had a predisposition towards virgins, and was imagining taking her by the hand up to his bedroom. But he had a violent wife who would take her revenge for him favouring someone more beautiful than herself.

Chapter Six

The Marchese Battagliero walked the poplar-lined avenue to the stables of Carrara marble from Michelangelo's quarry, where the head groom was brushing down a magnificent white stallion.

'Is this the mount for Il Duce?' the Marchese asked.

'It is, Excellency.'

Zeus, a Lipizzaner, wasn't only the finest horse in the stables, but one of the finest in Italy, and the Marchese had refused offers of many lire to mate the white stallion with mares from other estates. The money would be useful, but his pride would be offended by the commercialization of the magnificent animal's semen. It would be like himself giving a baby to the girl who scoured the pots in the kitchen.

'Make sure you choose a comfortable saddle,' he directed the head groom.

'That's all taken care of, Excellency, and the stirrups also.'

On his way back down to the castle the Marchese stopped to extract a cigarette from his gold case. Gisela had been really clever, persuading Il Duce to come to stay with them, he mused as he flicked his lighter, fashioned out of a shell, a souvenir from his participation in the Great War.

But there was something missing, the Marchesa lamented as she and her husband sat down to coffee.

'I'd have loved to ask a photographer, because we could have had our pictures in the newspapers and magazines,' she told him, since it would have maddened his fellow members of the aristocracy vying for the attention of Il Duce.

'He may bring a photographer, Gisela.'

'We'll see.'

At five o' clock that evening Mussolini arrived in a limousine, escorted by a phalanx of motor cyclists and an entourage. He didn't have his wife with him, because she preferred to stay at home with their children. As the guest embraced the woman he had had several times on the mosaic floor of his office, the Marchesa felt the power in his arms. He shook hands with his host, and was led into the library. The archivist and his assistant had stopped work early, and had watched the arrival of Mussolini from a high window.

'History is being made today – at least for this family,' the archivist observed. 'Look at the Marchesa: it's a wonder she's not down on her knees in supplication.'

Angela was surprised at his cynicism, having assumed that he was a Fascist.

'You don't admire Mussolini?' she prompted cautiously.

He spread his hands ambiguously, not wishing to risk putting his thoughts into words. He despised the jump-up with the puffed-out chest, like a turkey cock's. The history of his country was the archivist's profession, his abiding love. It had often been turbulent, with brigands as well as saints, and it had taken a long and bloody time for it to become a unified nation. But the brutal Fascist leader had already undone history and the work of patriots like Garibaldi by dividing the united country. His supporters and henchmen in Rome were well provided for, but the people of the countryside had been reduced to poverty and a state of terror by his laws. He was a gangster, not a statesman.

Mussolini was now in the *salone*, being served a cocktail by a footman. He had only glanced at Raphael's Madonna, but smiled when he saw the large photograph of himself addressing the multitude from the balcony of the Palazzo Venezia in Rome. He moved on to a full-length painting of Garibaldi.

'It would be a great honour if you would sit for a painting for our gallery,' the Marchese proposed. 'It would match this portrait of the great Garibaldi, with his worthy successor.'

'It can be arranged, when I have the time.'

'Of course it would be by a major artist.'

But that had been taken for granted by the man who was posing, a glass in hand, as if there were a photographer at work in the room. He didn't find it ironic that a person of his background should be standing in the *salone* of one of the oldest aristocratic families in Italy, because he knew that he had been chosen by destiny. His life was like an epic film in the making, with scenes on balconies, on horses, in aeroplanes, wielding implements in harvest fields, culminating in the barbaric victory in Abyssinia. But the life had been heavily edited, with the seduction scenes in his palatial office excised, and his mistress having no part. Hitler had featured, and would feature again, but as an understudy.

The great man was asked if he wished to rest, but answered that there was no time, and that he would retire to work on the portmanteau of papers which one of his entourage had carried up to his private sitting room. It was too dangerous for his hostess to join him, though as she watched him in her *salone* she craved his muscular body with a passion which her husband had never been able to satisfy. But Gisela, for all her astuteness, didn't realize that she was one of many who had been taken with bare buttocks on the cold marble of the symbolic bull mosaic.

Il Duce didn't take precautions, but the Marchesa did. Every time she returned from Rome with his seed within her, she invited her husband into her bed until he was exhausted. When she announced that she was pregnant with her second child Eduardo, the Marchese was delighted, but would never know that his handsome sixteen year old heir would shake the hand of his real father in welcoming Mussolini to the castle. Even if Il Duce were revealed as the father, the Marchese would probably have been proud of this addition to his genetic history.

The Marchese knew it had been a mistake as soon as he saw his guest's face. The glass case which the dictator was now examining contained the mummified corpse of the Cardinal who had been a collateral member of the dynasty. The small man in the brocade robe and petit oriental slippers, the skull cap askew on his head, rosary beads in his stiff fingers, lay in the raised glass-lidded coffin, so that at first Mussolini believed it was a marionette, until his host enlightened him, the dictator's face expressing disgust at the ridiculous thought of an afterlife. Or perhaps it was a reminder of time the leveller.

To match the magnificence of the banquet given in the castle that night for fifty guests, the archivist would have had to go back through piles of documents, to a visiting Pope. It looked as if Il Duce's chest was going to burst out of his starched white front, sending the diamond studs (a gift from a grateful seduced countess) across the table. There was a footman in attendance behind his chair, to transfer the fare from the golden dishes on to his Sèvres plates, and the butler hovered to pour a wine laid down long before the guest of honour was born. The owners of neighbouring estates who had been invited were wearing the Fascist uniform. The *Ciociaria* was the name of a traditional region of Central Italy without a defined border, or historical identity which had been adopted by a Fascist movement of Frosinone, as an ethical denomination for the province of Frosinone, when it was created in 1927. The name was said to have been inspired by the footwear worn by some sheep and cattle herders in the Central Apennines. The *Ciociaria* leaders were sitting round the Marchese's table, listening to Il Duce reminiscing about meetings with Hitler between mouthfuls of the pig slaughtered in his honour.

'I'm told that I've been an inspiration and a model to him.'

'As you have been for us all,' the Marchese added, rising to turn his adulation into a toast.

The guest shared his vision for Italy's future, making it sound as if those at the table were privileged. There would be even more highways, more modern buildings in cities beyond Rome; and even a new city. But Il Duce was careful not to imply that the old architecture, such as the castle he was dining in, had had its day. There was a place in Italy for the old and the new, for Catholicism as well as Fascism, with, naturally, Fascism predominant. 'This wonderful castle is part of the precious heritage of Italy' - this appreciation coming from a leader who had ordered ancient buildings in Rome to be bulldozed.

His conversation turned into a lecture, and at one point his fist smote the table, spilling choice wine from his neighbour's crystal glass. A hand in a white glove, like the disembodied limb at a séance, produced a napkin to absorb the spillage.

After riding the Lippizaner the dictator left the castle before lunch the following day, with the servants as well as the archivist and Angela with the host and hostess lined up at the door as Il Duce entered the limousine.

'We'd better get down to work this afternoon,' Dr Murino advised his assistant.

From Angela's journal for Thursday 20 October 1938:

> It has taken several weeks of instructions before I can attempt to read the old writing. I love undoing the ribbons and blowing the dust off the documents, unfolding them so carefully before laying them on the desk to start making a transcription. There are many unfamiliar words, but Dr Murino is so patient with me, coming

round from the other side of the desk to instruct me. Last week I undid a bundle to unfold sexually explicit letters written by a courtesan in Rome to a seventeenth century Marchese. Dr Murino noticed my hesitation and read over my shoulder. 'I'll work on these,' he told me gently, lifting them away. 'When you come across other correspondence like this, let me know. Despite my long experience, even I'm embarrassed reading them, and some of the words are so obscene they're not in any dictionary.' He told me that most of the Marchese's ancestors kept lovers in Rome, and some of them brought the estate to near ruin because of their mistresses' demands, amounting to blackmail, for money and jewels. Dr Murino came across one document showing that one courtesan had died in mysterious circumstances, possibly poisoned on a Marchese's instructions because she was blackmailing him. He said: 'I wonder if times have changed that much among the present-day Italian nobility with regard to such adulterous affairs.'

I am wearing Christopher's locket, but hidden, inside my high-necked blouse, beside my gold cross.

Angela's letter to Cavaliere Grillo, Saturday 29 October 1938:

The archival work is so interesting here, and I'm having a wonderful insight, not only about life in an aristocratic family, but also about the troubled history of Italy before unification. I was trembling with excitement the other day when Dr Murino gave me a letter to hold, signed by Garibaldi! (He was thanking the Marchese of his time for hospitality and political support.) Dr Murino the archivist tells me that there is correspondence with D'Annunzio, since the Marchese was at Fiume with him.

I hope that you are well, and I look forward to beginning a doctorate under you when I return to Glasgow next year in time for the start of the university in October.

With Kindest Regards,

Angela

She wrote regularly to Christopher Murchison, telling him about Mussolini's visit and the thrill of seeing Garibaldi's signature. She had sealed a letter to him and was undressing for bed when the door opened and the Marchese came in without knocking.

'You're very beautiful,' he complimented her as he advanced unsteadily into the room, having consumed brandy on top of wine.

The archivist in the room next door didn't only study old documents, but also human beings. He had seen the way the Marchese watched his assistant when he came into the library that morning, on an excuse to ask a question about the archive. Dr Murino sensed that a late visit was likely, which was why he was lying, fully dressed, on his bed. When he heard Angela's raised voice he swung down his legs. He knew that if he opened the door into her room, then he would be dismissed from his archivist's position because he had seen the Marchese, so he knocked and called out: 'Angela, I need to speak to you about something. I'll wait in my room until you're ready.'

He returned to his bedroom and heard her door opening, then the Marchese's footsteps hurrying down the stairs. When he went through he found her distraught, pulling down her blouse.

'He attacked me!' she blurted out.

He sat her down on the bed beside him, holding her hand.

'I thought that this would happen because of the way he's been looking at you since you arrived here. I'm afraid he's inherited the brutal way his ancestors treated women. You must leave here, but not abruptly. You'll ask the Marchesa in the morning for the weekend off, go to your aunt and uncle's at Cassino, then write to the Marchese to inform him that you're unable to return because your aunt is ill and requires your help.'

Chapter Seven

When Angela alighted from the cable car at Montecassino with her suitcase on an overcast afternoon in November 1938 she didn't go down to her uncle and aunt's house. Instead she went into the monastery and asked to see Dom Pietro. When he came he asked her what was wrong, and she told him that she had left the Marchese's employment because he had tried to assault her.

'What should I do?' she asked her uncle. 'Should I write to my parents and tell them that I want to come home?'

'Let's go into the basilica and pray for guidance,' he advised, and both went down on their knees in front of the altar while he said a prayer. Afterwards they sat in a pew.

'You'll have to give your parents a reason for wanting to go home,' her uncle pointed out. 'And if you tell them what happened at the castle, they'll be very distressed. I presume you would make your own way home, if your mother's busy in the café, so she'll be deprived of seeing Beatrice and myself after all those years. The Lord is telling me that you needn't take such a drastic step. You're away from that brute the Marchese, and Benigno and Beatrice love having you to stay. Tell your uncle and aunt that you didn't like the people at the castle, and that you would like to stay here until your mother comes for you, as arranged. Tell them that you're going to look for a job in Cassino.'

Her uncle and aunt were delighted to have her back and told her that she could stay for as long as she pleased. The following day she went down to Cassino. She posted the letter to the Marchese, informing him that her aunt was ill, so she wouldn't be returning to the castle, 'regretfully.' She went into shops and hotels until she found employment, as a tablemaid in a small hotel of ponderous dark furniture and depressing drapes. The proprietress was Signora Faustino, a severe woman with foul breath, in a dark tight-fitting costume, a leather belt at her waist which would have suited a holster. On the wall of the front hall was a blown-up photograph of Mussolini in military uniform on the roof of the Palazzo Nicolini Sereni in Rome, wielding a pick to begin the demolition of the Via dell'Impero, to clear the route for its successor, the Via dei Fori Imperiali, symbolically running in a straight line from the Piazza Venezia where the dictator had his office, to the Colosseum. Forty thousand square yards of one of the most densely populated and historically significant parts of the city were obliterated, including the monastery of Sant'Urbano ai Pantani and the nearby convent of Sant'Eufemia.

Signora Faustino tapped the photograph as she lectured Angela. 'Il Duce is clearing from Rome what he's called centuries of decadence. It'll be the greatest capital city in the world with its modern buildings and new streets, greater than Berlin or Paris. Look how generous he's been to the Roman Catholic Church, which lost its land holdings in the unification of Italy in 1870. Mussolini gave it 750 million lire in compensation, and one billion lire in state bonds, as well as one hundred and nine acres in Rome to create a new

Papal State, the Vatican. The Pope even has a small army.'

If Angela could have found another job she would have left, but she couldn't live off her aunt and uncle, so, when she wasn't serving at table, she endured the daily lectures on the greatness of Il Duce, hearing him compared to Julius Caesar. She found that the best strategy was to listen without responding, and after a while the Signora would go away to deliver her lecture to other members of staff. Sometimes Angela had to work late because Fascist officials from Rome sat on, eating and drinking at the state's expense. She loved approaching the dusty track to the lighted windows of her aunt and uncle's house, where, even though they were in bed, there would be a plate of supper in the oven for her, and a glass for wine at her place at the scrubbed board. After her meal she played with the kitten before carrying her upstairs in her arms to her bed, where Annabelle slept under the covers close to Angela's heart. In the early morning there was the intense pleasure of going to greet the four mules, bringing them gifts of food and talking to them.

It was now December and bitterly cold, with the surrounding mountains white. Her bedroom had no heating, and when she woke in the dark morning the hieroglyphics of frost on the window pane hazed the lights of the monastery as the monks began their day of devotion, the same ritual of sung services of canonical hours day after day, but never wearied of, from Matins to evening Compline.

Though there were no winter visitors to Monte Cairo, Benigno's four mules still had to be lct out of their stable, otherwise Samuele drummed his hooves in protest on the stable door. Angela walked them along the track to Augusto's house, where his grandmother came out to greet them. Since there wasn't much to do on their smallholding, Augusto would walk her back.

'What will winter be like in Scotland?' he enquired.

'I had a letter from my mother last week. She says that it's very cold, but so far, no snow. Do you get white Christmases here?'

'Sometimes. I don't celebrate Christmas.'

'Why not?' she asked in surprise.

'Because I don't believe in the birth of a saviour from Heaven. We have a saviour born on this earth.'

'Who is that?'

'Josef Stalin. Along with Lenin he's one of the saviours of Russia, liberating the people from centuries of oppression under the Czars and the nobility. The people rose up against those who had made them serfs, keeping them in poverty, without education.' He clenched a fist. 'I hope the people of Italy will do the same against that monster Mussolini. I would be willing to pull the trigger if I could get close enough to him.'

'That would be a mortal sin,' Angela pointed out.

'I don't care what you call it, so long as Italy is freed from Fascism, because if Mussolini dies, then his movement collapses. It would be the same with Hitler in Germany.'

Such talk depressed her as they walked with the docile mules, stopping to allow them to crop the sparse grass of the wayside. Why couldn't he acknowledge and celebrate the beauty and mystery of creation, the white mountains, the sun on the high monastery, instead of always preaching revolution and violence? He was an attractive intelligent man denying the existence of his soul with his obsessions. But she knew that there was wisdom in what he said about the evils of Fascism.

Beatrice began the preparations for Christmas by cleaning the house while Benigno whitewashed the fire surround. Angela helped her aunt prepare food for the holy day.

'I'm making *crispelli di Natale*, Christmas fritters,' she explained to her niece. 'An old relative who lived at Ripi gave me the recipe for the first Christmas of my marriage, saying that it was as good as a blessing and would please my husband and ensure that he would never leave me for another.'

Beatrice laid out the ingredients, a kilo of flour, a tablespoonful of salt, traditional dry yeast, a cup of raisins, a cup of warm water and a teaspoon of sugar. Under her aunt's watchful eye Angela mixed the ingredients and worked them into soft malleable dough while accompanying Beatrice in the carol she was singing.

'We'll rest the dough for several hours,' Beatrice advised, taking the ball from her niece.

When they returned to the pleasant festive task the ball was twice its original size.

'This is how you make the *crispelli*,' Beatrice

demonstrated, pulling off a piece of dough and making a hole in it. Angela fashioned fritters from the rest of the dough and Beatrice fried them in hot oil until they turned golden brown.

'We'll let the excess oil leak out,' Beatrice advised, laying the *crispelli* on a towel. The fritter was still warm when she sprinkled on sugar and handed it to her niece.

'It's delicious,' Angela enthused.

'Of course it's delicious. It's Italian.'

Benigno led the way with a lantern up to the monastery for Christmas Eve Mass in the basilica, with other local families in attendance. For Angela it was the most uplifting experience of her life, with the singing of the monks, the beautiful vestments of the Abbot celebrating at the altar, lifting the glittering chalice in the candlelight as the wine was transferred into the Precious Blood. When the wafer was placed on her tongue she felt that she was in communication with the One whose body had been transfigured.

From Angela's Journal for Sunday 25 December 1938:

> *When we came home last night we ate the crispelli di Natale by the fire, leaving the remainder for today, when we attended another Mass at the Abbey. I bought Uncle a shirt, and Aunt a blouse in Cassino, and I received gloves and a hat which Aunt knitted. I was reflective this afternoon, thinking wistfully of my family celebrating Christmas in Glasgow,*

the café closed, Papa in the flat above cooking traditional Italian festive fare, including polenta into which he puts a secret ingredient handed down in his family. It's a dish that many regular customers come to the café to enjoy. There will be holly and presents and Mass at St Peter's in Partick. Christopher sent me a Miraculous Medal in gold, but I bought nothing for him, to my shame. However, a prayer for him is a special gift.

Will I marry and have children? Sometimes - and this is one speculation I haven't shared with Papa and Mama - I wonder if I should become a nun. That doesn't necessarily mean being shut away for life in a convent, not able to speak, except to Christ. Nuns of the Notre Dame order taught me in the convent school I attended in the west end of Glasgow, where I was very happy, so I could perform a valuable service teaching the young, then, at the day's end, retire into contemplation and prayer. But like Uncle Peter surely I would be given permission to continue my Dante studies.

Spring came to the Cassino area, and the mountains shed their snow. The frost evaporated in the sun, leaving the soil soft for planting. The mules spent the day out. Angela worked in the hotel in Cassino, and when she came back in the early evening it was light, so she could walk the mules before their bedtime. The birds paired off and began to nest, and a robin which Angela had fed throughout the winter sometimes graced her hand. In late spring small whitish flowers appeared on the olive trees.

Angela constantly exchanged letters with Christopher, reading them in her bedroom. On Sundays she met her uncle Dom Pietro Contadino after Mass. Though it was a monastery devoted to prayer and contemplation, the monks were aware of events in the world beyond their massive walls, and listened regularly to the wireless. Hitler's rants were heard in these silent corridors of individual cells where men, for their own reasons, had given their lives to God. They had to rise in the pre-dawn for the first office of the day, and when they weren't at prayer, they tended bees, practised calligraphy, and taught in the boys' school in the monastery. But there were feast days, and days which were a holiday (*dies non*) from the strict ritual of their lives. When they passed away they were assured of an elaborate Requiem Mass, followed by burial in the cemetery within the monastery's bounds.

But this freedom and the constant protection of prayer didn't mean that they were unconcerned by current events in the world. They understood the threat that Hitler posed, not only to the Jewish population, but also to European peace. They were wary of Mussolini, but were careful not to express their opinions of the dictator to visitors. The most they could do was to pray, and their collective appeals to God in the form of amplified chants in the great basilica always had a powerful effect on the listener.

'It's good that your mother is coming to take you home shortly,' Dom Pietro told his niece after the uplifting Mass on Easter Sunday in April 1939. 'Mussolini has invaded Albania, so God knows what kind of conflict Italy could be plunged into, if other European powers chose to intervene. Imagine doing this at Easter. He's a godless tyrant, and he only tolerates the Catholic Church because he knows that it would be too dangerous to move against it, since this is a Catholic country. And in violation of the Munich Agreement which gave Germany the Sudetenland, Hitler has invaded the remainder of Czech territory.'

Dom Pietro knew that in expressing his contempt for Il Duce to his own flesh and blood, he could trust her not to repeat it in company, but at the same time he didn't want to frighten her.

In June the hotel down in Cassino became busy with tourists, mostly Germans, and Angela had to work longer hours at the reception desk, as well as helping to serve supper in the dining room where Signora Faustino patrolled among the tables, snapping her fingers to summon a member of staff when dishes had to be removed, or more wine poured. It was getting dark as Angela arrived back at her uncle and aunt's house. The four mules were quiet in their stable, having taken a party up Monte Cairo. Benigno was counting the money he had received from them.

'These Germans are very mean,' he complained. 'They never give a tip. I much prefer the English, but they seem to have stopped coming because they're frightened that war will break out. Poor Vincenzo had to carry a very fat man today because he was out of breath in the first few minutes of the ascent. I suggested through the interpreter that he waited for us until we came down, but he was determined to conquer the mountain, in the same way that his leader Adolf Hitler is determined to conquer Europe.' He took another swig of wine. 'Well, my dear, your aunt and I are certainly going to miss you when you go back home in September. Maybe I'll try to persuade my sister to let you stay another year.'

'I'd love to, but I can't, uncle, because I have to resume my studies. Maybe I can come back after I've completed my doctorate.'

'You'll always be welcome here. You're the daughter we were never blessed with. And the mules love you. That's just as important, because animals know when a person is good. Sometimes I wish they would give the Germans a good kick.'

Chapter Eight

Rosa Boni heard the news of the German invasion of Poland on the wireless in the family café in Glasgow on the first day of September 1939.

'You were right about what you said about Hitler having his sights on Poland,' she reminded Professor Henderson, the political theorist and government advisor, when she put his coffee in front of him the following morning. 'Is it still safe for me to go out next week to bring Angela home?'

'Oh I think so. You're going by sea after all.'

Rosa took comfort and confidence from the opinion of a customer she trusted, and went back through to the kitchen. Two days later, on the Sunday morning, as she was leaving Mass, she heard a woman at an open window shouting down to a neighbour in the street that Britain was at war with Germany.

On the Monday morning customers in the café were talking about the sinking by a U-boat of a liner which had left Glasgow on the Friday. The disaster was in the Late News box of that morning's *Glasgow Herald*, and when the first edition of the *Evening Times* appeared on the street, the vendor outside the café was shouting about the sinking of the *Athenia* in the rapid contorted language which only Glaswegians could decipher. During the week Rosa learned that the *Athenia*, which had sailed from Glasgow for Montreal via Liverpool and Belfast, with over a thousand passengers, Jewish refugees, Canadians, American and British citizens, had been torpedoed two hundred nautical miles northwest of Ireland with the loss of one hundred and twenty eight passengers and crew.

'I hope this isn't going to affect me going out to Italy to bring Angela home next week,' Rosa said anxiously, showing the newspaper to her husband.

'Wait and see what Professor Henderson has to say when he comes in for his coffee tomorrow morning,' Joe advised.

But the professor had been summoned to London to help plan Britain's strategy in the war.

'What are we going to do?' she asked Joe, who was busy meeting the demand for his famous ices.

'You're working yourself into a panic,' he cautioned.

'But other liners might be sunk,' she said fearfully.

'Let's make ourselves coffees and take them into the kitchen,' this equitable man advised, putting the young woman assistant on the ice cream counter. When they were settled at the kitchen table with their cups he began: 'So you're booked to sail next week, spend a fortnight with your sister at Cassino, then come home with Angela at the end of this month in time for her to start at the university. But if you're so worried about how safe it will be to sail, with a war on, then you don't need to go next week. Angela can come home by herself. You've already booked her ticket, haven't you?'

'I have.'

'So what you need to do now is to go down to the shipping office this afternoon, cancel your own sailings and get them to change Angela's reservation to one as early as possible. Does that make sense?'

She took a tram into the city, even though they were short staffed in the café. But there was a queue at the Orient Line Agency in West Nile Street, with intending travellers anxious about their reservations, and others, following the sinking of the *Athenia*, worried about the safety of relatives due to visit them from various countries. The number of people and their raised voices made Rosa nervous as she pushed her tickets across the desk to the elderly clerk when her turn came eventually.

'I want to cancel my reservation to Naples next week, and the return at the end of the month. My daughter's due to sail back with me, but I would like her to come home on the next sailing.'

'These are the instructions we've received,' the clerk responded, reading from a sheet on his desk. '"All sailings are subject to change, deviation or cancellation, without notice. Passengers are requested to register their requirements."'

'What does that mean, "register their requirements" when I've already paid for these tickets?' Rosa demanded to know.

'You'll get a full refund, of course, madam. "Register your requirements" means that we can take your details – which we have already, and to which I'll add your request for a reservation on the earliest possible sailing from Naples – and get in touch with you when the situation becomes clearer.'

'But I need to get my daughter home from Italy as soon as possible,' she protested.

'I appreciate that, madam, but I can't do anything about it. Will I contact you by telephone when I have news about sailings from Naples?'

'Yes please,' she replied, without optimism.

She was serving in the café the following morning when one of the regulars, a lecturer in French, remarked how tired she looked.

'I'm so worried about my daughter Angela,' she disclosed. 'I've been trying to get her home from Italy by liner, but the sailings seem to have been suspended due to the war.'

'Have you considered her coming home by rail, Mrs Boni?' the lecturer suggested.

'I never thought of that. What would that entail?'

'Travelling out of Italy and across France. Why don't you go and see the French Consul here? I have the telephone number in my head, if you bring me a piece of paper. Phone and make an appointment to see him, using my name.'

She was given an appointment at Woodside Terrace the following morning. The consul, Comte Alfred de Curzon, was a charming sympathetic man, and when she told him about her predicament with regard to her daughter, he responded that 'it's possible to travel by train from Rome to the Channel ports, though if this war is anything like the last, you can expect the cross-Channel steamer services to be reduced. But the trains are still running to and from Italy, since it's not involved in this war.'

He went to the large map of Europe opposite his desk and traced a possible itinerary for Angela across Italy and

France.

'It's a long journey, with a number of changes. She may have to stay overnight in places, which means booking accommodation. But I'm sure a travel agent would still be able to work out a route for her and book tickets. If she has a problem, I could send a wire to our consul in Rome.'

When she returned to the café to transmit the reassuring conversation she had had with the Count her husband informed her that Cavaliere Ernesto Grillo had been in to the café.

'What did he think about Angela's situation?' her mother wanted to know.

'He appreciates that you're worried, which is why he came. He said that he'll drop in this evening on his way home from the university after we're closed to speak with us.'

The immaculately dressed Knight Officer of the Crown of Italy favoured an expensive Brazilian coffee, a tin of which Joe kept exclusively for him, without charge, because he was so caring of Angela. When the three of them were settled at a table, with the door locked, Grillo spoke to Rosa in Italian.

'You're worried about Angela being stranded in Italy?'

'I want her home, because of the war.'

'But Italy isn't in the war, and won't be,' he responded.

'I know, but I want her home. I saw the French consul today, and he says if necessary he'll help to get her home by train through Italy and France. She needs to come home, for our peace of mind, and because she has to resume her studies for her doctorate with you next month.'

'That was the original arrangement,' the Cavaliere agreed, tasting his black brew with the palate of a connoisseur. 'You have a genius for making coffee, Giuseppe.' He turned to Rosa again. 'Your daughter doesn't have to come home for the sake of her studies. I would be very happy if she spends a further year in Italy.'

'There's no university at Cassino,' Joe pointed out.

'But there's the monastery, and your brother, Mrs Boni, is a monk there, and a scholar who has published important papers on Dante, the subject of your daughter's doctorate. Dom Pietro, with whom I've corresponded, can supervise her studies and send me chapters for checking as they appear. I'll write today to my friend the Marchese Battagliero, whose archives your daughter is helping to catalogue, and ask him to release her from her duties for two days a week so that she can study with Dom Pietro at Montecassino.'

'But she's no longer working for the Marchese,' Rosa pointed out. 'She's working in a hotel in Cassino.'

'The Marchese hasn't informed me of this,' Grillo said peevishly. 'So your daughter is staying with her aunt and uncle near to the monastery? That means she can devote even more time to her studies with Dom Pietro.'

'But Italy has a pact with Germany and could enter the war,' Joe came into the conversation.

'I'm in touch with highly placed government officials in my home country, and I can assure you that Il Duce has no intention of committing our country to support Germany in this war,' Grillo emphasized. 'Were Angela my daughter

– which would be a great privilege and blessing – I would rather leave her in safety at Cassino than bring her home by a complicated arduous train journey, involving changes and probably delays – if not danger.'

'We're immensely grateful to you for the interest you take in our daughter, Cavaliere,' Joe told their visitor. 'Now that the matter's decided, let me pour you more coffee.'

From Angela's Journal for Monday 18 September 1939:

I'm in the habit of visiting Augusto's grandmother after lunch on Sunday because I like the old lady, and conversations with her improve my colloquial Italian and give me new and interesting words relating to the flora and fauna of the surrounding countryside. Augusto was at home, in an excited state. 'Do you understand what Britain having declared war on Germany means?' he asked me. When I told him that I didn't he said that it means that Europe will be in turmoil. I asked him if Italy will join in, and he replied: 'I hope not, but Mussolini's capable of anything.'

Now that war has broken out I've written to Mama, asking if I should try to make my way home by myself. When I went back down to the hotel this morning to serve breakfast, I found Signora Faustino poring over a map of Europe at the reception desk. 'This is Great Britain, which is at war with Germany,' she pointed out to me. 'And across the English Channel is her ally, France. This is Germany, the country they are fighting, and which has already invaded Poland.' When I asked her if Italy would go to war, she pointed out that 'Il Duce and Hitler share the same political philosophy.'

When I came up from the hotel this evening I found a letter from Mama, telling me that she has received a full refund of our fares from the shipping company. I must stay at Cassino for the present, on the advice of Cavaliere Grillo, who will arrange with Uncle Peter up at the monastery to start me on my doctoral studies on Dante until I can get home in safety to resume them with Professor Grillo. I'm relieved by my parents' decision. 'Who knows, the Poles may drive Hitler out of their country, and then Britain and France will turn on him and destroy his army,' Mama writes. When I told Uncle and Aunt about Mama's letter before I came up to bed, Aunt said: 'We don't want you to go. I've written to your mother to tell her that you're the daughter we would have loved to have, and that we intend *keeping you for as long as possible.'*

Angela's letter to Dr Christopher Murchison of Wednesday 20 September 1939:

Isn't it terrible that we're at war again with Germany? I've been so looking forward to going home with my mother to my father and my brothers and sister, and to seeing you again, of course. But my mother won't be coming out now because of the international situation. Professor Grillo has advised my parents that I should stay here for the time being, rather than attempt to get home by rail by myself. I'm to begin my doctorate under the supervision of my uncle, who is a monk in the monastery here and an authority on Dante.

I hope you're well.

With Blessings,
Angela

You're a bloody fool,' George Murchison chastised his son. 'And you,' he turned to his wife, 'stop crying and I'll sort this out.' He turned to his son again. 'Why did you go and join up when doctors are exempt from military service?'

'Because I want to do my bit.'

'Your bit? Let others do that. Fortunately I know some senior officers, so I'll get them to withdraw your name.'

'I don't want that,' his son told him. 'I want to serve.'

'And be killed!' his mother wailed.

'For God's sake be quiet, woman! Why did I spend all that money on your education for it to turn out like this?' he confronted his son. 'How many of your medical friends have joined up?' his father continued the interrogation.

'I don't know.'

'You know full well that none of them will have.' He put his forehead into his hand in exasperation. 'I'm going to have to sort this out.'

Christopher had learned down the years not to answer back, otherwise the attack would increase. But this time he spoke up.

'It's my decision, and I don't want it sorted out, as you put it.'

But he didn't tell his male parent that, having been informed that he wouldn't be sent overseas, he had told the officer that he wanted to go with the troops, to wherever they were sent.

Chapter Nine

Il Duce learnt with the rest of the world that Germany had invaded Poland. He was on the telephone, making one last effort to halt the war he knew must come by proposing yet another peace conference between Italy, Britain and France.

But he was too late, and the next person who took the long walk to his desk was an orderly who brought a translation of Chamberlain's declaration of Britain being at war with Germany. Mussolini realized that by his speeches he had alienated Italy from Britain and France, and was therefore vulnerable to attack from either or both.

The next important message was from Hitler.

> Even if we now march down separate paths, destiny will yet bind us one to another…If National Socialist Germany is destroyed by the Western democracies, Fascist Italy will also face a hard future.

Il Duce was tempted to toss the communication into the wastepaper basket, filled to overflowing with official papers which had bored him. He swung his jackboots up on to the desk and considered the situation. That little bastard in the absurd moustache who looked like Chaplin and whom D'Annunzio, now dead but still revered, had called a 'ferocious clown,' was tempting him. *Come in with us; we'll see that you get a fair share of the spoils.* But this wasn't a comedian he was dealing with. A dangerous man recognizes another. If Germany goes down, they'll drive Fascism out of Italy.

The Italian dictator was now drumming his fingers on the desk. It was risky, because Britain and France were a formidable alliance, and America might back them. But if Italy stood on the sidelines, wouldn't that look like weakness or even cowardice? After all, Hitler and he were Fascist brothers.

He was going to have to think this one out. The boots swung from the desk and hit the marble. He picked up the phone to call for his driver. A session in the floral boudoir with his mistress would help.

When Angela reported for work at the hotel on the Thursday in the last week of September Signora Faustino was waiting to inform her: 'I heard history being made yesterday. I was listening to a Polish pianist playing a Chopin nocturne on Polish radio when the music was cut off by German artillery. Warsaw has surrendered.' She moved her finger on the map spread over the desk. 'This is the Polish border and that's Warsaw the capital. This is the distance the Germans have moved since they invaded Poland on the first of this month and set siege to the capital city of the country. Mussolini and Hitler have signed a pact not to attack each other, so we should admire the might of the German army. This is the greatest army in history.'

'What will happen to the Jews in Poland, Signora?' Angela asked, after their treatment in Germany.

'Why are you so concerned about the Jews? Have you ever met one?'

Angela told her that an old Jewish gentleman came into her family's café in Glasgow every day for coffee and said that his brother's shop in Munich had been smashed up by the Nazis.

'He's well off, this old Jew in Glasgow, is he?' the proprietress asked.

'He's a businessman, Papa says,' Angela told her.

'The trouble with the Jews is that they like money too much,' Signora Faustino complained. 'I'd go further and say that they adore money. They can never get enough of it, and they hoard it. They cheat people by selling them shoddy goods. So let's not be concerned about the Jews of Poland. They'll survive, as they've survived for centuries.'

Angela wished that she were at home in Glasgow with her brothers and sister, in their flat above the café. Rosa wrote to her daughter:

> The sister of a woman who was one of the passengers on the *Athenia* which a U-boat sank on the first day of the war sits in a corner of the cafe. She orders two coffees and a lemonade, and when I ask her who's coming to join her, she says: "My sister and her wee boy." She doesn't believe that they've both been drowned, and thinks they were picked up by another ship and will walk through the door of our café and that everything will be all right again. I serve the poor soul the two coffees and the lemonade, but only charge her for the one coffee, which she doesn't drink anyway.

Do you wonder that I worry about you, day and night? I know you're safe with your aunt and uncle where you are in Italy, but one simply doesn't know what's going to happen next.

Take care of yourself my dearest child and always say your prayers, not only for yourself, but for those who are suffering because of this war. Pray for that little boy and his mother lost on the *Athenia*, and pray that his aunt will get peace.

Com tutto il mio amore, Mama

Count Galeazzo Ciano, Mussolini's Foreign Minister and his son-in-law, with the looks of a Hollywood film star, was having an audience with Il Duce at the end of January 1940.

'The people grumble, and we must take into account the food restrictions,' he warned his Foreign Minister, who had to suppress a smile at the next statement: 'The Count of Torino is setting a bad example by hoarding soap. For what? To help wash his 35,000 whores, though what he does with them in his state of health, I can't imagine. I'm very disappointed in the Italian people. They're an unadventurous race, a race of sheep. For almost eighteen years I've been leading them, but that hasn't been enough to change them. It could take a hundred and eighty years – maybe even a hundred and eighty centuries. Only force will keep them in their place. Beat them and beat them and beat them,' he worked himself up, emphasizing his words with a fist on the table.

On Sunday 10 March 1940 Ribbentrop arrived in the

holy city with an entourage of thirty-five, including his gymnastics instructor and two barbers, presumably to take turns shaving his smooth Aryan skin. As he was being driven from the station he boasted to Ciano: 'The fine weather we're enjoying is bringing the moment for action nearer. Within a few months the French army will be destroyed and the British on the Continent will be prisoners of war,' a threat he repeated to Mussolini in the conference.

Ribbentrop brought with him the promise of a welcome gift from Germany – not a signed photograph of the Führer, but consignments of coal overland, since Britain was blocking shipments by sea of this vital fuel for Italy.

'The Führer wishes a meeting soon with Il Duce to tell him more about his plans,' the German Foreign Minister reported.

Hitler would come as far as the Brenner Pass to meet Mussolini.

'I'm not being given time to breathe, to think,' Il Duce complained to Ciano.

Four days later the two leaders exchanged salutes at a railway station at the Brenner Pass high in the Alps close to the border between their two countries. A snowstorm was raging, and in his heated railway carriage the Führer opened the subtle psychological assault on this vain Italian, so easily read. He told Mussolini with a shrug of his tailored shoulders: 'If Italy is content to remain a third-rate power in the Mediterranean, you should go home and attend to domestic affairs. On the other hand, if Italy is to become a world power, join us in the struggle against the democracies of the west.' The German dictator knew that silences were as important as rants. He revealed, with the timing of a consummate actor, and with the prophetic look of victory in his compulsive eyes: 'We're going to mount an attack on France.'

The whirl of the blizzard against the carriage window was like the activity in Mussolini's brain. In tactical powers it was certainly inferior to Hitler's, but he had the limited cunning which often accompanies ruthlessness. One difference between him and the leader of Germany was in his public persona. Mussolini looked and sounded like a thug, whereas Hitler had more elegance of presence, as if the one-time Vienna vagrant had enrolled in an academy which taught deportment and table manners.

'Yes, we'll enter the war on Germany's side, but only if your attack on France is successful,' he pledged.

'I think I can give that guarantee,' the Führer said with his treacherous smile, and after a short meal he prepared to return through the blizzard to his obsessive poring over maps of Europe in his mountain eyrie, where the goddess was Eva Braun.

Dom Pietro had begun to learn the organ while a pupil at the monastery school, and had been sent to Rome for advanced lessons. He practised most afternoons because he expected to succeed the old monk who was the organist. The Bach cantata was on the music stand, and it seemed to the fifty year old monk that he was drawing strength from a source other than his hands and feet to transform the score into sound which took on a power, a harmony, and a life of its own.

After he had ceased playing Dom Pietro went down on his knees in front of the altar in the basilica, praying for the safety of his niece and all his family. He feared for them from the reports on the wireless, and the discussions of the monks, several of whom were historians and who saw in Mussolini the bellicose tendencies of other leaders from Italy's fragmented past, notably Garibaldi. The charismatic poncho wearing hero of the Risorgimento, with his mantra: 'Here we make Italy, or we die!' had suggested that he be made a 'dictator.' But Dom Pietro knew, from consulting old dictionaries, that the word, which formerly meant the assignation of extraordinary powers in a time of national emergency, was being redefined if not corrupted in the reign of terror of Mussolini.

Abbot Diamare had told the monks that they must devote more of their energies to prayers for peace, from the moment in the dark before dawn when their feet found their sandals on the floor beside their bed, through all the services and offices of the long day, to when they retired for the night after Compline, prohibited from speaking, except to the Lord.

'If only we could pray during sleep,' the Abbot said wistfully, unaware of the significance of the researches into the unconscious, its storage and retrieval abilities being carried out by Carl Jung. 'Whatever we're doing in the course of our day, whether working with our hands or our heads, we should pray constantly for peace in this troubled world.'

Dom Pietro spent much of his time in the library, because he was writing a book on the turbulent history of Montecassino. He had already transcribed from an early chronicle bound in vellum the details, scant as they were, of the time, circa 529, when St Benedict founded Montecassino. He gave his niece Angela a lesson on the history of the Abbey after Mass one Sunday, when he had invited her to stay for coffee.

'It wasn't the first settlement on the mountain. In prehistoric times its heights were a place of heathen sanctuary, and when Benedict – under guidance from God, assuredly – chose the mountain as a place to make a new beginning, a heathen deity still stood on Montecassino. From being a place of human sacrifice it became a site of piety and respect for man as well as the veneration of the Lord. When the monastery was built it was looked up to as a place of holiness, culture and art. Pilgrims from all over the world came to visit it, on foot from as far away as Britain, having to cross forests filled with wild animals and robbers to get here, some of them mauled or murdered.'

'It's such an inspiring history,' Angela enthused.

'Yes, but the peace and prosperity didn't last. Around 577, according to the chronicles, the monastery was destroyed by the Longobards of Zotone, the surviving monks fleeing to Rome, where they remained for more than a century. It must have been a tragic sight to travellers raising their eyes to a heap of stones on the mountain. But Montecassino has always had its guardian angels: early in the eighth century Pope Gregory II commissioned its rebuilding, the beginning of a period of great splendour for Montecassino. The year 787 was one of the most important in the monastery's long history, because Charlemagne, head of the Holy Roman Empire, granted it vast privileges.'

Dom Pietro turned a fragile page damaged by insects to the year 883, when the Saracens invaded and, after sacking the monastery, burned it down. They caused the death of Bertharius, the saint Abbot, founder of the town of Cassino. The surviving monks fled, and monastic life was only fully resumed towards the middle of the tenth century, thanks to Abbot Aligerno.

'Do you require any help in transcribing documents for your history of the monastery?' Angela asked her uncle.

'That would be very welcome, though you won't be allowed in the library. I can arrange with the Abbot for us to use this room. But we must make time to begin your doctoral studies on Dante. I've had a letter from Cavaliere Grillo, and he expects to see initial chapters in due course.'

Chapter Ten

On the penultimate day of May 1940 a policeman came into the café, but instead of sitting down he asked the girl behind the counter, ten year old Maria, to fetch her parents. Rosa was frantic, thinking that something had happened to Angela in Italy, but the policeman explained that the Home Office had issued a directive, requiring all aliens over the age of sixteen to be in their homes between 10.30 p.m. and 6 a.m. from the following Monday.

'But we're not aliens,' Joe protested. 'We've been in this country for over twenty years.'

'As Italians you're classified as aliens,' the policeman responded abruptly. 'If you want to keep a bicycle or a motor vehicle, you have to apply for a police permit.'

'We don't have a motor vehicle,' Joe informed him. 'Our sixteen year old son has a bicycle which he rides to school. Surely these regulations don't apply to a schoolboy?'

'They do, so he mustn't ride his bicycle until he gets a permit. Here,' he said, thrusting a notice at Joe. 'These are the new regulations; read them and make sure you don't contravene them.'

'At least these restrictions don't affect our opening hours, since we live above,' Rosa observed to her husband when the policeman had gone. 'But they're still very harsh, and we thought that this was a good country to come to, far safer and fairer than Italy.'

Angela began work on the Montecassino archive. The old calligraphy wasn't a challenge after her archival work for the Marchese Battagliero, and Dr Murino's training. She transcribed the information that the eleventh century had been one of the high points of the history of Montecassino. Abbot Desiderius, who became Pope Victor III, had rebuilt the monastery and enriched it with many treasures - precious manuscripts, gold and enamel objects. He also hired expert Byzantine mosaicists to embellish the rebuilt abbey church to the glory of God.

As his niece worked at the wide table opposite him, Dom Pietro was writing up the black year of 1349, when the earthquake struck. He tried to convey in his prose the terror of the monks as the mountain rumbled as if it were going to explode, ceilings crashing down on Brethren at their devotions. There was no suggestion in the chronicles that this was divine punishment for their sins. Only a few walls remained standing, and so the pilgrim on his way to Rome by way of the Liri Valley with his staff and satchel lifted his eyes, crossed himself and said sadly: 'Lord, these ruins on the mountain top were once a monastery that was one of the wonders of the world. Why did You make the earth shake, bringing down the walls?'

Dom Pietro had already devoted five years to his task, and knew that it would take several more before he reached the triumphant story of the monastery he was sitting in, when it accumulated the treasures, some in the form of exquisite illuminated manuscripts, which he carried through from the library to show his niece.

Freud would have found Dom Pietro an interesting study on his couch, a devout monk whose contributions to the Latin prayers came from the heart, an exceptional organist and sensitive interpreter of Bach, an internationally acclaimed authority of Dante, a monk who cared deeply for people, and yet a man of God, armoured in daily prayer, whose sleep was disturbed by demons. They didn't have forked tails or carry tridents, but they bore an alarming resemblance to Mussolini, and they had skulls of steel and outsized fists. Some nights the monk rolled on to the floor in his nightmare and lay there sobbing, as if he had been assaulted.

Angela carried her writing pad out into the brilliant sunshine and sat on the slope below the house, within sight of the mules, who meandered up to nuzzle her neck and to push the straw hat from her face as she opened the pad on her lap and uncapped her fountain pen. The nib hesitated and she looked up to the monastery for inspiration before beginning to write in the script that Professor Grillo had complimented her on, telling her that it was a joy to read Dante in such a script.

Angela's letter to Dr Christopher Murchison of Wednesday 5 June 1940:

Dear Christopher,

Thank you for your latest letter, informing me that you volunteered for war work and have asked to be sent overseas. Being in the Medical Corps is very worthy, because you'll be able to help wounded soldiers - if this war descends into big battles. I will pray that you are kept safe. Never underestimate the power of prayer. Remember that each of us has a guardian angel who is with us constantly, listening to our prayers and helping us in sorrow and adversity. How I would love to see mine, though the radiance would dazzle me!

I'll remain here with my aunt and uncle until it's safe to make the journey back to Glasgow. Sorry about the blot, but one of the mules has just pushed my arm as if to protest that, instead of writing, I should be playing with him and the others.

I go up to the monastery regularly to study Dante with my uncle, and when I'm kneeling in the beautiful basilica, all my family and you are constantly in my prayers.

With Blessings,
Angela.

She put the envelope into her pocket for posting. But she was uneasy despite the weather and the affection of the mules. As she stood up for the Angelus bell from the monastery, she saw Augusto coming along the track with his dog. Everyone else in the neighbourhood would be bowing their head to the bell, but not him, because Communists didn't recognize God, he'd told her in no uncertain terms. She found him uncommunicative. That was a pity, because he had a great knowledge of the creatures and the flowers of the surrounding countryside, having roamed since childhood, and she would have asked him to share his knowledge with her. But in his favour, he was very devoted to his grandmother and could be amusing as well as aggressive in company.

'What are you doing today?' he enquired as he came down the slope to her.

'Writing a letter home,' she disclosed, patting her pocket.

'But will it reach its destination, with the war?'

'I've faith that it will.'

'Delivered by an angel flying over war-torn Europe, is that the way?'

'Why not? We need angels, not only in wartime. It's a pity you don't believe.'

'Oh I believe all right. I believe in the equality of man, love for people and for animals, respect for the countryside. Isn't that enough to be going on with?'

On Monday 10 June 1940 the Marchese summoned the castle's staff to the *salone*. Two footmen had carried the wireless from the Italian aristocrat's own sitting room and set it up with an aerial at one of the windows, with its view of the distant monastery of Montecassino under a cloudy sky.

It was like one of the theatricals which the castle's owners staged from time to time in the same room, using the services of the itinerant showman who arrived at the castle, his props strapped to two docile mules. The Punch and Judy show was erected, and as the pair – nicknamed Stalin and Hitler - boxed and abused each other, the servants laughed, tears rolling down their faces.

But this morning was a solemn occasion. The Marchese had taken a phone call from Rome, alerting him to the broadcast, and two minutes before it was due to begin, he entered in his Fascist uniform, as though he were an actor in a drama. All that was missing was a drum roll.

'Il Duce is about to make a momentous announcement,' he told his staff.

The voice of the dictator came through from the balcony of the Palazzo Venezia in Rome, intimating that Italy was declaring war on France and Britain. The speech, faint as it was because of the poor reception caused by mountains, echoed D'Annunzio's rant at the time of the occupation of Fiume when he claimed to hear Christ calling out to Italians to 'rise up and be not afraid.'

Standing beside the wireless, the Marchese raised his arm in the Fascist salute, and his lady and servants followed.

'This is an historic day,' he told the company. 'Italy will need fighting men, and I expect all of you to do your duty. I'll be with you in our triumphs. No one is exempt, because everyone has a contribution to make.'

As he was making this point he was watched by the archivist, who was standing at the edge of the gathering, beside the glass case containing the embalmed body of the Cardinal, collateral ancestor of the man standing before him in the Fascist uniform. The archivist had read enough of the family papers to know about the ruinous wars, at home and abroad, which the Marchese's forebears had instigated and entered, but it was too dangerous for him to pass on his researches to the gathering. Sometimes he wondered why powerful men built up archives, since they chronicled disastrous judgements, the deaths of heirs in duels over whores, the forfeiture of extensive estates through being on the losing side in campaigns which had almost bankrupted the family. As for himself, with his age, weight and unstable heart, the archivist was confident that he wouldn't be summoned to serve as a soldier, but would probably be put in charge of stores or some similar mindless post.

During the broadcast the Marchesa had been standing close to the wireless, and what those in the room took to be her audible delight at Il Duce's truculent voice was actually a deeply thrilling orgasm.

Father Borelli, the castle's chaplain, who had been standing on the fringe of the gathering, listening, was asked to come forward, to say a prayer for the success of Il Duce's war, which he did, since he was a spiritual opportunist, too well sustained on his patron's fine food and wines to voice his doubts. He was twenty stone and his cassock was splitting at the seams.

The retreat to the coast had been frantic: thousands of men of the 51st Highland Division hurrying along dusty roads, some of them hobbling, others sinking down by the roadside because they could go no further and knew that they would soon be prisoners. Lieutenant Dr Christopher Murchison, travelling in an ambulance, wanted to stop, to offer comforting words and medical assistance to the injured and exhausted. But the Colonel was sitting in the vehicle beside him and wouldn't permit the driver to stop, because that would hold up the other vehicles behind, and would almost certainly mean captivity. The Colonel wanted home to his wife and family in Sussex after the disaster of France, and he wanted to play his part in defeating the Germans, rather than sit uselessly in a POW camp. The young Lieutenant sitting beside him, waving to those left behind on the verges, and throwing one a packet of cigarettes, was thinking about his beloved in Italy, not his parents in Glasgow.

They reached the utter confusion of St Valery, where men were lowering themselves down the cliff on to the shore by their belts to try to reach the rescue craft offshore. Either the Germans shot them, or their belts parted and their spines were shattered on rocks below. But Lieutenant Murchison had scaled the Inaccessible Pinnacle on Skye with fellow students from Glasgow. Now he was going down the cliff, his fingertips bloody but holding, his boots kicking to create a step. He dropped the last ten feet, rolling on the sand, and now he was running, bullets spurting sand around him. It wasn't the tramp steamer waiting offshore he had his eyes on: it was the image of Angela Boni, with tinsel in her hair, partnering him at the Scottish country dance ball in St Andrews Halls. He had to survive. He was splashing through the shallows and shinning up the rope ladder slung over the side of the steamer. As the boat swung out he looked back and saw the body of his Colonel on the shore.

Dom Pietro had begun to tutor Angela for her doctoral thesis on Love in *The Divine Comedy*.

'This is a big theme which Cavaliere Grillo has set you. First of all you have to define Dante's understanding of Love. Is it the Love that God has for us, or the Love that we should have for Him? Is it Love between persons, and is this Love emotional or physical, or can these be separated? For example, consider what Virgil his guide tells Dante in Canto XX11 of *Purgatorio*:

> '*Amore,*
>
> *acceso di virtù, sempre altro accese,*
> *pur che la fiamma sua paresse fuore'*
>
> (Love,
>
> kindled by virtue, aye another kindles,
> provided outwardly its flame appear).

'Then again, in Canto 111 of *Paradiso*, when the narrator is talking to Piccarda Donati, who was an actual thirteenth century Italian noblewoman, he remarks: *ch'arder parea d'amor nel primo foco* (she seemed to burn in love's first flame). But what type of love is this, and what kind of woman is Piccarda? She's the first person Dante encounters in Paradise. As a nun she was forcibly removed from her convent by her brother, to marry her off to a Florentine man to further her family's political interests. She died soon after her wedding. Though her marriage was forced on her, she broke her vows to God, and is therefore only on the sphere of the moon, the lowest sphere in Heaven. She's important in Dante's poem because through her we learn the nature of

Heaven, and the revelation that souls there are much more beautiful than they were on earth. So what is the nature of this love she is burning with? I leave you with this question for our next tutorial, Angela.'

Chapter Eleven

From Angela's Journal for Tuesday 11 June, 1940:

Signora Faustino was waiting for me at the reception desk this morning, to tell me about Il Duce's declaration of war. 'Your position is now very difficult,' she warned me. 'You're now an alien in this country.' I pointed out that my mother and father are Italian by birth. She told me that since I was born in Britain, I'm a British subject. 'However, you're an efficient worker, and since my husband is a Fascist official, he should be able to persuade the authorities to let you remain working here - at least for the time being.'

As I was listening to Signora Faustino I had the terrifying sensation that I was looking into the face of a dead person, the harsh eyes closed, the grim mouth relaxed; or perhaps it was a trick of the light in that sombre room without windows. Instead of going to Uncle and Aunt's, I went into the basilica of the monastery for Compline, kneeling to pray for the safety of my family and Christopher in Glasgow, and to give thanks to God for my being in such a beautiful peaceful place, and for the mysterious unaccompanied chant of the unseen monks in their stalls.

Augusto came to supper this evening. Uncle had shot two hares, and over their stew, flavoured with herbs, the conversation was about Italy's entry into the war. 'I suppose you can't go back to the hotel,' Aunt said to me. I told them that Signora Faustino said that I could keep on working for her for the time being, with the hotel busy with Fascist officials. Uncle warned Augusto that he was likely to be called up as he poured them both more wine. 'I won't go.' 'They'll come for you,' Uncle warned him. 'I'll hide up in the caves on Monte Cairo,' Augusto said.

I watched the young confident guide. It's summer now, but what will happen if the war continues into winter when snow covers Monte Cairo? 'I don't want to kill anyone,' Augusto told the table. 'That is, except only one person - Mussolini.'

'Neither did I when I was called upon to fight in the Great War,' Benigno said. He told us how he was sent to the Julian Alps against the Austrians because he was a mountain guide. He said that you lose resolutions when you're in battle, which is about survival. 'I'm still saying Ave Marias for the Austrian soldiers I killed, and only my death will stop me,' Uncle said.

He warned Augusto that he won't be able to escape military service - and killing people. 'Mussolini has enough of an army already,' Aunt entered the discussion. She recalled that when she was in Rome two years ago visiting a friend she saw soldiers marching through the streets. Mussolini was up on a balcony, saluting them. 'I can still hear the noise their jackboots made,' Aunt said, fear in her voice.

'Let's change the subject and have a little music,' Uncle advised, warmed by the wine. He asked Augusto if he had brought his flute. He produced it from inside his jacket and began to play. His selection of tunes was slow and reflective. He's a complicated person, angry at the world one minute, sensitive and considerate the next. That's what makes him appealing. I believe that he has great integrity, but may pay a price for it.

'I've got a headache with all this talk of war, so I'm going upstairs to bed as soon as I'm finished down here,' Aunt announced as she cleared away the supper dishes. She warned Uncle to lay off the wine and keep a clear head, because he's going to need it. 'There won't be many more games of morra with your friends over flagons of wine.' She turned to Augusto: 'Don't you

*go doing anything foolish. Wait until you
see if you're being called to fight, and we
can talk about it further.' Augusto said
that he had to go because he was taking a
party up Monte Cairo tomorrow morning.
Uncle told him that it may be the last
trip for some time because tourists aren't
going to come to Italy to go up mountains
with a war on, so he and Augusto would
lose their livelihood.*

*When I came up to my bed a short time
ago I carried my zupei so as not to disturb
my sleeping Aunt. The monastery above is
in darkness because all the monks are in
their cells until the first devotions in the
pre-dawn. I have said my prayers, for my
family, and for Christopher and Augusto.
The kitten has grown and still shares my
bed.*

It was hot in Glasgow, so Joe left the window of the front
bedroom open as they were going to bed after an exhausting
day, cooking and making ice cream.

'Someone's breaking into the café!' Rosa called out,
terrified at the sound of smashing glass.

Joe ran to the window. A crowd of about twenty had
gathered on the pavement and were beginning to chant.

'Tally scum! We'll teach you!'

'I'm going down,' Joe told his wife.

'No! No!' she clutched his arm. 'They'll harm you.'

He broke free and ran down the stairs, but when he emerged on to the street his arm was twisted up his back and he was punched in the face. Blood streaming from his nose, he was forced to watch a sledgehammer wielded by one of his customers smashing the big window engraved with BONI'S CAFÉ while a crowbar was inserted into the door to burst the lock to gain entry.

The crowd pushed into the café and went behind the counter. Cartons of cigarettes were tossed out, and women swept shelves of chocolate boxes and bars into bags they had brought for the purpose. Chairs were passed out, tables reduced to firewood by the sledgehammer. The man with the crowbar smashed the till and emptied its contents into his pockets. Joe saw the expensive new coffee machine ripped from its water supply and carried out. By the following evening it would be dispensing coffees in the café of a Scottish owner.

The three Boni children were watching the looters in the street below from their parents' bedroom window, the youngest, Maria, screaming. Their mother dragged them away, shouting: 'We need to get out of here in case they set fire to the place!'

She shepherded them downstairs, but as they emerged the crowd began to jostle them.

'Haven't you caused enough damage already?' Rosa challenged them. 'What have we done to you?' She pointed to a woman. 'We gave you credit for your husband's cigarettes and you never repaid the debt.' She confronted a male customer. 'You've been coming into the café since the day we opened it, and now you're helping to wreck it. Why, in God's name? And you?' The finger pointed again. 'You kneel beside me in the pew in St Peter's, yet you've got one of the chairs from the café.'

'No more, Rosa!' Joe called over, his arm still twisted up his back.

'Plenty more!' this formidable woman replied. 'They're wrecking our lives as well as our premises.'

'You lot should be put up against a wall and shot!' a woman shouted.

'Tally bastards!'

'Hitler supporters! I lost my son in France.'

As a police car arrived the crowd scattered with their loot.

'We'll take you to the Infirmary,' one of the officers offered.

But Joe shrugged them off and went into the café. The fluted dishes he had served his famous ice cream in crunched under his shoes as he surveyed the wreckage of the café which he and Rosa had taken years of hard work to build up into a thriving business.

'But why?' he turned, opening his arms wide to the policeman standing on the trampled front door.

'Because your country's at war with us.'

'But why should they be at war with me?'

The policeman turned and went out to the car.

Even the telephone had been stolen from the café. There wasn't one in the flat, so Joe had to go to an Italian friend's house to find a glazier to replace the smashed window, but as soon as he gave his name he was told: 'We don't do business with the enemy,' and the receiver was put down on him.

He was in the café, trying in his despair to clear the wreckage when two policemen entered.

'You're coming with us.'

'Why? I haven't done anything wrong. Look at the wrong that's been done to me.'

'Do we have to take you by force?'

'I must tell my wife.'

But he was bundled struggling into their car and taken to a police station, into a small room, with a detective sitting behind the table.

'What's this all about?' Joe demanded to know.

'We're detaining you under the Aliens Act.'

'I'm not an alien. My wife and I are naturalized British citizens.'

'That doesn't make any difference,' the detective said. 'You're a friend of Ernesto Grillo?'

'Not a friend. Occasionally he comes into our café for a coffee.'

'He teaches your daughter?'

'He taught her Italian at the university.'

'And he arranged for her to go out to Italy for a year to work with the Marchese Battagliero.'

'He did, because he thought that a year in Italy would

benefit her studies for a doctorate.'

'The Marchese Battagliero is a leading Fascist.'

'I didn't know that. What has that got to do with my family? I need to get back to my business, to see if it can be reopened after the attack.'

'Grillo is certainly a Fascist. He's been lecturing and writing for years on what a great man Mussolini is.'

'This is news to me, and has nothing to do with me. I told you, I'm a naturalized British citizen. My wife and I have worked hard since the day we arrived in Glasgow. We've always paid our taxes and our debts and abided by the law.'

'Your daughter is still in Italy?'

'Yes, but she's no longer working for the Marchese. She's working in a hotel in Cassino and living with her aunt and uncle.'

'Why didn't she come home when war broke out?'

'She couldn't get home. I need to get back to see if I can get our café open again, after the destruction.'

He rose to go, but the constable standing behind him in the interview room put his hand on his shoulder and pushed him back into the chair.

France had requested an armistice, but before dictating the terms, Hitler wanted to confer with Mussolini. The meeting took place in Munich on 18 and 19 June. The German dictator wanted a swift reasonable peace with France, without laying down too drastic conditions, to avoid an uprising of the French Navy in support of Britain. It was made clear to

Mussolini that since Italy had made no contribution towards the campaign in France, it would not be able to participate in the peace negotiations. The Italian dictator wanted to add Nice, Corsica, Tunisia and French Somaliland to his empire, but Hitler was adamant: neither France nor any of its possessions would be carved up for Italy. He could make a concession to his Fascist brother, however: he would refrain from signing an armistice until the French had signed one with Italy. This gave Mussolini little time to seize any territory from France. On 21 June he launched a general offensive against France all along the Alpine front.

'Look what Rommel achieved in Normandy,' a rueful Mussolini reminded Count Ciano. 'He forced the enemy into the sea. Hitler has had great triumphs, but where are our victories?' Il Duce appealed to his son-in-law. 'Our troops were stalled by a snowstorm in the Little St Bernard Pass, and our assault along the Riviera was halted a matter of five miles from our border.'

As he brooded in his cavernous office where he had enjoyed violating female admirers on his self-serving mosaics, Mussolini was realizing a humiliating truth: Hitler had enticed him into a war in which Italy only had a minor role. From now on the German dictator wouldn't share his territorial ambitions or acquisitions with the man he had hailed as his Fascist brother.

Not even a night with his mistress, who was wearing a new and alluring perfume, could relax the dictator, though he was being administered fellatio by scarlet lips. All he could think about was that treacherous German bastard.

Kapitänleutnant Günther Prien was frustrated that July morning in 1940, but not because he spent so much of his life under the sea in the steel shark which had set course for Germany instead of continuing to patrol the Atlantic since he was almost out of torpedoes. Aged thirty-two, Prien was a hero in Germany, having sunk the *Royal Oak* in Scapa Flow, his view of life and sense of achievement now measured through a periscope. The sight of a ship going down satisfied him even more than a night with Zarah Leander, the Reich's favourite *femme fatale*, her photograph pinned above his bunk, would have done. He was frustrated because Captain Endrass, one of his students, was about to overtake him, to receive an award for the highest tonnage of ships sunk within that month. Prien was 5000 tons behind his student, with no deck ammunition and only one seemingly faulty torpedo to close the gap. A hoisted periscope was a torment when there was no prize, with a liner steaming into the lens bisected by a cross with no spiritual associations for the predatory remorseless eye at the glass. He gave the order to fire the faulty torpedo, more in frustration than hope.

Joseph Boni had been taken from Glasgow and interned on the Isle of Wight before being put aboard the *Arandora Star* at Liverpool. He lay on the floor of the two berth cabin which he was sharing with five other men on the liner, converted to a troop carrier. It had been painted battleship grey for camouflage, and the promenade decks where tourists had strolled and lolled in deckchairs on peacetime voyages had been separated from other parts of the ship by double fences of barbed wire, because this was no cruise. The liner was taking over 1,000 alien males, Italians and Germans, to internment camps in Canada.

The porthole of the cabin had been boarded up, so the Glasgow café owner couldn't see if it was morning. But his watch showed that it was just after 7 a.m. He was striking a match for his cigarette when there was a violent explosion. The lights were out on the ship, and no alarm was sounded. As Joe reached the lifeboat station, one boat was already being lowered, with only four people in it, but the occupants paid no attention to the cries of 'Wait! Wait!' from the deck above because they wanted to get away from the crippled ship as quickly as possible in case they were sucked under.

Prien punched the air before closing the periscope and ordering the U-boat to submerge.

Men were throwing rafts and benches into the sea and leaping overboard to cling to them. Some had become caught in the barbed wire fences at the promenade decks and were bleeding profusely as they struggled to free themselves. The deck was becoming a steep slope, and the café owner couldn't keep his frantic footing. He heard a boiler exploding before the ocean engulfed him.

Chapter Twelve

Lieutenant Dr Christopher Murchison, R.A.M.C., was home on compassionate leave because his father was dying. The prominent lawyer and, later, hardline Sheriff was lying in his ornate bedroom. Despite the best endeavours of the leading cancer specialist in Britain, the malignancy in the sheriff's stomach was the size of a grapefruit and still growing. The specialist who had been summoned from London had pronounced the tumour inoperable. It had sent out secondaries to the brain, but not in such strength as to impair his judgement. Above the doomed man's bed a naked winged Cupid in plaster was firing an arrow towards the window where his son was standing in his uniform.

'You were so fortunate to get away from St Valery,' his father spoke in the weakened voice that, when he was a student, used to shout insults at the Celtic team when Rangers was playing them. 'I heard on the wireless that the Germans took thousands of prisoners. They're a race of bastards, and I hope we bomb them into the ground.'

'I was lucky, father.'

'I was looking forward to going with you to football matches when this bloody war was over,' the voice, strengthened with anger, said.

'Maybe you'll recover, father.'

'I've never believed in miracles. They're for the Catholic Church. The water at Lourdes making the cripple throw away his crutch - my backside! One of the few mistakes I made was hiring a Catholic secretary. She assured me that she was a Protestant, but one day I caught her crossing herself, and she was out the door.'

He was listening to his father and thinking: *I always found what you said about Catholics offensive, but I never had the courage to challenge you because I was frightened of you, and also because I was afraid that you would cut my allowance. Do I love you? Yes, but not because you are a loveable personality. I pity you because you could never see past your bigotry to the fact that one's religion doesn't matter; it's character that counts. I've learned that in this war.'*

The Lieutenant looked at his mother, sitting at the opposite side of the bed, holding her husband's emaciated hand.

You're just as prejudiced. When the agency sent a new maid and she told you she was a Catholic you went on the phone and gave the woman at the agency hell. You spend half an hour getting dressed for church because it's a show of fashion to you, not a spiritual experience. The two of you tried to show me love; you thought that rewarding me with material things for being first in subjects at school was sufficient. The army has changed me, made me grow up. I'm having to learn to take decisions myself. It's time to stand on my own feet, to choose my own path in life, not to have it laid out for me.

'I can rest easy, knowing you'll never marry a Catholic,' the voice from the bed said.

'Save your strength, father,' the Lieutenant spoke as a

doctor.

His mother came out on to the landing with him.

'Will they give you leave for the funeral?' she asked anxiously.

'It depends how long he lasts and where I am.'

'At least he's seen you. He's so proud of you.'

On Sunday, when Angela went to Augusto's house, she asked him if he had heard any news on his neighbour's wireless about any attacks on Britain.

'Don't worry about your family, they'll be safe. Most of the war news from Germany is lies. They're claiming successes because they want to frighten the people of Britain and France into believing that they're losing the war.'

'Who's winning?' she asked wearily.

'I don't know. They're not only fighting this war with bombs; they're fighting it with words as well, and sometimes words can do more damage than bombs.'

Angela continued to work in the hotel in Cassino. There were no tourists, but officers from Rome came to stay to consult with local Fascist leaders, and one afternoon Angela saw the Marchese entering in his uniform. She hoped that she wasn't going to have to serve him in the dining room. But he hadn't come for a meal; he was preoccupied with the war, as if an ancestral instinct for conflict had been revived in him. When Italy triumphed – and he was confident that that would be the case – then he could expect a reward from Il Duce himself, hopefully a grant of land confiscated from someone who hadn't supported the Fascist cause. In the dining room of the Faustino hotel the Marchese sat with local officials, studying recruitment figures and drinking the wine he had brought along for his sole consumption. The box of corona cigars in front of him wasn't offered round the table.

There had been very few volunteers, and a significant number were refusing to fight.

'What do we do with them?' one of the officers appealed to the Marchese.

'Any man who won't fight for his country is a traitor. If they refuse, shoot them.'

'Is this an order from Rome, Excellency?' a voice asked nervously.

'Are you doubting my authority?' the Marchese rounded on him.

'Of course not, Excellency.'

On his departure the Marchese recognized Angela behind the reception desk, but hurried out, averting his face, though not through shame.

From Angela's Journal for Friday 5 July 1940:

> I am 23 today. It seems that I have been in Italy for years, yet it's only two years since I left Glasgow. Uncle and Aunt asked some of their neighbours round for a meal to celebrate my birthday. Augusto didn't come, and we were beginning to wonder if he or his grandmother was unwell when

he appeared, with the news that he had received his call-up papers this morning. He's supposed to report to Naples in three days' time. He told the company that he wouldn't be going, and that it's his intention to hide out on Monte Cairo until the war was over. 'You won't survive,' Uncle warned him. 'I won't survive in the battlefield if I refuse to shoot.' Aunt told him: 'You certainly can't live on the mountain.' He insisted that he could, in a cave. So what was he going to eat? Uncle asked. 'What I can shoot.' 'And where are you going to get a supply of ammunition to last you for God knows how long?' Uncle confronted him. Augusto informed us that he had already bought two boxes of bullets in Cassino. 'How long will these last?' Uncle asked. Augusto said that he was being subjected to an inquisition, and that he can take care of himself. He revealed that he has already taken items from his grandmother's house up the mountain. 'What does she think of your idea?' Uncle asked. 'I told her that it won't be easy for her,' Augusto answered him, 'but it'll be better than me being shot in battle and her being alone for the rest of her life.'

From Angela's Journal for Monday 8 July 1940:

Augusto came this evening to take his leave of us. We sat among the laden olive trees. I told him that I was worried about him going up Monte Cairo to hide in a cave. I also told him: 'You're an active man, so being confined to a cave day after day will be a tribulation for you, and on dark nights coming down to your grandmother's house for food, even with a lantern, will be dangerous, especially if the weather is bad.' But I didn't put into words my thought that it may be better for him to go to the army, on the chance that he may not be posted to the battlefield.

'I love this landscape,' he told me as he sat beside me. He said that he has a sense of foreboding that the war will sooner or later come to Italian soil to destroy the peaceful way of life in the shelter of the great monastery above us. We watched Nico the monastery's resident raven performing aerobatics in the twilight. 'How are you going to pass the time in a cave?' I asked. 'I won't stay in it all the time. I'll go climbing to keep myself fit.' I put it to him: 'Suppose you're seen?' 'There won't be any people out on the mountain, now that the tourists have stopped coming.' I pointed out: 'But you'll have to have a light with

you when you come down at night.'

He reached over and took my hand, and I realized tonight that he has strong feelings for me. Why have I not noticed this before, or have I ignored the signs, his eyes on me as he entertained us with his flute, as if sending me the message that the tender tune was for me? I am a mature woman of 23 and must acknowledge such feelings, so I let him take my hand. He kissed me on the cheek before I watched him with his dog going through the olive grove, turning and waving to me before he disappeared. I stood for some time before I went into the house and upstairs, sitting on my bed, my rosary in my fingers as I looked up at the monastery, praying for the safety of Augusto and for the world in turmoil through war. I sat watching the huge dominant building fading into the darkness, as if it had become part of the mountain.

Augusto told his grandmother that he would come down the following evening when it became dark.

'If anyone comes looking for me, tell them you don't know where I've gone. Don't let them harass you.'

'I want you to take this.' she said, putting a small box on the table beside him. 'It was given me by your grandfather as a wedding present.'

Augusto opened the box to find a silver rosary, with Christ in mother-of-pearl on the cross. Though he admired its workmanship, he had no faith in its powers; but he couldn't bring himself to say such a thing to the pious old woman who had always been so kind to him. So he replied: 'I'm frightened I'll lose it.'

'You won't lose it if you take care of it. You're going to need it as much as you're going to need that lantern, because you need to pray often, to ask for protection. You don't know what the future will hold for you, up on the mountain. You'll be cold, and there could be wolves about, and when you come down to me in the darkness you'll need more than a light to guide you. It's all very well to climb a mountain in summer, and descend to your own bed, but it's a very different matter if you're living in a cave in the darkness of winter, with the mountain covered in snow.'

'I'll survive,' he reassured her. 'I'm going to take Jupiter up with me. I don't want to deprive you of his company, because I know you love him as much as I do,' he added, fondling the dog's ears.

'Take him,' the old woman urged.

He left before it was getting dark because he didn't want to light the lantern in case it could be seen by someone who would report it. He ascended the slope he had taken so often with tourists, but when he reached steeper ground the moon emerged to guide him, and within the hour he was at the cave to which he had already carried bedding, and a box with coffee and other provisions. He could fetch water from a stream a quarter of a mile's traverse.

He opened the box and sat eating on a rock at the entrance to the cave, his arm round the neck of his dog as he looked down on distant lights, trying to work out if one of them was Benigno and Beatrice's house because that was where Angela would be sleeping, peacefully he hoped.

Because Italy was at war with her country Angela didn't expect to receive any more letters from her family or from Christopher. How would she know if something happened to any of them? Suppose that Glasgow were to be bombed? Suppose that Christopher, away on medical service with his unit, was to be wounded or even killed?

After her next tutorial on Love in *The Divine Comedy*, her uncle Dom Pietro observed: 'you can read Dante according to the beliefs and morals of his time, but what makes him probably the greatest poet that the world has ever known is his relevance to each new generation, and never more so than the turbulent time in which we live. Consider this quotation from the Canto XXXI of *Inferno*:

> '*chè dove l'argomento della mente*
> *s'aggiunge al mal volere ed alla possa,*
> *nessun riparo vi può far la gente.*'
> (for where the instrument of the mind is joined
> to evil will and potency, men can make no
> defence against it.)

'The narrator is confronted with the Nephilim, the Giants, sons of earth who made open war against Heaven. But they could also be Mussolini and Hitler, whose intellects are joined to evil will and power, and against whom the people of the conquered countries of Europe can make no defence. And like the Nephilim, these two dictators will end up in Hell. Hitler joins the ranks of the ruthless highwaymen Pazzo and Corneto who, as Dante says in *Inferno*: *che fecero alle strade tanta guerra.* How would you translate that, Angela?'

'Who on the highways made so much war?'

Chapter Thirteen

Angela spent her time between the hotel in Cassino, the monastery and the farm. The mules required exercise, and she walked the four of them along the track, allowing them time to graze the verges as she talked to them in Italian, calling them '*bambini.*' She stopped at Augusto's grandmother's house and had coffee with her in the quaint old dwelling with its earthen floor and low roof. The old woman shared her home with a goat called Sergio which wandered in and out as he pleased, and lay down by her bed at night.

'He looks after me, with Augusto away,' she explained. 'If anyone came into the house during the night he would have to deal with Sergio's horns. Animals are very wise, some of them much wiser and more loyal than people. They don't betray you, like people do. Though I'm sorry that Augusto took Jupiter with him, the dog will be good company for him in the cave. He'll keep Augusto calm, and alert him if anyone comes to the cave who means him harm. I know you're missing Augusto, like I am, but you'll see him again, be sure of that.'

An hour after Angela had gone a gloved fist seemed as if it would split the door that had been in place at the time of the birth of Garibaldi, before Italy was unified. The old woman took her time shuffling towards the summons because she knew without having to resort to any psychic abilities what it was. Centurione Faustino, jackbooted and in breeches, demanded peremptorily: 'Where is he?'

'Where is who?' the old woman asked, as if her mind were beginning to wander. But it had the clarity of a twenty-year old, with the distilled wisdom of an octogenarian who had paid attention to the lessons of life. In another time, another place, she could have been an inspirational teacher, urging peace and tolerance.

'Your grandson,' the Centurione stated. 'He was supposed to report for military service a fortnight ago, and is now registered as a deserter. Deserters are shot, but if he turns himself in, I'm prepared to overlook his crime.'

'He left.'

'Left for where?' the caller asked in exasperation, sure he was dealing with a mentally retarded peasant.

'I don't know. I got up one morning and he was gone.'

'Without saying goodbye?' the Fascist asked sceptically.

'Perhaps he thought it was better that way.'

'I don't believe you.'

She was pushing the door shut, but he inserted the toe of his boot.

'I can no longer protect him from the firing squad.'

'Would you not be better to be away fighting this hopeless war instead of tormenting the innocent?' the old woman challenged him.

'This hopeless war?' he repeated menacingly. 'You could be in a lot of trouble for using such a defeatist phrase. Italy will triumph under Il Duce.'

'I'm not going to hold my breath. Now if you clear out I've got chickens to feed.'

'We'll find him, you old bitch,' he vowed as he withdrew his boot.

Back in his office in Cassino the Centurione summoned his squad, who were loitering in the yard, smoking and discussing the progress of the war which they learned about from others because they couldn't read the newspapers. In any case they were full of Fascist propaganda, distorting the ignominious progress of Italy in a war it was now apparent it should never have entered. Several of the Centurione's squad had pre-war prison sentences for violence and drunkenness, and one of them was a murderer whom Faustino had had released from prison because of his physical strength and blind obedience. Another was the son of one of D'Annunzio's *Arditi* who had turned the peaceful port of Fiume into a place of gratuitous violence and sexual excesses.

The heels of their boots clicked together and they saluted as they stood in front of his desk.

'I want Augusto Faccenda found. Search the grandmother's house first, and then the houses around, to make sure that a neighbour isn't hiding him.'

'What shall we do with him when we find him, Centurione?' the confident murderer enquired.

'I want him brought in alive,' Faustino stated, 'though if he tries to escape - '

The rest of the sentence was left to their discretion, since they were armed. They were turning to carry out his commands, but he wasn't finished.

'If you don't find him I want his house watched. If he's still in the district he has to feed somewhere.'

The old woman was eating a small bowl of olives when the latch was burst. Four men with guns came into the two roomed house, but because she had been expecting them she continued calmly with her scant meal, spitting out olive stones, one of them landing on a black boot. The intruders overturned the two beds and tumbled out the contents of the cupboard.

'I hope you'll clear up after you've finished,' she said calmly, aiming another olive stone from her mouth at the intruders.

'We'll find the deserter,' one of them vowed.

She turned in the chair to stare at the speaker.

'It's Stefano, isn't it?'

He didn't answer.

'You were Augusto's best friend. You sat side by side in the school and played football in the same team. I remember him telling me what a good player you were, one of the cleanest on the pitch. No dirty tackles from you, no elbow in the face when the referee wasn't watching. Why have you come to this?'

It seemed as if the person she was addressing was rooted to the flagstones, though another of the thugs was tugging at his sleeve.

'Was it the attraction of the uniform?' the old woman continued, because she had nothing to lose, wars having already taken from her precious members of her family. 'I must say, you look smart in your polished boots, and that pistol in your hand is certainly impressive. I'm afraid to move in case you shoot me. Of course I forget, you're acting on the instructions of Il Duce, and would do anything for him – including killing a person, whatever their age or sex. Take care, though: this insane war is going to be lost, and then some of the team you played football with will come looking for you, and you'll find the tackle getting very dirty indeed.'

The goat came rushing in, head down, butting the former footballer. As he fell backwards he drew a pistol, shooting the attacking animal in the head. The old woman wailed, dropping to the floor, cradling the goat's head, blood spurting into her lap. The four men roared away on motorcycles requisitioned, or rather, stolen, because Il Duce had been photographed on a motorcycle, and thunderous exhausts were intimidating in the psychological campaign of Fascism. The Führer preferred motorcades, marching boots and banners, to show the world the muscle of the Third Reich. Faustino's mounted thugs braked their machines outside the next house and burst open that door also, ransacking the rooms to the screams of children and the curses of the parents. When they rode up to the De Santis homestead they saw a young woman pinning washing to a line, her figure accentuated as she stretched up out of her *zupei*.

'What do you want?' Angela challenged them, though her heart was beating fast.

'I know what I would want from you, if we had the time,' one of them replied, winking at the others.

They went up to the house, where Benigno was repairing a stool.

'What's this?' he demanded as they clattered up the stairs to overturn the beds.

'We're looking for Augusto Faccenda.'

'He doesn't live here.'

'But he's a friend of yours,' the football teammate of the fugitive reminded him.

'Everyone in the district's a friend of mine. What do you want him for?'

The footballer sat down at the table and removed his cap, but not out of respect.

'You know why, De Santis, and if you're concealing him anywhere, it'll be the worse for you as well as him.'

'Come with me,' Benigno said boldly, leading them out of the door and into the stable. He lifted the hay for the mules and shook it out. 'There's nobody hiding under it. Look up and you'll see there's no loft. You couldn't hide an infant in here. Have you been to his house?'

'That niece of yours, she's an alien, isn't she?' the footballer asked menacingly.

'She was born in Britain to Italian parents, and she speaks perfect Italian. She's working in Signora Faustino's hotel.'

They sped away on their motorcycles, but instead of descending to Cassino they wheeled the machines among trees up at the monastery and sat with their backs to the trunks, smoking, and waiting for nightfall.

The fugitive was sitting outside the cave, his dog Jupiter beside him, watching the lights of the monastery coming on, lamps being lit in farm kitchens where families would soon be sitting down to supper, reminding him how hungry he was. Time dragged when you had nothing to do, when it was too dangerous to take exercise in daylight, in case the mountain slopes were being swept by binoculars; too dangerous also to play your flute, in case the sound carried and betrayed you. He thought about Angela, but it was too risky to visit her.

When it was still light enough to go down the mountain without the guiding beam of the lantern he descended to his grandmother's house, signalling his arrival, as arranged, by three raps. When she opened the door he saw the dead goat lying on the floor.

'I had a visit from a group of Fascist brutes, your school friends, looking for you. One of them shot my protector and friend.'

'Is there nothing these bastards won't stoop to?'

'You can't stay here; they could come back at any time,' she warned him.

'I'll bury the goat after I've had something to eat.'

There was only one bowl of polenta on the table because she knew it was too dangerous, setting out two meals.

'Hurry up,' she urged him as he was sharing his supper with his dog.

'If they're going to come we'll hear their motorbikes.'

'Don't count on it.'

'I'm sorry you've been frightened by them,' he told her, kissing her forehead.

'I'm not frightened. I'm angry that such brutes should be given the power of life and death over people. At the beginning we thought that Mussolini was a great man, a socialist who would share out the worldly goods of Italy and make life easier for us all in the country, because he was photographed helping with the harvest. Then we began to hear rumours of the beatings and the murders, and he was visited by that devil Hitler who recognized that Mussolini could help to serve his purpose in making Germany the greatest power in the world – far greater than the Russia you admire so much. Look what's he's done, taken our loved ones to fight a war which we can't win. And look what Hitler's done – made a pact with your hero Stalin, another brute.

'You know what you should do? You should turn your back on Italy and make for Switzerland. You'll take the little money that I've saved. Switzerland isn't involved in this insane war, and you can work as a mountain guide there. Go tonight: I'd rather know you were climbing a mountain in Switzerland than facing a firing squad in Italy, because that's what will happen to you when you're captured.'

'I won't be captured.'

'Oh yes you will, because this war looks as though it could go on for years. You can't live in a mountain cave for months, never mind years, like an animal, because the snows of winter will soon arrive, and it'll be too treacherous to come down here for food, even if you survive the freezing cold and the hungry wolves in your cave. Go tonight.'

'I can't.'

'Why not?'

He shrugged.

'Oh I've known for some time that you're in love, the way you've been going about, in a dream state, spending so much time at the De Santis's, and inviting Angela here. Have you told her you're in love with her?'

He shook his head.

'So you don't know if she has feelings for you? For all you know, she has a boyfriend at home in Scotland. She's a very fine, caring young woman, and you would be blessed indeed to have her as a wife. You can't hang around here because of Angela, because you're in danger, not her. Go to Switzerland and, God willing, at the end of the war you can see if you still have strong feelings for Angela. If so you can come back here and tell her, or stay in Switzerland and make a living as a mountain guide.'

He knew that she was talking sense, and for the first time in his life he was feeling depressed in his inertia. He grasped the goat's carcass by the hind legs and was about to drag it out to bury it when the door was trampled down and his footballer friend who had never made a dirty tackle put a pistol to his head.

He was hauled before Centurione Faustino.

'I could have you executed for desertion, but you're said to be a good shot, and you also have stamina from climbing mountains. So I'm going to send you to the army, with a recommendation that you be put in the front line.'

'I don't want to fight a war for the Fascists.'

'In which case I'll have you taken out and shot,' the Centurione told him. 'I've already had two men executed in the past fortnight for evading military service. But if you're dead, what's going to happen to your grandmother? Who's going to look after her?' He lifted back his black cuff to consult his watch. 'I'm going to give you three minutes to decide.'

The old woman dragged the goat outside. But she didn't have the strength to bury it, so she left the carcass for the ravens.

Chapter Fourteen

Angela was working in the garden when she saw a figure coming along the track in the uniform of the Italian army. Thinking it was Augusto, she dropped the rake and ran to meet him. It wasn't him, but one of his friends, Umberto, come to pay a call and to give them news of Augusto, once he was settled at the kitchen table with wine, with Angela leaning over eagerly to hear how Augusto was faring.

'He's sorry he can't get leave, but sends you all his love,' his friend since schooldays began.

Leave back home was granted only for marriages, to undertake university examinations, and to take part in selection for national or civil service.

'I got leave because I'm getting married. Lucia and I were going to wait until this war is over, but there's no end in sight. She wrote to me and said we should get married. I wrote back and warned her, I might be killed, and then you'll be a widow. If that's God's will, then I'll be proud to be your widow, she wrote. Ask for leave. Tell them you have a fiancée whose heart is breaking.'

'And are you married yet?' Beatrice wanted to know.

'Yesterday, in a very quiet ceremony. I have a week with my wife before I have to go back to North Africa.'

'How is Augusto?' Angela asked.

'As well as can be expected. The climate gets everyone down. It's scalding by day and bitterly cold by night in North Africa. The landscape's bare sand that seems to go on forever.' Umberto didn't tell them that one afternoon when he was collapsing through thirst he had seen a water hole and staggered towards it, but when he reached it it wasn't there, and he went down on his knees and wept.

Nor did he tell Angela, her uncle and aunt that many Italians had been killed, showing how dangerous the alliance with Germany was proving to be. He kept to himself how, after Italian soldiers were buried, the wind blew the sand off their unstable graves, and they lay staring at the sky like men in deep contemplation until the next wind covered them over again. Some of the corpses were boys who had started on the route to premature deaths with wooden rifles in Fascist youth battalions.

'Augusto asked me to bring him news of his grandmother.'

'She's still mourning Stefano the goat's murder, as she calls it,' Beatrice told the caller. 'Benigno and Angela harvested her olives for her, and he took them down to Cassino to sell. Angela helps her with the animals. She visits her almost every day, and stays with her some nights.'

'You can tell Augusto that Centurione Faustino, who hounded him into the army in the first place, sends one of his men up with a little food from time to time to the old woman, so he must have a heart under that black uniform,' Benigno told the returned soldier. 'Well, are we going to win this insane war?'

'I was told yesterday in Cassino that the Italian Navy had been badly hit by British planes,' Umberto reported. 'But the people I spoke to didn't blame Mussolini. They blame the war, as if it was started by someone else.' He rose from the table. 'Thank you for the wine. I must go and see Augusto's grandmother. I'll take back to him your love and blessings.'

Angela walked some of the way with him, to try to get more news of Augusto.

'He keeps on talking about you. He admires you very much,' Umberto disclosed as they parted.

The sudden gust blew the tent flap aside and sand formed a film on the stump of the newly amputated leg of the soldier lying on the operating table. The surgeon looked over his mask towards his assistant, Lieutenant Dr Christopher Murchison, who handed the severed limb to an assistant before attempting to remove the sand from the stump. The Lieutenant was weary, having assisted in dozens of operations, some of them unsuccessful because of the horrific wounds inflicted by Rommel's shells. The soldier was lifted from the table and replaced with another, his brain exposed. This was going to be a long and dangerous operation, but the doctor cared that these soldiers should survive, and somehow be returned to their families. That was why he concentrated on the complicated surgery, sustained by his love of Angela.

That Christmas of 1940 Rosa Boni didn't know where she was going to get the money to buy presents for her children. She knew that even if she had the funds to open the café again, another brick would come through the window, and the contents would be looted. To make ends meet she was cleaning and cooking for the Macfarlanes, an elderly couple in the west end of the city, leaving her sixteen year old son Tony, who was still at school, to look after his siblings, Armando aged fourteen, and Maria, newly eleven, in the flat above the shut café when they came home from school and while she was at work.

'One of the girls in my class said that Italians are dirty because they eat worms,' Maria told her mother one evening.

'I know what she meant, because I've had the same,' Armando disclosed. 'It's because we like spaghetti.'

Tony was silent. He appreciated that his mother had sufficient worries already, so he didn't tell her that he had been called a 'fucking Tally' by the school bully. Tony had advised him to take back the insult, and when the bully wouldn't, he had thrashed him. After that, some of his schoolmates had not treated him so badly, as they would have liked to have done the thrashing themselves. One of them had even said that he was sorry for being nasty to Tony. But others still looked on him as an enemy. He had applied for a permit so that he could ride his bicycle to school, and one afternoon when he came to collect it from the shed, found that somebody had slashed his tyres.

Dr Macfarlane was retired from his medical practice in the city and spent most of his day in his study, listening to the war news on the wireless because he had served abroad as an army doctor in the Great War. One evening at Ypres a long line of soldiers had stood outside the medical tent in the incessant rain, waiting for his attention. They had bandages round their eyes after a gas attack. The doctor had known they would never see again, but they stood patiently, a hand resting on the shoulder of the man in front, like a game of blind man's bluff that had come to a halt. After that the wounds inflicted by razors and bicycle chains which he had seen in his career as a police surgeon after a gang brawl in Glasgow were like scratches compared to the damage done by shells – if the victim was unfortunate enough to survive.

As she dusted the doctor's study, with the skeleton hanging in a corner appearing to be leering at her with its pronounced molars, Rosa talked to Dr Macfarlane about her daughter stranded in Italy, and the loss of her husband on the *Arandora Star*.

'That was a terrible thing to do, sending those defenceless men across the ocean in a liner that was a sitting target for a U-boat,' the doctor said sadly. 'We were pleased enough to have these Italians and Germans working for us, contributing to the economy, but as soon as war broke out they became aliens. Have you informed your daughter in Italy about the loss of her father?'

'No I haven't. A letter wouldn't get to her because of the war and besides, it would upset her too much. And I can't write to my sister to tell her. She lives at a place called Cassino. Have you heard of the monastery of Montecassino?'

'I have, but I've never been there. They say it's a very beautiful building, full of treasures. I'm sure your daughter's going to be safe, Rosa. From what you tell me she's a very level-headed young woman, and she has your family out there.'

Mrs Macfarlane was very fussy about her house, and even after Rosa had polished the furniture, she would draw a finger over it, particularly her rosewood grand piano which was her pride and joy, and which she played for an hour each evening after supper, mostly Chopin, while her husband listened to his wireless. She was also particular about food, and was always complaining about the shortages the war was causing.

'I can't get my favourite brand of coffee from Coopers,' she lamented to Rosa. 'They say that the U-boats are preventing supplies getting to us, but I think they're arriving all right, and that the coffee's being drunk by all those people in London who're working for the War Office.'

Mrs Macfarlane had had a man dig up her back garden, and had planted winter vegetables which Rosa had to scrub and cook. Rosa had to queue for a small portion of meat from the butcher for lunch and supper for the elderly couple. The Macfarlanes appreciated that she had children to attend to, and always asked after them, sometimes sending them small sums of money. At six o' clock they had the supper she cooked for them, and after she had washed up the dishes she had to walk through the blacked-out streets half of a mile to home. She thought sadly of how it might have been, if there hadn't been a war and her husband had lived.

Some nights she turned into St Peter's, kneeling in front of the Blessed Mother's statue to pray for Angela's safety and happiness, and asking that the war be over soon, though life could never return to the way it had been, with Joe gone.

Mrs Macfarlane gave Rosa two pounds for Christmas, so she was able to buy her children modest presents, and to have a chicken for dinner. Though the family sat in their paper hats, trying to be cheerful over their meal, there were the two empty chairs. Rosa didn't think she would ever get over her spouse's death. She was beginning to wonder if God wasn't listening to her, perhaps because there were too many people to listen to in this awful war, with the casualties rising every day until, as Dr Macfarlane said, they would be higher than the Great War, in which millions had been slaughtered.

Rosa continued to go to the Macfarlanes, passing shops with sandbags in the doorways, adhesive tape criss-crossing the window panes, because there had already been enemy action over the city, with buildings damaged and some people killed. The family café was boarded up, and she was going to have to find a buyer soon, though what was a wrecked business worth in wartime?

Rosa had agreed to work late at the Macfarlanes on a day in the middle of March 1941, because they were expecting relatives to stay. Bedrooms had to be made ready, vegetables dug from the garden and prepared. She was washing the supper dishes when the plates began to vibrate on their rack on the draining board. She turned to the kitchen clock and saw that it was ten, time to head for home. As she was taking off her apron the first explosions shook the Macfarlanes' house, terrifying her.

The German bombers from Denmark had been guided to Glasgow by the full moon shining on Loch Lomond, and once they picked up the silver ribbon of the River Clyde they followed it up to the shipyards. Mrs Macfarlane heard the sirens above the Chopin serenade she was playing on the grand piano in the drawing room, and came rushing through, shouting that the city was under attack, and that they were going to be killed. The doctor was calm as he came through from listening to his wireless.

'We'll go down into the basement,' he advised the two women.

'I have to get home to my children,' Rosa told them in panic.

However, she saw the elderly couple safely down to the basement, making sure they had bedding, with food and drink to last the night, and then she went out. The sky, usually blacked out, was lit by the fires already burning on the river side. The trams didn't seem to be running. As she ran she heard the whistle of a bomb and thought that it was coming towards her, but it hit a street down at Clydebank.

She met a policeman who advised her to take shelter, but she told him that her children were alone, and ran on. She could see herself clawing at the rubble of the building to get at her children, and it flashed through her mind that Angela was safer in Italy than in this hellish city, with the sky illuminated as if it were day. She stumbled up her stairs and into the flat. The children hadn't gone to bed, but were sitting in a circle on the floor round Tony as he told them a story which she had told him as a small boy and which he was recounting to his siblings to calm them in the distant rumble of detonations from the German raid.

Rosa stood outside the open door, listening to her son telling in Italian how Rocco, a fourteenth century French-born boy of noble birth, had shown great devotion to God, but had been left an orphan. Rosa had sat on her mother's knee in their home close to Montecassino, listening to the same legend.

'Rocco gave away his fortune to the poor and became a pilgrim, travelling in Italy which was in the grip of the plague.'

'What's the plague?' Maria, the youngest, wanted to know.

'A terrible disease that killed millions of people.'

'Could I catch it?' Maria asked anxiously.

Her mother had to put her hand to her mouth to suppress a laugh as Tony explained that the scourge had died out centuries before.

'Everywhere Rocco visited, the plague disappeared through the miraculous powers given to him by God. Then he himself caught the plague. People saw the open sore on his leg, and even though he had cured so many of the plague, he was banished from the city. He slept on leaves and drank water from a small stream. And then a miracle happened. A dog that refused to eat brought the sick Rocco bread, to keep him alive.'

'I want a dog,' Maria said with determination; then, spying her mother, ran to greet her.

Next day when Rosa went to work for the Macfarlanes horrific stories of the Clydeside Blitz were being recounted on the tram. Entire streets in Clydebank had collapsed, burying the occupants. People were going about with the possessions they had salvaged piled on prams, like the refugees after the Germans had attacked Poland. Dogs whose owners had been killed were roaming in packs and had to be shot.

The Macfarlanes had come up from their basement. The doctor went out to his club and brought back more heartbreaking stories of mortally wounded people lying in the corridors of the city's infirmaries, too many to be treated with such shortages of blood and morphine.

'And I thought the last war was bad,' Dr MacFarlane said, shaking his head. That evening he called Rosa into his study.

'Listen to this,' he said, turning up his wireless.

'Germany calling, Germany calling,' the sneering English voice announced. 'Last night the shipyards on the river Clyde in Glasgow were almost totally destroyed in a bombing raid.'

'That's a man they call Lord Haw-Haw,' Dr Macfarlane explained. 'He's a traitor who lives in Germany and broadcasts propaganda to frighten people. The shipyards weren't destroyed. In fact, comparatively little damage was done to them, though a lot of people were killed in Clydebank.'

That night the bombers took advantage of the bright moon to return, but this time Rosa walked slowly home. When she opened the door of the flat Tony was continuing the story of Rocco, with his brother and sister sitting, listening intently.

'The dog used to leave a nearby castle with bread in its mouth, and its curious owner, a nobleman, followed it to the cave and saw the dog standing by the weak Rocco to let him take the bread out of its mouth. The nobleman took pity on Rocco and brought him to his castle, where he was looked after until he was cured.'

'What happened to the dog?' Maria asked anxiously.

'It was loved by everyone for saving Rocco's life. When Rocco died a voice from above said that he was such a good man, he was in Heaven. He's one of the Saints of the Catholic Church.'

'Was the dog made a Saint?' Maria persisted.

'No, because only people can become Saints, though you should remember the dog in your prayers for its kindness to Rocco,' Rosa explained, hugging her small daughter.

'Could I become a Saint, Mama?' the child asked.

'You never know, if you grow up to be a very good person who helps others.'

Entire families had been lost under the rubble of Clydebank, and mothers had fled up into the hills, breastfeeding their infants under the stars, like the tribes who had inhabited Strathclyde in ancient times. For days afterwards Rosa could taste the dust of the bombed tenements in the oppressive atmosphere of the stunned city.

Chapter Fifteen

Easter, the greatest feast day in the Catholic Church, was celebrated in Montecassino in 1942 with a Mass, the scent of the incense, combined with her uncle's organ music, making Angela light-headed with ecstasy. Now it was May, feast day of the Madonna Della Rocca. Her statue was in the ruined castle above Cassino, constructed in the ninth century as an outer defence for the monastery above. As Angela, her uncle and aunt went down the winding road from the monastery they saw the glow from the castle of hundreds of lights in honour of the Madonna. They joined the procession up to the castle where Mass was said, and Angela knelt by the statuette to pray for the safe return of Augusto from the furnace of North Africa.

At twenty-five she was an even more beautiful woman, her figure filled out, her Italian indistinguishable in its fluency from the local dialect. When her aunt made cheese from the goats' milk it was her niece's chore to trade it for maize at a farm near to Cassino. She took the little food there was to spare along to Augusto's grandmother, because the occasional loaf or little polenta from Centurione Faustino had more or less stopped.

'Have you had any word from Augusto?' Angela asked.

'Nothing. I don't know if he's alive or dead. We're told that the Italians are having great victories in North Africa, yet it's a different story on the wireless from abroad, my neighbour says. He tells me that the other side is winning.

Why don't we surrender if we're doing so badly? Where's the shame in that, I ask you? It would save so many young lives.'

'Augusto will be safe,' Angela tried to reassure the old woman.

'All I can do is to pray that he'll be sent back to us both. He's in love with you.'

Angela blushed at this revelation.

'Oh yes, I know these things. I'm sure he's thinking about you, wherever he is. I pray for you both, that'll you'll both survive the war and marry – if it's God's will.'

Angela was deeply pensive as she went back to her aunt and uncle's. So that accounted for the surreptitious glances he had been giving her since she had first arrived?

The Fascist official who banged on the door of Augusto's grandmother's house had a briefcase with him, and at first she thought that he had come with bad news about her grandson. But he was looking at her hands.

'Your wedding ring,' he said peremptorily.

'What about my wedding ring?'

'It's required for the war effort.'

'Are they going to start making guns out of gold?' she asked sceptically.

'It'll raise money to equip our soldiers.'

The ring, slipped on to her finger by her husband over fifty years before, was beginning to sink into her flesh, as the memories of the man she had loved and lost in war were embedded in the heart of this loyal devout woman who venerated the dead and loved the living.

'I can't give you this,' she told the official.

'So you're not interested in helping your country?'

'I've helped my country for long enough,' she answered indignantly. 'My husband gave his life for Italy, and so did one of my sons in the same war. God knows, my grandson may already have given his, and my daughter-in-law, Augusto's mother, died of a broken heart as well as influenza at the death in battle of her husband.'

The official undid the buckles of his briefcase and handed her a steel ring.

'This will replace it.'

'Nothing will replace my wedding ring. If you want it, you'll have to cut off my finger;' and she held out a steady hand.

The official left, muttering about 'unpatriotic people,' but by the time he returned to Cassino there were only two gold rings in his briefcase.

From Angela's Journal for Wednesday 19 August 1942:

> *Rationing has been introduced, and last night Aunt was lamenting the lack of salt to me as she made a pot of broth from the bones of a mountain hare shot by Uncle. Tonight when we came down from the monastery after Compline Uncle lifted*

some of the small portion of pasta from his supper plate and transferred it to mine. 'You're a young woman and need to eat,' he told me. I keep praying for Augusto, asking his guardian angel to take care of him.

From Angela's Journal for Monday 24 August 1942:

When I came home from the hotel in Cassino last night I saw Uncle spreading a net on the grass. I asked him what it was for. 'To trap birds.' But why? I wanted to know. 'My father trapped them to sell them.' Alive? I asked. He explained that some of them were, to sell as songbirds in cages. Others were eaten. Thrushes were particular delicacies. He needed to catch them because we're short of food and money, and he can sell some of them in Cassino. 'But you love birds,' I reminded him desperately, and I added: 'So do I. I love to be wakened by their singing.' His weary answer was: 'I know, but we have to eat.' He asked me to hold the poles so he could get the net up. I couldn't sleep last night for thinking about wee terrified birds struggling in the mesh, and I prayed that they would evade it when they started flying in the dawn. I have just *been outside and the net is empty! Now I need to go up to the basilica, to thank God for this deliverance.*

From Angela's Journal for Wednesday 2 September 1942:

Autumn is here in a burst of colour. I try to make my contribution to the food shortages by going out in the early morning with a pail to pick fruit from the bushes. But the little lanes, always deserted in the past, are now crowded even at that early hour with families who came up from Cassino in the dawn to supplement their meagre fare with fruit. The children fight as they pick, elbowing me out of the way, a small swift hand helping itself to the contents of the pail on the crook of my arm. But there's enough in the pail for me to make a tart for supper, rolling out the precious dough in the shortages of a war which now seems as if it could be prolonged for years. I helped Uncle to spread sheets under the olive trees before he shook the trunks to bring down the harvest, the same Fascist official who had appropriated the cheeses and part of the harvest standing by. He returned to watch the golden oil oozing from the press before having most of the containers loaded on a lorry.

Sleep, when it could be snatched, was full of an endless expanse of sand, and when he was awake his eyes, nose and mouth were full of the same abrasive substance. When a shell landed it sent up a fountain of sand, obscuring the relentless sun. Augusto Faccenda had helped the German and Italian forces to capture Tobruk, and he was with them when they reached El Alamein and attacked the Allied defences.

But that had been in the summer of 1942, as if anyone were counting the days, weeks, and even years now. It was November, and the ferocious assault by the Allies was threatening to break the enemy lines at El Alamein. Everything was in disarray in this shifting landscape. The nights were freezing, and before snatching sleep Augusto's numb fingers slipped from its little leather purse the mother-of-pearl rosary which his grandmother had given him as a talisman. He tried to move his lips to say his prayers, the first time since childhood, but sand sealed them, as though he were already a dead man. He had in his wallet a photograph of Angela hugging the mules, taken before the world seemed to fall apart. But the wind snatched the image, precious as a religious relic, from his freezing fingers and when he rose to chase after it a hand on his shoulder restrained him.

'There are snipers about.'

He lay down again, trying to close his sand-filled eyes, cursing Mussolini and Hitler, because the German dictator had started the war that had engulfed so much of the world, and Mussolini had followed him into battle, for personal aggrandizement and territorial spoils. Augusto hoped fervently that Hitler's invasion of Russia would prove to be as disastrous as Napoleon's had been. But so little news of great events filtered down to the soldiers sprawled in the sand of North Africa. Besides, how was one to separate truth from propaganda?

These topics were too dangerous for Augusto to discuss with his compatriots lying beside him, though he hadn't heard much enthusiastic support for Mussolini. Men were more concerned with their loved ones than national pride. Weeping was the only thing that soothed his eyes, washing out the grit. He wasn't weeping out of pity for himself, but for the engulfed world, and as he wept the photograph of the woman to whom he hadn't had the courage to openly profess his love was carried by the wind across to the British lines, to be blown against the side of a tank and in the dawn found by one of the crew, who put it into the pocket of his battledress before climbing into the killing machine.

Augusto never felt the shell splinter that struck his head.

On an evening in early May 1943 Benigno came up from the town with the momentous news that German and Italian forces in North Africa had surrendered.

'Thank God!' Beatrice exclaimed, sinking to her knees and crossing herself. 'I thought it was never going to end. That means that Augusto will be home soon.'

'He may not,' her husband cautioned. 'One of my friends heard on his wireless that the British and their Allies have captured several hundred thousand German and Italian soldiers and are likely to put them into prisoner of war camps.'

Angela hurried along to tell Augusto's grandmother the good news. She found a neighbour sitting by the old woman's bedside.

'I've sent for the priest. I found her lying behind the door this morning. My husband carried her to her bed. I think she's had a stroke.'

'I'll fetch the doctor from Cassino,' Angela said.

But the old woman raised the arm that wasn't paralyzed to signal that she shouldn't bother. The stroke had deprived her of speech, but she had nothing to say to the two women in the shaded room with her. She pointed to Jupiter, her grandson's dog sitting, looking sad, by her bed, and the neighbour nodded, indicating that she would take him.

'Augusto will be home soon to look after you,' Angela assured her.

But either the figure on the bed didn't hear, or didn't have the strength to linger on in the hope that her grandson would return. She had been born with few expectations into the poverty of a smallholding, and all that had sustained her in an arduous life was her faith. She had raised animals which she had come to love, only to have to slaughter them in order to feed her family, and she had lost a husband and a son to war. But she had a gift which she had never spoken about.

She knew who was going to call at her door even before that unexpected person had set out, and she had observed passing her house the funeral of a man she could see in the distance harvesting his olives, and who waved to her. Many nights she sat by her fire, trying to see across an immense distance, to determine if her grandson were still alive with the Italian army in a land of endless sand and beasts with humps on their backs ridden by men in flowing robes who looked like spectres, where, only a few kilometres away, a gun was sending a thunderous shell a mile in a matter of seconds. But the old woman's paranormal gift couldn't be induced, and so the fate of her grandson was hidden from her.

The previous week she had seen a funeral wending its way along the track to the burial ground. She had seen the corteges of neighbours in the past, the coffin being carried on the shoulders of black-garbed men, but this time she knew that it was herself in the rough box in her vision.

She signalled to Angela to come close, taking the young woman's right hand in hers. As she held it she looked into Angela's eyes. Was she trying to transmit that she approved of her as a wife for Augusto?

In the balmy evening in July 1943 the shepherd boy was watching the sky darkening as if Mount Etna was erupting, shooting ash towards the sun. But it was a cascade of parachutes as over 3,000 American airborne troops drifted down. The boy could see the soles of the boots of one as he descended, scattering the flock of sheep, one going over the ridge in its terror. The paratrooper was reaching into a pocket, and the boy thought that his young life was going to be ended by a pistol shot on the darkening slope on Sicily, but the warrior from the sky produced a packet of chewing gum, put a portion into his mouth and handed the rest to the boy. They were soon chewing together. Five minutes later he was gone, leaving behind his parachute, as a moth sheds its casing. The boy bundled it up and ran home with it, and three years later his sister would be married in the pale billowing silk.

The statistics were terrifying. Around 140 gliders had taken off from North Africa, but half of them fell into the sea, drowning their passengers. Over 2,500 ships carrying 600 tanks and 14,000 mechanized vehicles approached Sicily which had variously been under the rule of Greeks, Carthaginians, Romans and Normans. Furthermore, 180,000 Allied troops and over 4,000 aircraft were deployed to drive the Axis forces out of Sicily, the island held sacred to Demeter, goddess of earth's fruits which the shells and bombs of the invaders would ripen prematurely.

Garibaldi had landed in Sicily in 1860, and had been able to expel the Bourbon King of Naples from Southern Italy, though his 2,000 poorly equipped volunteers were paltry compared to the aerial invasion of the American paratroopers.

Chapter Sixteen

From the raised dais covered with red brocade Mussolini was addressing the Grand Council in the Room of the Parrot in the Palazzo Venezia in July 1943, reviewing the major errors of the war: Alamein; Rommel's miscalculations in North Africa; Tripoli; the loss of the island of Pantelleria; and now, the humiliation in Sicily; troops fleeing to their homes; units routed throughout the island; anti-Fascist sentiments among the people.

'And what does the General Staff forecast for the immediate future? Perhaps an enemy attack on Sardinia where there are 160,000 men, or in the Dodecanese and other Mediterranean islands, in order to prepare, not for a landing on our peninsula, which is thought improbable, but a long-range manoeuvre either in France or the Balkans.'

Mussolini spoke for almost two hours, praising the generosity of German aid to Italy and scorning his critics. He refuted the accusation that 'the people's heart is not in the war' by arguing that the people's heart had never been in any war, and that such 'psychological fluctuations' were to be expected. The most perceptive analysis in his speech was his admission that 'at this moment I am certainly the most disliked, or, rather, loathed man in Italy.'

Count Dino Grandi, chairman of the Grand Council of Fascism, rose to put his motion. Did he have two hand grenades in his pocket to defend himself, or perhaps even to assassinate Mussolini as he argued that the dictatorship and not the army was responsible for the disaster Italy found itself in? The people had been betrayed from the day that Italy's destiny had been thrown in with Germany's. The Count called for the restoration of all the organs of state and the transfer of the command of the armed forces to King Victor Emmanuel III.

Mussolini's supporters lost the motion, and the King demanded his resignation. When he left the royal audience he was confronted by two carabinieri officers and was told by one of them: 'His Majesty has charged me with the protection of your person.' The dictator was driven in an ambulance to carabinieri barracks.

From Angela's Journal for Tuesday 27 July 1943:

As I went into the hotel this morning to begin my shift, I met Signora Faustino stamping up and down in front of the reception desk, shouting: 'A traitor, that's what he is!' I asked her what had happened. 'The King's a traitor. He's ordered the arrest of Mussolini.' The news had already reached Uncle and Aunt when I came home this evening. Aunt has made a big pot of polenta, and neighbours have come, some of them with wine they have been hoarding for good news. 'Augusto will be home soon,' Uncle predicted. I sang 'The Road to the Isles' while the schoolmaster beat on the table with his spoon. Before the food was served the schoolmaster said grace, and I shall remember his moving words. 'There are young people who were here with us at happy gatherings before this terrible war which we could never win. Some of them, including my own son, are lying dead in graves in North Africa where I can't visit him. Let's say a prayer for them before we continue with the celebrations.'

Uncle went round pouring more wine as I sang love songs by Robert Burns, and the accordion played for dancing, zupei clattering on the flagstones as if the war has only been an inconvenient interruption and not a prolonged national disaster. Perhaps it will be over soon, with the British and Americans having landed in Sicily a fortnight ago. But they have bombed the airfield at Aquino, a few miles away from us. There are German soldiers in Cassino, with several of the officers lodging in the hotel. They are arrogant, as if Italy is now a colony of Germany, and we are all their slaves.

Up in the monastery Dom Pietro Contadino was sitting with Abbot Diamare.

'This is a terrible war,' the old man lamented, 'with so many people suffering and in despair, not only in Italy, but across Europe. That's why we must all pray as much as we can. Only prayer can stop this war, since Hitler won't listen to reason because, now that he's launched this catastrophe, he can't retreat without losing face. The dictators have their positions in history to consider, because they want to be remembered as victors. Hitler is even more dangerous after his disastrous invasion of Russia. I want you to arrange for the Brothers to meet me this afternoon so that we can talk about the latest situation. How is your niece, Dom Pietro?'

'I saw her on Sunday after Mass, Abbot. She's very worried, like we all are, but she's very brave.'

'It's a pity she wasn't able to get home to Scotland before the fighting started.'

'I don't think she regrets having to stay here, Abbot.'

Dom Pietro shared the Abbot's pessimism. His dreams continued to be disturbed, and he knew that he wasn't giving of his best when tutoring Angela for her doctorate on Dante. It seemed to him that the traumas of shells exploding in other countries were being felt in the monastery, destabilizing the foundations of his faith. Wasn't the Abbot being too optimistic about the power of prayer, against such destructive guns and killer submarines? Couldn't God bring about peace, or was He leaving the armies to battle it out, to teach the world a lesson? But surely there had been a terrible lesson in the Great War which had ended only twenty five years before, and in which the monk had lost a brother? It was man, not an uncaring God, who was responsible for these slaughters, since man had free will.

From Angela's Journal for Thursday 9 September 1943:

When I went down to the hotel this morning the front door was locked. The bell was answered by the cook, who let me in. 'There's been a terrible tragedy, signorina,' she wept into her apron. Evidently Signora Faustino was listening to the wireless when it was announced that Italy has surrendered unconditionally. She unlocked the cupboard in which her husband keeps his guns and shot herself through the mouth with a pistol because she couldn't bear the shame. Her husband the Centurione was in his Fascist uniform as he sat in the reception room, phoning for an undertaker. The suicide of his spouse has shaken his adulation of Mussolini. His wife boasted to me that they believed Il Duce was going to lead Italy to glory with the tanks and battleships that D'Annunzio praises in his writings. No doubt the Centurione believed that he would get a share of the spoils of victory. But now his world is falling into ruins, with Mussolini deposed and his wife dead by her own hand. 'We'll close the hotel, but I need you to stay on and sort out the paperwork,' he told me.

Great celebrations tonight on the news of Italy's surrender. Uncle did his famous clown's dance. If only Augusto were here!

From Angela's Journal for Friday 10 September 1943:

The schoolmaster came last night with the news that the British and Americans have landed at Salerno, south of Naples. Today I was going through papers at the reception desk in the hotel when I heard a droning sound. I went out on to the street and watched as planes appeared over the mountains, a sight which chilled me because of their size and the noise they made. A man standing beside me said that their wing markings were American. As they began to drop bombs on the outskirts of the town, people were running about, screaming. The hotel wasn't a safe place, so I closed the door and ran through the dust and noise. Instead of going to Uncle and Aunt's I went into the basilica to pray for the terrified people of Cassino.

People spent the rest of that disastrous day searching the rubble for family members. When they uncovered the corpses, or the heaviness of the broken masonry they were trying to shift showed that rescue was hopeless, they salvaged what possessions they could, including food, piling them in prams. Some of them travelled north to other parts of Italy; others journeyed south, braving crossing the Allied lines and being interrogated as spies. Many used intact doors as stretchers for the sick and wounded, before heading for the steep winding road up to the monastery because the cable car had been knocked out of action after a German plane had earlier become entangled in its wire. At the gate marked PAX a monk was arguing with the growing mass of refugees.

'There's nothing left of my house, and my little girl is dead!' one woman was wailing. 'We never had a chance. The planes came over as we were rising, preparing to face another day of fear and uncertainty, and many elderly and infirm people must have been killed in their beds. I beg you, let us into the monastery for shelter. We've nowhere else to go, and surely God will make one of His many houses available to us. They won't dare bomb the monastery.'

News of the disturbance at the gates was brought to the Abbot, who was conferring in his office with Dom Pietro.

'How many are there?' the Abbot enquired of the bearer of the news.

'Hundreds, with more arriving every minute.'

'Go and arrange to let these poor people in,' the old man instructed Dom Pietro wearily. 'It's fundamental to our founder's rule that we give shelter to the poor and needy.'

'But where shall we put them?' the monk needed to know.

'Where you can find space.'

The guest in the ski lodge in the Apennine Mountains had no desire to descend to the world again on the funicular railway. He had enjoyed the height of power, but now it was time to retire, to devote himself to his mistress and his horses. Perhaps he should write his memoirs, though he would rather that they ended in victory. The deposed Duce let his coffee grow cold as he contemplated ravens drifting with the thermals. He was telling himself on that peaceful September morning three days after the Salerno landings that he wanted freedom from his responsibilities and the severe strain of conducting a war. But the ravens turned into gliders in the sky, and when paratroopers swept in, he hailed them with renewed fighting spirit: 'I knew that my friend Adolf Hitler would not desert me.' Now he would deal with those little men who were unworthy of Italy's destiny.

From Angela's Journal for Monday 13 September 1943:

The schoolmaster, who seems to spend all of his spare time listening to the wireless, came last night with the news that Mussolini had been rescued by the Germans. After we got over our anger we felt despair, because this could prolong the war. After the bearer of such bad news left us, we were sitting talking when there was a knock on the door which I answered. Augusto was standing there, with a filthy bandage round his head. I hugged him, and he put his arms round me, but his embrace seemed half-hearted. When I took his hand into the light we saw that his army uniform was in tatters. When he took off his boots from his bare feet and I saw the blisters I began to cry, and couldn't be comforted by Aunt. When Augusto was settled at the table with a plate of polenta and a glass of wine he told us about his head wound. 'If I hadn't had my helmet on the shell splinter would have killed me, rather than concussed me. I don't remember being evacuated to a hospital in Italy.' Uncle said that no one knew he was in hospital. 'The Fascists aren't as efficient as they say they are,' Augusto told us. He was sitting by his bed in the hospital when word came through that Italy had surrendered. 'I didn't say anything. I took the money I had in my locker and decided to clear out. How is my grandmother?' The suddenness of the question took the three of us by surprise, and I appealed to Uncle. He told Augusto that she had passed away. 'There was no way of getting the news to you. Anyway, what good would it have done?' Augusto pushed his plate of polenta away. 'What did she die of?' he asked, his voice trembling on the verge of tears. It was Aunt who answered, telling him: 'She was old and weary. The war got her down." He seemed to be losing his voice as he whispered: 'I couldn't get leave to be with her. Did the Fascist bastards harass her?' Aunt told him how they had come looking for gold wedding rings for the war effort, but Augusto didn't seem to be listening. 'I'm going to have to settle the score,' he said, his voice increasing. 'That's not what the old woman would want,' I told him. I shouldn't have spoken because he turned on me: 'How do you know what she would want? You hardly knew her. She was like a mother to me, the last close relative I had. They'll pay for this,' he vowed, getting to his feet. Aunt pled with him to stay for the night. He said that he had to go and check the house, besides, there were German soldiers about. He was going to have to hide.

You can hide here,' Uncle offered. 'No, it's too dangerous for you,' Augusto said. 'I'll go back up to my cave on the mountain.' Aunt said that he couldn't go without meeting a friend. She went out and when she came back she had Jupiter the dog with her. The animal barked in ecstasy, his paws up on his master's shoulders, washing his face with his long *tongue. It seemed to me that he gave the dog a more loving welcome than he had given to me. Or is that the sin of pride? He had other matters on his mind than me. He was foremost in my prayers as I knelt by my bed tonight.*

Augusto went home without a light because he had been walking that track since he was a child. The door of the house was open, and when he saw his grandmother's bed, still rumpled from when her body had been lifted from it, he sat on it and stuffed the blanket in his mouth to stifle his anguish. He opened the food cupboard and saw a small bowl of dried-up olives, but shut the door again as if the cupboard were a tabernacle containing the Host. He went through to the other room and found his bed made up. He lay down on it after his exhausted walk of many miles, Jupiter stretched on the floor beside him, but he knew that he would have to rise in the small hours and climb up to the cave on Monte Cairo, before the German soldiers were on the move.

As he ascended he thought that the sun rising in the mist was causing the same kind of mirage he had experienced in the desert. It seemed to him that Cassino was crumbling, but when he stopped to scrutinize the town he saw that its suburbs had been bombed, its walls jagged, familiar buildings gone.

Angela didn't sleep that night. She lay, confused and anxious, as if a different man had come back from the war, a man with eyes which had lost their intensity. She could appreciate what he had been through, and that it would take time for him to try to forget those violent days in the desert. He wasn't going to get the time because with the Italian surrender the country's soldiers were no longer the allies, but the enemies of the Germans. What disturbed her and made her lie awake was his determination to avenge the death of his grandmother, because he was convinced that it was the Fascists who had killed her. God knows what he was going to do, but it was bound to be very dangerous to himself and others.

She needed to speak with him and rose in the dawn, walking to his grandmother's house, but he had already gone. She sat on his bed, wishing she were back in Glasgow, with her parents and her siblings. But though the Italians were out of the war, it was still raging in Europe, and there was no way home for her.

'We need to leave Augusto alone at present, until he works the anger out of his soul,' Benigno advised his wife and niece.

'But he's talking about taking revenge,' Angela pointed out.

'Against the Germans?'

'No, against the Fascists, who took Italy into the war in the first place.'

Angela went up to the monastery, to confession, telling the priest on the other side of the latticed screen that she was frightened that the Fascists would harm Augusto. She was beginning to have strong feelings for him, worried about his physical frailty after the hardships of North Africa, and moved by his grief for his dead grandmother.

Chapter Seventeen

Benigno shot more hares to exchange for salt, but on 10 October, the night before he intended to go down to the black marketeer, more Allied bombers arrived over Cassino, bringing down the roof on the trader's calculating head, and by that evening, when the dust had settled, children had looted his entire stock, and rats had begun to share out the marketeer's corpse.

The majority of civilian refugees from the damaged and destroyed houses from the air raid of the previous month had been evacuated from the monastery to outlying villages, but there were still around 150 in the building, which they used as an alternative place of safety to the caves they were also occupying on the surrounding mountains. The Abbot had put Dom Pietro Contadino in charge of looking after the refugees. It was a large responsibility for the monk, but he fortified his exhausting duties with frequent prayers on his knees in the basilica and therapeutic sessions on the organ, since Bach cleansed the soul and restored one's faith in an optimistic future.

On 13 October Italy declared war on Germany, and from his vantage point at the cave on Monte Cairo Augusto deduced from the line of chanting people, preceded by an accordionist, in the countryside below, that something momentous had happened. That night, when he descended to his house, he found a note from Angela on his bed, informing him that Italy was at war with Germany, and there would be celebrations tonight at the De Santis house.

From Angela's Journal for Wednesday 13 October 1943:

The kitchen was crowded with neighbours drinking and singing. I was asked for a love song by Burns, but I excused myself and sat watching the door, hoping - no, willing - Augusto to come. When he opened the door I ran to greet him and led him outside, into the moonlight. 'Isn't it wonderful news?' I enthused as I hugged him. I was waiting for him to kiss me, but instead he spoke. 'It's dangerous news. The Germans aren't going to quit Italy just because we've officially become their enemies. They regarded us as that when we surrendered to the British and Americans, and they're going to build up their numbers to stop the Allies from getting to Rome.' I pointed out: 'But at least the local Fascists won't betray you.' He said that the Germans are far more dangerous than thugs like Faustino, because they regard Italians as traitors to the German-Italian pact. 'We're going to have to organize resistance.' I told him that that would be very dangerous, and I blurted out with passion: 'I don't want you killed.' His response was: 'But you want

Italy liberated, as all of us do.' He turned to the lighted windows of the house, where Uncle was performing his famous clown's dance. 'They've got something to celebrate tonight, but tomorrow could be very different.'

I pled with him: 'For God's sake Augusto, don't do anything foolish!' Why is it, when I express my feelings for him so strongly, he answers like a politician? 'War is foolish, Angela, but it's got to be won.' I reminded him that he was once a pacifist. 'That was before a gun was put to my head by one of my friends and I was sent to fight. It's different now: they taught me to kill.' I spoke to myself: Why can't you tell me what your grandmother told me, that you love me? Why are you out for revenge, endangering your life?

There would be resistance fighters down in Cassino, but Augusto couldn't trust anyone any more, and had to act by himself. He had his hunting rifle up in the cave with him, and shot game to feed Jupiter and himself, and when he ran out of ammunition he went down into Cassino under cover of darkness, to the gunsmith's store where he had purchased ammunition in the past. He broke the hasp of the lock and stuffed as many boxes as would go into his army haversack before going back up to the cave.

In his headquarters at Frascati Field Marshal Kesselring was briefing his senior commanders.

'This is the map of the defences of the part of the country under my command which my staff have drawn up,' "Smiling Albert" explained, his finger moving as he spoke. 'The enemy has crossed the Volturno River, breaching our defensive line there, so I've ordered our troops to retreat to the Barbara Line on the Tyrrhenian Sea side of the Apennine Mountains. But we can't be complacent, so a much stronger line, the Bernhardt Line, forty miles north of Naples, is being fortified, and in the unlikely event that the enemy succeed in breaking through the Barbara and Bernhardt lines, they'll encounter another, more formidable line, called the Gustav, along the Garigliano and Rapido rivers and anchored on the monastery of Montecassino. This line is being fortified with gun pits, concrete bunkers, turreted machine-gun emplacements, barbed wire and minefields. The enemy has superior forces, but we're more professional, as we've proved time and time again in the course of this war. We'll make them fight for every metre.'

Centurione Faustino had buried his wife, worshipper of Il Duce. The windows of their hotel had been blown out by the aerial bombardment of the town's outskirts, and his office in Cassino, from which he had conducted a campaign of intimidation and extortion against the local population, had also been damaged. He had originally joined the Fascist Party, not because he believed particularly in its doctrines, but because he was attracted by the uniform and the authority bestowed on him, since he was by nature a bully. After the Armistice he had tried to flee north, but had been intercepted by the Germans. He was now one of 700,000 Italian military personnel to be transported to Germany, to be used as slave labour, and where the former Fascist official would be among the many to die, lungs choked with the dust of the stone he was breaking for another monument to the Reich which expected to last a thousand years, despite its reverses in the snows of Russia and in the hot sands of North Africa.

After Mass a monk stopped Angela at the door of the basilica and told her that the Abbot wished to see her, leading her along a corridor to a room where Dom Pietro was sitting with the Abbot.

'I need you to do something for me, at the suggestion of your uncle,' the Abbot requested. 'I appreciate that you want to advance your studies of Dante with him, but would you consider giving up your time with him to starting a school for the children of the refugees, to keep them occupied, and so that they may continue to learn in these times of confusion and distress?'

The old man, who had believed that he would end his life in peace and contemplation in his beloved monastery, his funeral Mass conducted by his Brothers, a space reserved for him in the cemetery, removed his spectacles, rubbed his weary eyes and cleaned the lenses with the hem of his garment, as if he required a clearer perspective on a world which was changing drastically and tragically by the day and which Scriptures didn't really help him to understand, because there had been no Panzer divisions, no dive bombers in the time of Christ, despite the cruelties of Herod and Caesar. Faith, as well as buildings, could be shaken, and perhaps also shattered, by explosions. The prophecy of Isaiah was not being fulfilled:

> *The law will go out from Zion, the word of the Lord from Jerusalem. He will judge between the nations and will settle disputes for many peoples. They will beat their swords into ploughshares and their spears into pruning hooks. Nation will not take up sword against nation, nor will they train for war anymore.*

Two days after the crossing of the Volturno River by the Allies, two German army visitors, a Lieutenant Colonel Julius Schlegel and a Captain Dr Maximilian Becker, both from the elite Hermann Goering Division, were waiting to see the Abbot. They had been there the previous day on separate visits, Schlegel warning the Abbot that his monastery had to be 'cleared out,' irrespective of the Abbot's opinion. Becker had told the Abbot that his monastery was likely to be caught up in the coming battle as the enemy advanced north, towards the prize of Rome, and that he wished to help to save the sublime archive of manuscripts and books, paintings and other treasures.

'But you are a doctor of medicine, are you not?' the bewildered Abbot enquired.

'Yes, but I also have a passion for archaeology, for paintings, for all things which enhance the human spirit. Your treasures need to be moved to a place of safety, along with your monks.'

'That isn't possible or necessary,' the Abbot informed him. 'Field Marshal Kesselring has given me his personal assurance that the monastery won't be used for military purposes, and the advancing British and American army certainly won't bomb the building.'

The doctor had mustered his arguments on the drive to Montecassino. If the monastery wasn't going to be used for military purposes, why were German soldiers digging at the base of the mountain it stood on? Granted, the opposing army might not bomb the monastery, but they would attack any German fortifications around it. Bombs and shells did not always hit their intended targets.

The Abbot was silent, as if he hadn't heard Becker's predictions. Then he spoke in a strong, clear voice, as if rejuvenated, not by a drug, but as though the doctor's words were an antidote to his depression. He wanted to know where his monks and the refugees, including nuns and orphans from the three Benedictine convents down in Cassino, figured in Becker's evacuation plan for the treasures. And he had a further question for his visitor. Would the doctor's General leave his soldiers in the lurch in battle?

'I'm the general here, the bishop here, the shepherd of

my people,' the Abbot said, as if quoting scripture. Even if the battle advanced to Montecassino, he was remaining with his monks and his refugees. 'That would be St Benedict's position also.'

The following day, as Schlegel and Becker waited to see the Abbot, to hear if he had changed his mind, the Lieutenant Colonel, an Austrian and man of nervous energy, was perambulating the room, studying the paintings on the walls.

'Come and see this,' he called to his companion.

They stood admiring an eighteen inch high exquisitely carved wooden statuette of the Madonna, with a crown on her head, carrying the Infant.

'How old do you think this beautiful piece is?' Schlegel asked.

The art connoisseur estimated the early Middle Ages. As he touched it he marvelled at how the creator's chisel had given the Mother of God such a serene countenance, and how beautifully Christ's tiny fingers, touching her cheek, had been executed.

'Now that would be something for the Iron Man,' Schlegel pronounced at the doctor's back.

Becker's heart seemed to malfunction under his stifling uniform. The Iron Man the name given to Reich Marshal Hermann Goering, the patron of their Division, who had agents all over conquered Europe, looting the choicest works of art for his residence, Karinhall, more a palace. So was that what Schlegel and his officer accomplices were up to? They wanted to loot Montecassino of its treasures and give first choice to the Iron Man, whose desire for artefacts was insatiable, like Mussolini's for women, taken with the same brutality and justification.

'What do you mean by that?' Becker confronted his senior officer.

'I thought you would have known that the Reich Marshal collects Madonnas.'

'I've no doubt he has a large enough collection of Madonnas already,' Becker observed, though he was still anxious about his companion's motives. He lied when he said that the one they were admiring was 'by no means the finest example that I've seen.'

They were being ushered into the presence of the Abbot.

'I understand that you're storing here works of art from the Museo Nazionale of Naples, along with artefacts from its archaeological museum, including items found at Pompeii,' the doctor began cautiously.

'Who gave you this information?' the Abbot demanded.

'Some 200 crates,' the doctor continued, without disclosing his recent source, an Italian guard at the gate of the monastery. 'I believe the Museo Nazionale has the only two Goyas in Italy, as well as a dozen Titians.'

'We could take the Naples paintings and artefacts to the Vatican for safekeeping,' Schlegel offered.

'That won't be possible,' the Abbot replied. 'These treasures of Naples are the property of the Italian State. You are forgetting that the Vatican isn't Italian soil, but an independent state.'

'We could move the Naples treasures to the north of Rome – say to Assisi,' Becker suggested.

'But suppose this terrible war was to reach St Francis's sacred town? What would happen to the Naples treasures if they were being stored there as you propose?' the Abbot challenged him.

'There's no danger of Assisi falling, but if there was any threat to the capital we would move the treasures to somewhere beyond the battle.'

'Could that mean removing them from Italy?'

'They'll stay in Italy, Abbot,' the Lieutenant Colonel assured the frail old man for whom he felt pity.

'What do you think?' the Abbot appealed to Dom Pietro.

'I believe we must listen to Colonel Schlegel and Captain Becker and take whatever help they can give us.'

The Abbot's melancholy was beginning to affect his health, and some days his colour – that of newly quarried marble – was so bad that Dom Pietro worried he wouldn't survive the day. But what comfort could the monk offer his superior when bombs had fallen so close?

'Is this plan agreeable to you?' Schlegel asked. 'We'll take the Montecassino treasures, and your monks, to the two Benedictine monasteries at St Paul's Outside the Walls and Sant' Anselmo in Rome. As for the larger amount of archives and art from Naples, the property of the Italian State, as you point out, they will be taken to the supply depot of our Division, the Hermann Goering.'

'Where is this based?' the Abbot wanted to know.

'At Spoleto, seventy miles north of Rome, a place of safety now and in the future,' Becker assured him.

'You need a sign from us that we'll keep our word,' Schlegel insisted.

He stood up, and the doctor followed. Both men placed their hands on their hearts and delivered a solemn pledge about the safety and security of the Montecassino and Naples treasures.

'You reassure me, gentlemen,' the Abbot responded.

'Work will begin tomorrow, since time is not on our side,' the Lieutenant Colonel told him.

But there was still the delicate matter of the safety of the Abbot.

'We can arrange to take you to Rome,' Schlegel offered.

'I repeat what I told you yesterday, I cannot leave Montecassino,' the Abbot said firmly.

'Then you must be prepared to die here with your monks.'

Becker frowned at the Lieutenant Colonel's insensitivity, but the Abbot took it with a shrug. However, he needed Schlegel's advice.

'If some of the monks stay here with me, would you show us a place within the monastery where we could hope to survive bombing – if it occurs?'

Dom Emmanuel Munding, being a German speaker, was detailed to show Schlegel round the building. The German army officer and his guide descended to beneath the basilica, passing chapels and crypts which Schlegel stopped to inspect carefully. They reached an arched room thirty feet underground, with a sixty feet stone tower above it.

'Here you will be safe from bombs.'

From Angela's Journal for Monday 18 October 1943:

I run my school in the mornings, beginning with prayers. I tell the children about my family in Scotland, and how they too will be suffering from the effects of the war. There aren't sufficient desks in the monastery's deserted schoolroom, so in the afternoons I make the children sit in a circle in the Bramante Cloister, with the adults standing at the back. I encourage the children to sing the songs and stories they've learned from their parents and grandparents. They stand up to tell tales of wolves and spirits of the woods and the mountains, and I'm enthralled.

I don't go down to Cassino now because of the bombing raids by the Allies. Uncle tells me that the Faustino hotel has been flattened. We're cut off from Cassino because of the cable car being out of operation.

Chapter Eighteen

The monks, with some of the refugees who were being paid with cigarettes and food by the Germans, were helping the soldiers in the carpenters' shop, sawing and nailing together lengths of wood into packing cases of different sizes for the treasures. The place was deafening with the sound of hammers, the air hazed with sawdust. When a case was ready it was carried along the corridors to the library. The treasures were being packed under the supervision of Lieutenant Colonel Schlegel, with Dom Mauro Inguanez the vigilant Maltese archivist explaining to the visitor that the Library which Charles Dickens had admired on his visit in 1845 contained over 40,000 books, illuminated manuscripts and ancient vellum scrolls with seals. 'A vital part of the history of European thought and civilization is within these walls,' the archivist revealed proudly. 'We have much of the writings of Tacitus, Cicero, Horace, Virgil and many other great classical writers. This is one of our treasures. It's an edition of *The Divine Comedy*, and the writings you see in the margins are notes made by Dante's son.'

He took down a large book from a shelf.

'This is a choir book from the sixteenth century,' the archivist demonstrated as he opened the cover to show a superbly executed coloured plate of the Virgin Mary with her child, with an angel hovering above.

'Exquisite,' Schlegel murmured as he turned a page reverently.

'Yes, but this book, of which we have a whole series, was not only made for its beauty. They were used in our Masses at important feasts such as Easter and Christmas.'

'It wouldn't only be a great loss to Italy if any of these came to harm,' the German officer pointed out. 'It would be a great loss to civilization.'

'This manuscript took Dom Alfonso thirty years to write,' Dom Inguanez disclosed as he unrolled a parchment. 'It's the story of the Children of Israel fleeing to Canaan, with the Red Sea dividing for them. It would take me a year to show you all of our treasures,' the archivist added. 'But we must get on with clearing the shelves.'

The hundreds of paintings from the Museo Nazionale, Naples, including works by Leonardo da Vinci, Titian, and Tintoretto which were being stored in Montecassino were being protected before transportation to safety. Becker was helping to handle Pieter Bruegel the Elder's canvas *Parable of the Blind*. The German doctor with his deep spiritual as well as artistic sense saw in this painting of six blind men, linked by staffs, stumbling and falling, a modern parable on the state of war-ravaged Europe and its leaders.

From Angela's Journal for Wednesday 20 October 1943:

> *Uncle Peter asked me to assist with the treasures that were being packed for dispatch to Rome because, he said, a woman's gentle hand was necessary among such fragile items, and besides,*

he wanted me to be part of an important event in the history of the monastery.

'Don't push them in,' Dom Inguanez the archivist, who wants the treasures to remain in Montecassino, warned one of the German soldiers who were putting parchments into a wooden case. 'You'll tear them, they're so fragile.' I went round showing everyone the object resting on my palm, a tiny prayer book that looked as if it belonged in a doll's house. The archivist told me to wrap it in a cloth and, with a description of what it was, to put it in a suitable box marked Fragile. One of the helpers was asked to place in one of the packing cases a mitre decorated with pearls and blue and red stones which had belonged to Pope Leo X. Instead, he was parading round the room, wearing the mitre on his head and making the sign of the cross over the workers in a moment of light relief until Dom Martino Matronola, the Abbot's secretary and chief assistant, gave him a scolding and retrieved the precious relic.

I helped to wrap a magnificent painting by Maestro del Tondo Miller, showing St Benedict and St Margaret of Antioch together. The objects were nailed up in the cases and carried along the corridor.

Lieutenant Colonel Schlegel fussed around the trucks, making sure that every space on every vehicle was filled before he would allow it to leave for its destination.

'It's going well,' Dom Emmanuel Munding the German speaking monk complimented him. 'It's a race against time,' the Lieutenant Colonel replied. 'The enemy's getting closer, and there are so many treasures in the monastery.' He revealed that he could get into big trouble, withdrawing trucks from the front, where 'they're shouting for transport and fuel.' He said that he had tried to take as much care as possible, selecting the drivers and warning them about the precious cargoes they're to be carrying. 'I've instructed them to keep a distance of at least 300 metres between each vehicle in case they're attacked from the air.'

I was holding aloft an exquisite wooden statuette of the crowned Wooden Madonna with the Infant, about eighteen inches high. Dr Becker, who was helping with the packing, said to Lieutenant Colonel Schlegel: 'It's the one you were admiring the other day when we visited here.' I was hugging the statuette when I asked Uncle Peter: 'Why can't we keep it here?' He said that it would be safer in Rome. Then Dr

Becker said in a low voice to Uncle Peter: 'I'm not so sure. I'm worried it could end up in the collection of Reich Marshal Goering.' The archivist asked if Goering was a Catholic and Becker laughed, then became serious again. 'If the statuette brings spiritual comfort it should be left in the monastery.' But Lieutenant Colonel Schlegel pointed out forcibly: 'Its safety can't be guaranteed here.' However, Uncle Peter assured him that 'we'll look after Our Mother.' He told me to take the Madonna and place her on a side altar in the basilica.

The Benedictine nuns who had been bombed out of their convents down in Cassino and who were sheltering in the monastery along with orphans in their care left on one of the trucks for Rome, the entire community of Montecassino - monks and workers – gathering at the gate to see them off. The Abbess, who was partially paralyzed, had to be lifted up on to one of the trucks.

The Abbot was giving them his blessing and wishing them a safe journey to their destination when Allied fighter-bombers appeared to attack the town of Cassino, the explosions making the nuns leap out of the trucks and run for shelter, though the German Lieutenant Colonel was shouting at them to stay where they were. The Abbot and some of his monks were kneeling under the trees, asking

God to turn the bombers back to their bases. The Germans went round inspecting the trucks, but there was no damage to their precious cargoes.

Dom Pietro trusted Schlegel, but items could go missing. A German soldier with a thin enough hand could push it between the slats of a crate and help himself to a small object, small but precious enough to give him the money to buy a house when he got back to Germany, the monk brooded. Or the trucks could be attacked by planes, despite Schlegel's instructions about keeping a safe distance between them. Look at the way they had come out of the blue to attack Cassino.

The Abbot asked Angela to translate an Allied broadcast, claiming that the Hermann Goering Panzer Division was busily engaged in looting the monastery of Montecassino.

'Have we made the wrong decision?' the Abbot asked in despair.

'I don't think so,' Dom Pietro tried to assure him. 'That's only propaganda. We need to trust Colonel Schlegel.'

'Then let us go and pray for the success of his mission,' the Abbot told the monks.

But Schlegel, who also heard the broadcast, was worried. He was thinking: *What will High Command have to say about me taking it upon myself to divert much-needed trucks from the front – trucks that should be transporting soldiers, not books and chalices? Will my mission to save the treasures of Montecassino be stopped, and will the items now safely on their way to Rome be diverted to Germany?*

Because he couldn't sleep Dom Pietro went outside. He stood on the terrace, wondering if that pinprick of light on the hillside was a German machine gun post. When the wind was in the right direction he could hear the sound of the guns at the Volturno River, forty miles to the south. But it was too cold and too depressing to linger. He went into the basilica and saw his niece kneeling in front of the statuette of the Wooden Madonna, and left her to her prayers, not only because of the Benedictine rule of silence after Compline, but also because he wanted to respect her solitary devotion.

The packing of the treasures continued, with the Abbot in the room, two boxes on the table beside him.

'These are the most precious treasures of the monastery, far too precious to trust on a truck to Rome without someone watching over them,' he instructed two of the monks. 'That's why you must take these boxes on the truck and never let them out of your sight for a second. They contain pieces of the bones of St Benedict and his sister St Scholastica. You know that the major bones of the Saints are buried here in the monastery. St Benedict's bones are under the basilica, where it's said that he was buried standing up, his arms raised in prayer, and his sister was laid to rest beside him. So let us all raise our hands in prayer and ask God for the safe delivery of these precious relics to Rome.'

After the Abbot had led the prayer he and his secretary Dom Matronola picked up the two silk-covered boxes wrapped in a blanket, containing the relics of the saintly brother and sister, carrying them out to one of the German trucks waiting at the gate. The old Abbot kept his hands on the two boxes until the truck was pulled away, as if blessing the relics, tears in his weary eyes.

In the back of Captain Maximilian Becker's little Fiat convertible were another two of the monastery's exceptional treasures, original manuscripts by Keats and Shelley contained in two metal boxes which the German doctor was himself driving to the safety of Rome. Dom Inguanez the archivist was travelling with him on the orders of the Abbot. Because of the frequent attacks by enemy planes it was too dangerous to drive the direct route to Rome, so Becker was taking a country route, via the Abruzzi Mountains.

Dom Inguanez asked his driver to stop at a farm owned by the monastery so that he could try to arrange a food supply for the refugees in the building. There was time to let the engine cool, to admire the panorama of the sunlit landscape so far untouched by the war.

'I pray every night that the British and Americans won't damage or destroy our monastery,' the monk confessed to his companion. 'Have you heard of William Gladstone?'

'He was Prime Minister of Great Britain.'

'He was indeed, and when the Italian state was going to take our archive into its custody, it was Gladstone who persuaded it to leave it in its true home of Montecassino, so surely the English won't destroy what they helped to preserve.'

'I wish I could give you an optimistic answer,' Becker

told the monk. 'But at least your treasures are now safe.'

'I find it hard to accept that a cultured man like yourself, a doctor of medicine and scholar of antiquity, serves a ruthless dictatorship which is looting the treasures of Europe, and causing such devastation and death,' the monk admitted.

Becker was silent, drumming his fingers on the steering wheel.

'Treat what I'm going to say as if this car is a confession box,' the Captain requested his travelling companion. 'I'm a British citizen because though my father was German, my mother was British.'

'I sense your disillusionment at this war,' Dom Inguanaz noted, giving the pensive physician time to reply.

'The war's lost, though it's treason to say it. Too many like Schlegel have built their reputations and expectations on it. They all want to be Field Marshals with jewelled batons like Goering. I'm a doctor, and I've seen too much blood spilt already. How much more is to flow before the British and the Americans thrust their way to Rome through the Liri Valley? That's what I ask myself.'

'There are ways of escaping, doctor.'

'You mean deserting?'

'Let's call it quitting. The Benedictines may be able to help you to relocate, shall we say.'

'I've a wife and child in Germany, and God knows what would happen to them if I deserted,' he said as if to himself as he restarted the engine of the Fiat.

Accompanied by Captain Becker, Lieutenant Colonel Schlegel told the Abbot that his work was now finished and that in under three weeks over one hundred truck journeys had conveyed to safety tens of thousands of documents and books from the Library, as well as paintings, with the majority of the monks. Nearly 200 cases of Neapolitan art had been taken to the supply depot of the Hermann Goering Division at Spoleto.

'You've earned our undying gratitude,' the Abbot said. 'What can we do in return?'

'Hold a Mass for myself and my soldiers in the basilica,' Schlegel requested him.

The basilica had three great bronze doors, the middle one dating from the eleventh century, when Desiderius was Abbot. It consisted of a set of panels with silver damascened lettering; the lower panel at the right, between two crosses, certifying that the doors' wings had been made in Constantinople in 1066 and were a gift from Mauro of Amalfi, son of Pantaleone.

'We have nothing like this in Germany,' Schlegel said in awe, his peaked cap in his hand against his heart as he entered the basilica.

After the very few remaining monks had sung Mass in their stalls behind the high altar, with Dom Pietro on the organ, the Abbott called Lieutenant Colonel Schlegel and Captain Becker to the altar and presented each with a parchment written in Latin, thanking them for saving the treasures of Montecassino. Schlegel wanted to repeat that the Wooden Madonna, which he had prayed to before the side altar before Mass, would be safer in Rome, but knew that he had been defeated in this matter.

'I'll personally escort you to Rome,' Schlegel told the Abbot.

'I can't leave Montecassino,' the old man replied.

'But it's unsafe.'

'I must remain here, whatever happens, otherwise it would be desertion.' Only to God in prayer would he confess that he was frightened, not for himself, but for the remaining few monks and the refugees. He had had a long and peaceful life of piety, and felt that he had discharged his administrative duties as Abbot to the best of his ability.

The German Lieutenant Colonel saw that the old Abbot's mind was made up and admired his resolution, which was like that of a soldier, except that he belonged in Christ's battalion and would not have any sins to answer for when this protracted war was over. Schlegel himself felt that his successful evacuation to Rome of the monastery's treasures would help him when he came to be judged, either after death in battle, or when this appalling war was over.

Chapter Nineteen

After the announcement of the armistice with Italy on 8 September 1943 Rosa Boni decided to refurbish and reopen the wrecked boarded-up café. She required a further loan, so she took the tram into her bank in the centre of Glasgow for an appointment.

'I can't advance you any more money. In fact the bank is planning to sell your property,' the official told her, sitting behind a barrier of brass inkwells, black and red for solvency and insolvency.

'But you can't do that.'

'Yes we can. You'll recall that you stopped repaying the loan instalments, and since we hold the title deeds as security, we need to recover our investment.'

His decision not to grant this woman a further advance was based, not on the viability of a café which had been busy and could be again, but on his loathing of all Italians, his only son having been killed in North Africa by an Italian sniper. The fact that the Italians had now joined the Allies against the Germans made no difference.

'When are you planning to sell my property?' Rosa asked.

'We'll put it on the market within the next fortnight. It may take some time to sell, given the present economic conditions. But it's a good site for a café because of the proximity to the university,' he added maliciously.

'I'm not going to let it go, after the hard work we've put into it,' Rosa told him resolutely. 'We came to Glasgow with nothing, and worked our fingers to the bone to realize our dream of owning our own place. I owe it to my late husband to find some way of keeping it in the family.'

'You won't get finance from another bank, since we hold the title deeds,' he cautioned her.

She was a determined woman, and on the tram going home she worked out what she was going to do. She was still cleaning for the Macfarlanes, and the next morning after she had finished her chores she knocked the door of the room in which the retired physician, veteran of the carnage of the Somme and Ypres, was listening to war news on the wireless.

'I need your help, doctor.'

He switched off the set and gave her his attention, as he had always done with his patients, since medicine was about listening as well as examining.

'I want to reopen our café, but the bank won't advance me any more money to fit it out. I need to replace everything: even the toilet bowl was stolen when Italy entered the war.'

'I'm sorry to hear this, Rosa.'

She came to the point, because time wasn't on her side, and she had no one else to turn to. 'I need a loan of five hundred pounds.'

'I see,' the doctor reacted cautiously.

'I'll keep the café open from morning till night seven days a week to pay it back.'

'But will you get back the customers you used to have?' he queried.

'I think I will, and there are the students just up the road.

Will you help me, even though I won't be able to work for you and Mrs Macfarlane any longer if I reopen the café?'

He admired this woman who had been left a widow by the war, and had been so badly treated by his fellow citizens. She had become more than a good and loyal worker to him and his wife: she was a valued friend, the way she had helped them down into their basement during the Clydebank Blitz.

He opened the drawer of his desk and took out his cheque book. Next morning she went to see the bank official behind his redoubt of inkwells.

'There are still good caring people in this world,' she told him as she passed him Dr Macfarlane's cheque, which he could have torn up in his fury.

The toilet bowl was replaced, the interior decorated, a new coffee machine purchased, tables and chairs from the sale of a city restaurant bankrupted by the war installed in the café. On the first day of reopening former customers came in to hug her and order coffees, and several of those who had looted the property of the cigarette stock bought their smokes from her in penance. Though ingredients were in short supply, Rosa managed to make ices for the university students. After two months she went to Dr Macfarlane, to give him the first instalment of her loan.

'Keep it, Rosa. We don't have any children to leave our money to, and yours is a most worthy cause.'

The bowls of the Abbot and the four remaining monks trembled on the tables in the refectory of Montecassino at another explosion, but the rule of silence at meals prohibited conversation. The Gustav Line to prevent the Allies moving north to Rome was being fortified. The monks could hear the clatter of drills as the surrounding mountains were packed with dynamite. The blasts gouged caverns to form observation posts, machine gun and artillery emplacements. In the valleys below, anti-tank ditches were being excavated, and miles of barbed wire rolled out. The autumn sun glinted on steel shelters being erected around Cassino, where there was a machine gun installation manned by two soldiers.

The blasting was incessant, breaking up the chants of the various offices of the Benedictine day in the basilica as cellars were excavated under houses, then connected by escape tunnels to other buildings. Houses constructed of Travertine limestone that would withstand artillery fire had their windows reduced to loopholes for gun emplacements, as in ancient fortifications where the weapon was the blunderbuss. In fields ploughed by cattle for centuries, the Germans sowed over 20,000 anti-personnel mines, their wooden construction preventing a metal detector from locating them. They were designed to detonate at the pressure of the lightest foot, to amputate it in the cruelty and cunning of war.

In early November Lieutenant Colonel Schlegel arrived at the monastery to say goodbye. The Abbot gave him a bottle of the monastery's forty year old wine, with his blessing, in gratitude for the German officer, along with Dr Becker, sending the treasures of the monastery to safety. In return Schlegel left a paper with his signature, stating that

Montecassino was under military protection, a pledge he truly believed, because he was an honourable man despite the uniform he was wearing and the orders he had to carry out in furtherance of Hitler's ambitions. His notice was nailed to the gate marked PAX.

From Angela's Journal for Friday 19 November 1943:

> Today sacred tapestries from a nunnery in Cassino were brought up to the monastery. One of the nuns accompanying them was tearful, telling me that the Germans had ransacked the nunnery, carrying away religious artefacts, not to venerate them, but to keep them as souvenirs, or to sell. 'Some of the locals who profess to be such devout Catholics have been just as bad, helping themselves,' the nun added sadly. 'The Sisters have prayed so hard for peace, and the world to return to the way it was, but it gets worse.'
>
> Uncle Peter is sad tonight, after a German chaplain came to the monastery with an old volume and valuable sacred vessels from churches in Santa Elia which have been abandoned by their priests because of the German presence.
>
> Uncle Peter has had to suspend writing his history of Montecassino because the manuscripts he requires have been sent

for safety to Rome. He wants to continue tutoring me for my doctoral thesis on Dante, but I told him that privilege on my part has to be postponed because of my commitment to the children of the refugees. I've been teaching them writing, spelling and maths, and pointing out Glasgow in an atlas. For recreation I teach them Scottish country dances, and because I don't have any music I've been singing Scottish songs which fit the steps as they dance. Also, I've chalked squares on the flagstones so that they can play hop-scotch, a game I used to play with other children on the pavement outside our café in Glasgow. The children teach me Italian games, though as yet I'm not very skilled.

When I'm not with the children or praying to the Wooden Madonna for peace on my knees in the basilica , I'm down at Uncle and Aunt's smallholding, helping where I can, since I'm not earning any money after the hotel closed. How I love slipping the stool under Darlene their cow and milking it as I sing to it in Italian, placing my forehead against her flank in an act of love and gratitude for the milk hissing into the pail between my feet as I tug the teats, keeping time with a song.

Two nights ago we were at supper when the schoolmaster knocked the door. Whenever he has news from the wireless or elsewhere, he shares it round the houses. 'The Germans are moving down the valley towards here, demolishing houses,' he warned us over a glass of wine. 'They took our neighbour's cow. We've hidden ours, and you'll be well advised to do the same.' After our visitor had gone to warn the next house I asked Uncle where we could hide Darlene. 'Take her up in the morning to the small wood near the monastery and tether her to a tree.' 'And leave her out all night?' Aunt said, shocked. Uncle said that it was probably the only way to save her.

This morning I led her up on a rope to the wood, talking to her all the way. 'I'm so sorry we have to do this to you, Darlene,' I apologized, hugging her. 'But we don't want to lose you to the Germans, not only because you're our only milk supply, but because we love you. But please, don't moo, or you'll attract the Germans' attention.' As I was milking her among the trees I heard a motor and saw a truck with flapping canvas sides bumping along the track. Gina, one of our neighbours, told me about women in the district having been raped (*brutalizzazione* in Italian) by German soldiers. She herself, fearful that she would be violated, had spread cow dung on her inside thighs, and I did the same with Darlene's dung before going down to the house. A German officer was standing in the kitchen, confronting Uncle and Aunt. 'You have to get out,' he ordered through an Italian Fascist interpreter. 'Why?' Aunt demanded. 'For security reasons.' What do you mean - security?' she repeated, as if she hadn't heard him correctly. 'This house has been in my husband's family for generations.' The German threatened: 'Get out, or my men will throw you out.' She asked him where we were to go, and he said that he would arrange a lorry to take us down to Cassino. 'What good will that do? We don't have relatives in Cassino,' Aunt told him. 'Besides, it's been wrecked by the bombing.' The officer warned us that he was giving us ten minutes to get out of the house, before going outside to sit smoking on the wall, constantly glancing at his watch. I thought: your training - and your ambition - allow you to exclude the human consequences of your orders, as if, like millions of your fellow soldiers and citizens, your brain has been programmed by the propaganda of the Nazis, the area relating to free will disengaged. 'Where are we to go?' Aunt asked helplessly. I told her that we would go up to the monastery, where Uncle Peter would look after us. All the time I was praying that Darlene up in the wood wouldn't give herself away, and end up in the meal tins of German soldiers. Aunt and I went indoors to pack suitcases. What do you take from a house when you get only ten minutes to vacate it? Clearly, some clothes. But Aunt lifted from the kitchen wall above the fireplace the crucifix which she said her grandfather had made when Italy was a peaceful, devout country.

Annabelle the cat was rubbing against my leg, as if telling me that she wasn't going to be left behind, so I picked her up under my arm. When we came down Uncle was with a soldier, who was opening the door to the stable. I hurried across to give him support. 'Are they yours?' the officer asked, indicating the four mules. 'They're my sons,' Uncle told the officer, putting his arms protectively round the necks of Gionata and Lucano. He told the mules to come with him because they were going to a new home, but the officer's arm barred his way. "What are you doing with my uncle?' I demanded. The officer signalled that Uncle and the four mules were staying. Beatrice heard the confrontation and came running. 'He's coming with us!' she shouted, hauling at Uncle's arm. The German officer struck her arm away.

What do they want with mules when they have so many tanks and vehicles?' Aunt was sobbing as we lugged the suitcases up to the monastery. 'Surely to God they're not going to eat the poor creatures. I would believe anything of the Germans now. How could Mussolini have got in tow with such a cruel race?' I was worried about Darlene, who would die if she was left tethered to a tree. We had to bang on the monastery gate for five minutes before a monk answered, and another five minutes before Uncle Peter arrived. 'The Germans have come to knock down our house, and have kept Benigno to help them,' Aunt told him tearfully. He said that they've done the same to a number of houses in the district, and were holding some of the men who can be useful to them. Evidently the Germans are strengthening their defences to stop the British and Americans getting to Rome. 'I can't arrange a room for you,' Uncle Peter apologized to us. 'There are the cells of the monks who have gone to

Rome, but the Abbot doesn't want them used. You'll have to join the other refugees in the cloisters.' I told him about Darlene the cow hidden in the wood, and he said he would send a lay Brother down to put her with the monastery cows.

Uncle Peter brought Aunt and me bread and cheese with the bedding. I shared my small portion of cheese with Annabelle and went to get her a saucer of water, telling her that I would try to get milk from Darlene for her later. Aunt was exhausted and tearful after the encounter with the Germans who were intent on demolishing her home where she had been so happy with Uncle. She lay down, using her suitcase as a pillow, but I couldn't settle and lay staring up at the stars and stroking the cat. It wasn't the smell of the protective cow dung smeared on my thighs that was keeping me awake; I'm asking myself why life has changed so drastically in the space of only one day. Is this God's plan? Or has He retreated in sorrow to let the nations battle it out to exhaustion? But surely this isn't a reason for stopping praying, though my pleas for peace must seem infinitesimal compared to the immensity of the conflict which has engulfed Europe. There must be millions *of dead to be prayed for, as well as all the living, maimed and terrified.*

Lying in the cloisters of the transformed monastery, it seems to me that I have entered another existence from the one I enjoyed in Scotland, with my loving family, the pleasure of setting down ices in front of lovers in the café, and with Cavaliere Grillo's eloquent insights into the soul of Dante. With his veneration of Fascism and Mussolini, is he being allowed to continue to teach at the university, to extol the genius of D'Annunzio? Where is Augusto? Is he safe or in captivity? I wish he was lying beside me.

Where will we put these tapestries from the convent in Cassino?' the Abbot asked Dom Pietro.

'I don't know. Is there anywhere safe in this place?' Dom Pietro appealed helplessly, exhausted with endeavouring through prayer to prevent his fears of destruction of the monastery from becoming reality. The hand that expressed his despair was gnarled through years of winters in the basilica, the fingers swollen with chilblains.

'We could put them in the crypt,' the Abbot suggested. 'Not that I think we'll be attacked. The Germans have given their promise.'

'What about the British and Americans? Have they also given you a piece of paper?' Dom Pietro asked.

'No,' the Abbot admitted, 'but I trust them not to bomb this holy place.'

At that moment the building trembled in an explosion.

'I didn't hear a plane going over,' the Abbot said anxiously.

Dom Pietro followed the Abbot outside. A man had run up the steep road, gasping for breath as he told the monk who opened the gate for him that the Germans were blowing up even more houses in Cassino and on the outskirts of the town. Another explosion shook the monastery, and a column of thick yellow smoke rose into the sky as if the sun had exploded.

'I must write to the Vatican, to report this latest development,' the Abbot said, hurrying away.

The number of refugees in the monastery rose and fell as further Allied air raids were made on Cassino. The refugees were now augmented by new arrivals who had trekked from outlying villages which the Germans had requisitioned. They lay down where they could find a space, their children huddled against them for warmth and reassurance. The village school they had adorned with flowers was occupied by a machine gun crew, the De Santis's friend and informant the schoolmaster in captivity, useful to the Germans because he spoke their language. Some of the refugees had brought maize and olives they had been hoarding, but most were being fed by the overworked monastery kitchen. They were mostly women, many of the men having been rounded up and sent to Germany as forced labour.

High up in his cave on Monte Cairo Augusto Faccenda, heavily bearded now, conscious of his body odours, his faithful dog sharing its warmth, had heard the explosions and seen the dust rising as more and more houses were blown up as part of the fortifications of the Gustav Line, and when he descended to his house, he found it a pile of rubble. He picked up the crucifix which had been on the wall above his grandmother's bed. Every night she had kissed the feet of Christ, but the Saviour's body had been broken in two by Fascist dynamite, and as he put the shattered cross into his pocket he once again vowed vengeance.

It had become too dangerous to sleep in his cave, because the Germans were going higher on the mountain, converting caves for observation posts, so he lay down by the ruins of his grandmother's house, and in the dawn moved through trees to where German soldiers were building part of the fortifications. Augusto thought of the horrors and wastage of the battles he had participated in in North Africa, where he had had to kill or be killed. He had grown sick of killing, and couldn't avenge his grandmother's death because the Fascist thugs who had caused it were having their bodies and minds broken by stones in Germany. But the Germans were the ruthless occupiers of his country, evicting people from their houses, so he rested the barrel of his rifle on the bough of a tree. It was as if his finger on the trigger had suddenly become paralyzed.

One of the male refugees who had evaded transportation to Germany had arranged football matches for the boys in the Paradise Loggia, using the cloister pillars as goal posts, while Angela showed the girls how to make dolls out of pieces of wood and rags. Beatrice could barely drag herself up from the kitchen in the evening.

Chapter Twenty

Dom Pietro went about as if the predicament of the monastery wasn't real, but a phantasmagoria. On the rare occasions when he had the basilica to himself he knelt at the side altar before the Wooden Madonna, praying for the safety and survival of the monastery and its inhabitants, though his requests were disrupted by the sound of detonating shells coming nearer and nearer to the massive building on the mountain. The Barbara Line had been breached by the United States Fifth Army, commanded by Lieutenant General Mark Clark, and the Germans had fallen back to the Bernhardt Line on the western side of the Apennines, in front of the main Gustav Line positions. The new German defensive position which was only a dozen miles from Montecassino was already under attack, the din of battle incessant in the monastery.

Dom Pietro hardly slept, worrying about the safety of his niece and sister lying with the other refugees in the cloisters under the stars, the nights freezing. He thought also of the soldiers of both sides huddled in the waterlogged valleys and on the mountains, short of sustenance, of hope, fearful that the next day was going to be their last, but without the consolation of faith, a belief in the protective power of prayer.

On a day towards the end of November a German Lieutenant arrived, demanding to see the Abbot.

'I want to go up to the meteorological observatory,' the Lieutenant requested.

'Why do you want to observe the weather when you know already that it's raining?' Dom Pietro, detailed by the Abbot to accompany the German officer, questioned him as they went up the steps of the tower, Nico the raven flying ahead.

'I want to see the Gaeta Mountains,' the Lieutenant disclosed.

'This is a weather station, not a military observation post,' Dom Pietro reminded the Lieutenant. 'We have a letter from Lieutenant Colonel Schlegel, stating that the monastery isn't to be used for military purposes. If you start using Montecassino as a lookout position to plot the movements of the enemy, then they'll attack the monastery.'

The Lieutenant made no reply as he turned his field glasses on the Gaeta Mountains, which were obscured by the rain. He was making a survey for the Gustav Line, and when he had written down his observations he asked to see the basilica.

'Surely not for a military purpose,' Dom Pietro reacted in alarm.

'Of course not. I'm interested in churches.'

The Abbot gave permission for the Lieutenant to be shown the basilica, and the visitor spent some time admiring the soaring marble. He stopped in front of the Wooden Madonna at the side altar, but didn't kneel in prayer to her.

There was excitement at the beginning of December when a van came up the winding road to the monastery, containing a mobile cinema sent from Rome by Lieutenant Colonel Schlegel to prove that the treasures of Montecassino had really arrived in a safe place. The screen was set up in the Benefactors' Cloister, the projector powered from a portable generator so that the refugees as well as the monks could watch. The film showed a line of trucks crossing the river Tiber, then stopping outside an impressive building in the centre of Rome.

'That's the Castel Sant' Angelo,' Dom Pietro whispered to Angela, pointing out the fortress built as a mausoleum for the Emperor Hadrian, and which had been used as a prison and a papal residence. 'I've visited there. Look: there's the German officer who came here.'

Schlegel was in the centre, between two German officers, one of them Major General Kurt Mälzer, who styled himself the 'King of Rome,' with a pugilist's face, notorious for his addiction to alcohol and brutality. Though the aesthetic importance of the Montecassino treasures was lost on this high-ranking bruiser, another of Hitler's calculated appointments, he was holding the scroll in which Abbot Diamare expressed his gratitude to the Hermann Goering Division for rescuing the treasures of Montecassino.

'There are the crates we helped to pack!' one of the audience called out.

The German soldiers carried drawers of precious scrolls to the gate of the castle, where they handed them over to Italian workmen. The camera showed soldiers in helmets and long coats standing beside one of the paintings from the monastery.

'Who do they look so grim?' Angela whispered to her uncle.

'Because they're Germans.'

Instead of being reprimanded by his superiors for arranging to transport the treasures of Montecassino to safety, Schlegel had been praised. Hitler hadn't erupted into one of his tantrums and ordered the officer's demotion, or even his execution, despite the fact that the Italian campaign against the British and American invaders was making the dictator nervous as his army was forced back. The Germans saw that the evacuation of the treasures could be used as propaganda in a newsreel shown round the world to demonstrate that the master race weren't barbarian looters. Arranging this film was a shrewd move on Schlegel's part, because it meant that the Germans couldn't appropriate any of the Montecassino treasures and send them to Germany, to add to Reich Marshal Goering's looted art collection.

'It's wonderful that our treasures are now in the safekeeping of the Vatican,' the Abbot enthused. 'It was good of Lieutenant Colonel Schlegel to send us this film, to reassure us. I'll sleep easier for the first time in weeks.'

But Dom Pietro feared what the British and Americans would conclude when they saw the newsreel – perhaps that the majority of the treasures having been saved from Montecassino, the Germans would occupy it as a fortress. Dom Pietro wanted to share his apprehension with the Abbot, but what was the point? Abbot Diamare was weary of the whole business. Monks shouldn't have to get involved in wars, the Abbot believed. They were supposed to be left in peace, to pray for the souls of people who were sometimes too harassed to do that for themselves.

In Dom Pietro's opinion the German General who had handed over Montecassino's treasures in Rome had been made to look like old Noah himself, as if he had saved civilization. But there was no one the monk could say such things to – except to God. There were aspects of theology Dom Pietro wasn't so sure of now. Monks weren't supposed to lose their faith, far worse than an ordinary person losing their faith, because monks had dedicated their lives to God and His works.

Dom Pietro knelt in front of the Wooden Madonna on the side altar in the basilica and asked: *Immaculate Mother, why would God allow Montecassino to get caught up in a war? I'm not saying that He should stop the war immediately, though that would be wonderful. But God could stop the British and American soldiers coming this way with their terrible weapons that can bring down substantial walls. He could show them another way to Rome, and once they get there, He could protect the treasures of the Eternal City, including those of Montecassino now in safekeeping there.*

Dom Pietro told his niece as they stood in the cloisters:

'There's been so much noise in the world these past four years, nobody has listened, Angela. They haven't listened to the voice of God. That's the only voice worth listening to, the only voice you can really trust. Instead people listened to the rantings of Hitler and Mussolini. Look where that's got us, four years of war, and when will it end? The fighting could go on for years around Montecassino until there's hardly a soldier left on either side.

'I was so proud that first day I sat at my desk in the school here. Of course there were disadvantages. The monastery was freezing in winter, which is why I have chilblains,' he demonstrated, holding up his hands. 'These are the hands of an old man, though I'm still in my fifties. I remember one afternoon after lessons I met the Abbot on the terrace. He asked me if I was happy at Montecassino, and if I still wanted to become a monk. I answered an enthusiastic yes to both questions.'

After he had said the last of his prayers for that day Dom Pietro went to the cloister, to see if his sister and niece were settled for the night. Their blankets were damp, but at least they had some shelter, unlike the soldiers of both armies out in the misery of the winter night.

Augusto was searching the ruins of Cassino for more ammunition for his hunting forays for food and for German soldiers. But it was a risky activity, even by nightfall, because of the presence of German soldiers, their field glasses focussed on the advancing army. A searchlight swept the mountainside as he crouched behind a rock, and then resumed his precarious descent.

Cassino was an eerie heap of rubble, with the stench of God knows how many corpses beneath the stones. It took him an hour to locate the street where the gunsmith had done his business, but another building had been blown on top of it, the blocks of masonry too heavy for one man to lift.

There was no other supply of ammunition, so he was either going to have to kill Germans for it, or use snares for his food supply. But where was he to find wire for snares? He didn't have a tool to cut the telephone wires that had been brought down by the bombing.

He sat on a slab of masonry which had once been the lintel of a house. Children had passed laughing under it, after playing in the intact streets, and gone upstairs to secure beds. The coffins of grandparents had been carried out under the same stone on which he was sitting. He would have liked accurate news of the war, to find out what the Red Army was doing to drive the Nazis out of the occupied countries of Europe. How much longer before Hitler was defeated? If he himself survived this war, would Angela stay in Italy and marry him – assuming that she too was alive at the end of the conflict, whenever that might be?

In all his time on the mountain and on the desert battlefield he had never lost the loving image he had of her. It was more secure than a photograph, which could be lost or destroyed, as had been the one of her which he had carried through the North African campaign. It was an image which gave him the strength and the courage to go on, with so many Germans in such close proximity.

He left the ruins of Cassino empty handed, but he had Angela's image in his heart, like a precious relic in a casket.

From Angela's Journal for Wednesday 1 December 1943:

Tenant farmers like Uncle and Aunt who have been evicted by the Germans or whose houses have been demolished to fortify the Gustav Line, have been bringing their salvaged possessions up to the monastery, in prams and slung across the backs of mules which have had to be turned loose at the gate, so God knows what will become of the poor creatures. Some of the refugees are squatting in the arched passage about sixty feet long that cuts through the foundations of the monastery. Uncle Peter tells me that it's called the rabbit warren because monks of the past kept for consumption these animals in cages. I go to services in the basilica when I'm not with the children, but the monks' sung devotions are made discordant by the constant roar of aeroplanes, and the organ notes get obliterated by the approaching artillery.

The Germans have been blasting rock to construct fortifications round the mountain on which the monastery stands. 'They're ruining the landscape,' Uncle Peter told me sadly as we stood watching a dam on the River Rapido being blown up, the spreading water submerging fields in case the opposing army reached here. 'There will be no crops sown this coming spring, no trees standing for the birds to raise their young in,' he said. 'How peaceful this countryside used to be, with only the creaking of carts, the braying of mules. Wild flowers can't grow in churned-up mud. Dante saw nature as the art of God. How we have defiled it!'

Chapter Twenty One

The man in the immaculate uniform relaxing in the armchair, with a Beethoven symphony playing on the gramophone and a crystal glass of whisky within reach, had a sharply hooked nose and high forehead, his eyes so heavily hooded that it was difficult to tell from the angle of his head if he had fallen asleep. But Panzer General Frido von Senger und Etterlin was very much awake in his headquarters, a rundown old palazzo at Roccasecca, at the southern end of the Liri Valley, fifteen miles from Montecassino. He had made his room as homely as possible with fine old paintings and cretonne covered furniture. Two of the canvases were religious scenes, one depicting the Madonna, and there was a crucifix, since he was a Catholic and a lay Benedictine.

Senger's ancestors had hailed from the country between the Black Forest and Lake Constance. His fine mind had been expanded as a Rhodes Scholar at Oxford, reading History and Philosophy, Politics and Economics. His gift for languages and classical learning meant that becoming fluent in English and Italian had been easy, and he had qualified as an interpreter in Italian.

Senger had a genetic inheritance of duty to the state. With the reorganization and reconstruction following the Napoleonic Wars, his family, lawyers and ministers serving the aristocracy, had lost their estates, and so he had become a career soldier out of economic necessity as well as loyalty to tradition.

The former cavalry officer was commanding the highly mechanized 14th Panzer Korps of five divisions consisting of 75,000 soldiers on a fifty mile front stretching from the west coast into the formidable Abruzzi mountain range.

As the General listened to Beethoven's *Pastoral* he envisioned butterflies floating between aromatic flowers in his garden in Germany, his wife Hilda, daughter of a Prussian General, kneeling with her trowel. He yearned for his home soil, for the welcoming arms of his life's partner.

At the beginning of December General Senger had phoned Field Marshal Kesselring, to make sure that he was adopting the correct strategy with regard to the monastery of Montecassino. Kesselring responded: 'High Command has promised the Vatican that we won't occupy the monastery. You must abide by this pledge.'

Senger had told his commanding officer: 'The monastery is such an obvious target, my troops will be safer in their existing dugouts outside it. I've studied the convex shape of the mountainside on which Montecassino stands, which dictates that the best position for observation posts isn't in the monastery, but below it on the mountainside, so we've no need to occupy the building.'

Kesselring ended the conversation: 'I'm sure that, as a devout Catholic, you're relieved that military tactics are against its occupation.'

The Beethoven symphony had uplifted the General and it was time for an aperitif before dining with his fellow officers.

Benigno's four mules were labouring up the track on Monte Cairo on which they had carried tourists on summer days before the war, treks that seemed to have taken place in another world of flowers and blue skies, the drumming of the white-backed woodpecker instead of the rattle of a machine gun. This time it was towards dusk on a winter's night, and instead of children or hampers of food and wine the mules were carrying boxes of basic provisions, the ropes securing the boxes to the wooden saddles abrasive on the mules' bellies as Benigno led them up to the German observers.

'I'm sorry, boys, but this is the only way we're going to survive, because the Germans will feed us,' he spoke to his beloved animals. 'They know that vehicles are no good in this type of countryside, with heavy rain at low level and steep mountain slopes, so they've requisitioned as many mules as they can find. I've seen trains of maybe forty labouring up Monte Camino, with boxes of ammunition which won't last an hour because the guns are spewing out shells day and night. These boxes of provisions (he tapped one on Samuele's side) are for the observation posts on this mountain. The Germans have a clear view of the countryside around, and if they can't stop the advancing army, then we'll be hauling up boxes of ammunition for a long time to come.

'But we have to keep going, boys. I know the loads are heavy and that your hooves must be sore, but there's nothing I can do about it.' He paused to point out the silhouette of the monastery on the mountain. 'At least Beatrice and Angela will be safe in there, thank God. (He crossed himself). 'Don't look down; look up and keep going. Tell yourselves as I tell myself that this war can't go on forever and that God loves mules as well as men and will protect us both.'

From the window of his room Abbot Diamare could see the hellfire on Monte Camino and Monte Maggiore. As Christmas approached he wrote to the German General Fries, complaining about the bombs and shells that were falling near the monastery. He pointed out that the Supreme Command of the German Army had set a 300 metre zone round the monastery, inside which munitions and weapons weren't to be permitted. The Abbot also wrote to the Abbot Primate in Rome, informing him of the German defensive work which was going on round the monastery and which was threatening the inhabitants as well as the building's safety.

Dr Maximilian Becker's Christmas was about to be spoiled. This time his little Fiat wasn't on its way to Montecassino, to wish the Abbot and the few remaining monks the compliments of the season. He was reporting to the chief medical officer of the Hermann Goering Division at a field hospital near Rome, but not to be given promotion for exceptional service among the wounded.

'What business was it of yours to become involved in the Montecassino affair?' his superior ranted at him. 'You're a doctor, not an art historian. You jump into your car and leave your unit without permission, visiting monks kilometres away when you should be helping to treat casualties. Do you understand that I can have you court martialled, with very serious, perhaps fatal, consequences?'

Becker wasn't listening. He was exhausted after the Montecassino business. Before the treasures were delivered safely to Rome he had seen a corporal from Berlin, Goering's representative, using a crowbar on a packing case to extract a gift for the Reich Marshal. Lieutenant Colonel Schlegel had soothed the distraught young doctor with the assurance that there would be no present for the art looter. And then there had been the confrontation with Jacobi the supply officer.

'You misled me, Becker,' Jacobi fulminated. 'When you came to me at first you told me that only two trucks would be needed to shift the Montecassino treasures, but it took far more – over a hundred loads, in fact. The Hermann Goering Division isn't a philanthropic institution: it's a fighting unit of the Fatherland at a critical time in the war, when we can't afford to divert transport to a monastery whose treasures were probably safe there anyway. So what are we getting out of it? A painting?'

'If anything is stolen from the Montecassino treasures, I'll go to Field Marshal Kesselring,' Becker threatened.

'Are you listening?' the medical officer shouted at their December confrontation. 'What have you to say for yourself?'

'I did it for European civilization.'

The medical officer's palm pounded the desk.

'Then you're in the wrong country. You should be in

Russia, treating our wounded and helping us to achieve victory if you want to save European civilization. I'm going to have you transferred to the Eastern Front.'

From Angela's Journal for Friday 24 December 1943:

The Blessed Sacrament containing the Host has been placed on the altar of the basilica, and I have been praying to its silver shape, like the rays of the sun. I prayed for my family in Glasgow, having not heard from them since Italy declared war. I wonder if Papa and Mama are struggling to keep the café open. I remember those Christmases at home, with midnight Mass, then a sleepless night before going through to the living room with my brothers - and later, little Maria - in the dawn to see our stockings hanging from the mantelpiece and containing modest presents from thrifty parents who were determined not to spoil us despite their comparative comfort. The candles on the tree would be lit for the festive lunch. Will Papa be making his famous polenta again this year? I also prayed that Uncle Benigno and Augusto are surviving out in that hostile countryside of snowstorms and artillery, far from these summer days when I picked a pail of cherries,

then walked Augusto and his dog home,
waiting for him to take my hand.

From Angela's Journal for Saturday 25 December 1943:

I am sad because I don't have a gift for
Aunt Beatrice this Christmas. The greatest
gift she could receive this day would be
for Uncle Benigno to knock on the door
marked PAX. Uncle Peter came to give us
his blessing. 'Do you know what I'd love
to do this morning?' he told us. 'I'd love
to ring the bells of the monastery so that
the soldiers in the mountains and valleys
would hear them and lay down their
weapons. Peace on earth and goodwill
towards men. But would they listen to our
bells? Would they listen to God Himself?'

Annabelle the cat is still with me, thank
God, because she is wonderful company.
I share my food with her and she sleeps
curled against my breasts, sharing her
warmth.

Father Desmond O'Brien, the Catholic Padre attached to
the RAMC, was helping to carry the wounded soldier into
the medical tent where the surgeon and Dr Christopher
Murchison, now a Captain, were standing beside the
operating table on Christmas Day. The surgeon looked at the
exposed guts and shook his head.

'Will you help me carry this poor man to my tent?' Father O'Brien asked Christopher.

It was the tent the priest slept in. He lit a candle on the upturned provisions box he used for an altar, put the narrow gold stole round his neck and anointed the dying man with oils. The young Captain was moved by the scene and knelt as the priest said a prayer.

'You look very tired,' Father O'Brien observed.

'I am very tired. There are so many men to treat, so few that we can help.'

'Come to my tent tonight and we'll have a chat. I've a bottle of Irish whisky that will help.'

The Captain went to fetch men to carry the corpse from the priest's tent. Wasn't it strange that they were probably not more than twenty miles from Montecassino, where Angela had been staying with her aunt and uncle before this hellish war?

He went to the priest's tent after supper, gratefully accepting the whisky.

'Are you a praying man?' Father O'Brien asked.

'Not really.'

'There's nothing stronger than prayer. You'll find when you get on your knees, that you'll have the strength and optimism to rise to the challenge of the day ahead. We may as well start you off now. Is there a particular person to be prayed for?'

'A friend called Angela, who's at Montecassino.'

'Then Angela's going to need our prayers, the way this battle is moving.'

General Senger's appreciative eyes were lifted to the mountain top as he was being driven up the road of double bends to Montecassino on Christmas Day. But there was no truce to mark Christ's nativity. Fighting continued as before, incessant, ferocious. An active man who loved to be out on the hills, the wind in his face, Senger liked nothing better than to kneel at a small wayside chapel, to pray for all the dead and for the preservation of the living in this dreadful war. He prayed for a cessation, even if it meant Germany surrendering. He visited the front line regularly and had learned from the Great War, reinforced in this conflict, that battle exhaustion had to be taken into account when assessing a situation, which was why he studied closely the faces of the gunner and the infantry soldier as he spoke to them, seeing in their eyes the loss of the will to battle on, and in their thin faces the lack of physical strength from insufficient sustenance.

He was returning from a tour of his men as he was driven up to the monastery. But there was a problem. The sentry on duty at the gate had strict instructions not to allow any military personnel to enter. The General appreciated that the sentry was doing his duty, and explained that he had to see the Abbot.

'Are you certain that the neutrality of the monastery is being strictly observed?' Senger asked the old man, after they had exchanged Christmas greetings.

'I give you my word. Will you join us in the crypt for Mass, and stay to share our simple lunch, General?'

'I'll be honoured.'

During the meal he refrained from looking out of the windows which gave a clear view of the combat zone below. The brief light was fading as he was driven back to the palazzo at Roccasecca, sad that men had died violently during that day of the miraculous gentle birth of Christ. After a pleasant dinner he relaxed in an armchair with a glass of wine, listening to a service of carols from the Vatican on the wireless as he thought with love of his family, wondering how they had spent this holiest of days. When the broadcast was finished he went through to the library, well stocked with volumes in many European languages. He selected a volume of the 'Duino Elegies' by Rainer Maria Rilke, echoing the Czech poet's *heartfelt appeal: Who, if I cried out, would hear me among the angels' hierarchies?* because the General's prayers for the ending of the war were not being answered.

Senger was reading Rilke's 'Sonnets to Orpheus' when an orderly came in to tell him that the show was about to begin. The General laid down the volume and followed the orderly through to the hall. He had already seen the newly released film *Der Weisse Traum* (The White Dream) several times, but as he settled back in his chair it was as if he was viewing the young skater's struggle for success for the first time as her blades hissed over the ice.

After the German General had departed Dom Pietro told the refugees to sit round in a circle and asked Angela to sit in the middle, to lead the singing of carols among the hundred and fifty or so in the Benefactors' Cloister, the numbers continuing to fluctuate as people came and went, some bringing provisions such as maize. The three bronze doors to the basilica were open, and Dom Pietro went through to the organ, to play *Tu Scendi dalle stelle* ('You Come Down from the Stars'), the music and the singing of the carol going out into the dark dismal countryside, hopefully heard by soldiers of both sides down in the valleys, mud solidified into treacherous ice.

The refugees felt as if a fire was burning close to them that Christmas, and had a sense of hope, as if they were going to survive, such was the majesty of the organ music and the optimistic voice of this young woman wrapped in a blanket in the centre of their charmed circle on this sub-zero holy day. She had lost too much weight because of the scarcity of food, and her lack of sleep due to trying to calm terrified refugees, especially children. But despite her thin face, she was still beautiful, and still she found the strength to sing.

On the ledges of the mountains and down in the valleys, men of both armies were smoking after their meals, the lights of their cigarettes too small for an enemy gunner to discern. They were spooning from tins the same cold food that they had been having for weeks while thinking of warm and loving past Christmases at home with their families.

Christmas dinner for the refugees was in the evening.

Dom Pietro and his sister carried up the big pots of broth that Beatrice had made from scraps of dried goat meat, and they ladled it onto plates for the refugees, with a small piece of polenta each. Angela wished that they had Christ with them to perform the miracle of the loaves and fishes on the food, because there was so little to go round, and so many old and sick people who needed nourishment.

'I wonder what kind of Christmas Benigno is having?' his spouse asked tearfully, recalling his clown's dance, his shadow moving across a wall on which a machine gun now rested.

From Angela's Journal for Tuesday 28 December 1943:

> Uncle Peter tells me about terrible scenes that he witnessed at the gate marked PAX. More refugees with their scant provisions and tattered clothes have laboured up the steep winding road to the monastery in the driven rain and sleet, searching for a corner to shelter from the war and the foul weather, but the German soldiers won't allow them to approach the building. 'It's like a scene out of Inferno,' Uncle Peter says, 'except that these terrified refugees are not sinners, but innocent men, women and children who have been driven from their homes by this hellish war.' He said that the Germans at the gate were using whips and clubs to drive the refugees back,

as if they were stubborn mules. A widow with a lame child had a piece of paper from her priest, giving her permission to enter the monastery, but after he had read it a soldier struck her in the face and tore up her paper.

Uncle Peter went out again to argue with the soldiers, telling them that they have no right to prevent people from seeking shelter in a Benedictine house of God, but they ignored him, as if they didn't understand what he was saying. He tells me: 'I don't want to provoke them in case they become even more brutal towards the refugees, who'll lie down in the open in the freezing conditions rather than go back down into the battle zone.'

Chapter Twenty Two

From Angela's Journal for Friday 31 December 1943:

This Journal, which began with such joy over five years ago when I first arrived in Italy and saw the wonder of Montecassino, is being written on the last day of another year of war, suffering and death. Yesterday a German dispatch rider roared up to the gate of the monastery, bringing in his pouch an official notice. Dom Emmanuel Munding translated it into Italian and Uncle Peter asked me to copy it, since it is part of the annals of Montecassino. The note, which has been posted outside the gate, reads: TRESPASS ON THE GROUNDS OF THE MONASTERY WITHIN A RADIUS OF 300 METRES IS FORBIDDEN TO ALL MILITARY PERSONNEL. THE SAME APPLIES TO THE ERECTION OF MILITARY FACILITIES. The Abbot is pleased with the warning, as he told me when I had the privilege of sharing the monks' treats of sweets and wine. Aunt was also invited, and I heard her wearily asking her brother: 'When is all this going to end?'

Uncle Peter warns that the war could go on for a long time yet, judging by the number of men and guns that are in the countryside below the monastery. He said sadly: 'Neither side can afford to retreat. This is a battle to the death, and innocent civilians are already getting caught up in it.' He warned that the monastery can't hold the number of people - some of them Montecassino's tenants - who've been driven from the woods and mountain slopes where they've been sheltering. 'Even if the German soldiers would allow them up to our gate, we can't offer them much food, or soft beds to lie on, but at least they'll have spiritual comfort.' For Aunt's benefit he predicted: 'Benigno and Augusto will both survive, because they know places to hide, and are both skilled hunters. But I fear for all those poor people huddled in the countryside around.'

The first days of the new year of 1944 brought drastic changes. The 300 metre protective zone around the monastery was abolished, and three lorries arrived to remove the refugees and tenants. Some of them resisted going on the lorries, though they were warned by the Abbot that if they remained, they would be in the battle zone. They accused the monks of betraying them, and several decided to take refuge in the scrub surrounding the monastery, rather than be pushed aboard the vehicles for an unknown destination, an unknown fate by former allies who were now their enemies.

The Abbot had persuaded the Germans to leave the sick in the infirmary, including Angela and Beatrice, who were helping with the nursing.

The Abbot and the few remaining monks were offered evacuation to Rome.

'The monastery must be in danger,' Dom Pietro surmised.

'I've been given an assurance that it won't be used for purposes of war,' the Abbot told his monks.

'Then why is it being cleared out?' Dom Pietro wanted to know. 'And why do the Germans want to buy our livestock?'

'To feed their troops presumably. It's not a disaster; we can't look after the animals, though we have a sufficient store of fodder, because our workers who do this have been evacuated with the refugees. Take no money from the Germans for the animals; they can, if they wish, make a donation to St Benedict. One day the entire world will know the truth about what happened at Montecassino,' the Abbot predicted, his pendulous lower lip trembling, eyes filling with the tears he had held back for months.

The monastery's donkeys had already been taken, the cows, sheep and lambs loaded on trucks. The Germans returned to take away nearly ninety more sheep, making payment for them. But the monks had brought into the monastery from their surrounding land thirty sheep for breeding, and the best milk cows, goats, pigs, chickens and donkeys.

'This place has become a second Noah's Ark,' Dom Pietro pointed out to Angela, who had left her temporary post as nurse in the infirmary when the German trucks had departed with the bleating flocks.

From Angela's Journal for Monday 10 January 1944:

I was in the infirmary, sitting by the bed, holding the hand of Lucia, the thirteen year old daughter of the cook. Why was the young girl, so close to death, smiling as she stared towards the door? 'What are you seeing?' I asked the serene patient. 'A lady standing in the doorway, with her arms stretched out. She's come for me.' I thought the child was having a hallucination as she passed on. Orazio her father was calm as he helped me to wrap the body of his beloved daughter in a sheet, and when I told him about the visitation of the lady, he smiled. 'That's my ancestor. She always comes to welcome members of the family to the next world, which must be better than this one.'

The body lay in the Chapel of the Crucifixion in the torretta, the monks kneeling before it. Uncle Peter helped to lay Lucia in the coffin which Dom Eusebio Grossetti, who is an artist in all things he touches, had finished making, and which he and Uncle shouldered to the cemetery at Sant' Agata, near the monastery on the side away from the front lines, where there are so many new crosses erected by Dom Eusebio, who has become the sexton as well as the coffin maker for refugees of all ages. 'How can a benevolent God permit such wastage?' Uncle Peter blurted out in my presence when he and Dom Eusebio had returned from the cemetery. 'This was an innocent child who had hardly lived.' Dom Eusebio said gently: 'I understand your anguish, and I too have doubts.' He revealed that he had been angry as well as tearful when making his first coffin of this war, until he told himself that God didn't equip these armies killing each other below us. 'He didn't manufacture the shells that kill innocent civilians,' Dom Eusebio said. 'I understand that you would like to get back to your scholarship, Dom Pietro, but God has given us a mission in this war, to comfort where we can, and to give the dead Christian burial.'

As I was putting my hand to my throat to touch my cross, I realized that the locket which Christopher gave me wasn't there. I have searched the infirmary where I have been most of the day, but can't find it. I am sad about its loss because it was given to me with love and hope. Perhaps it will turn up.

Dom Martino Matronola, the Abbot's secretary, dipped his pen in black ink and wrote in copperplate in the annals:

11 January, 1944:

This evening, at nine o' clock, the first Anglo-American shell hit the monastery.

He blotted before proceeding with his tragic narrative. The following day he would record that the cloister had been partly smashed. It was Reich Marshal Goering's birthday, but among the art treasures presented to him there was nothing from Montecassino from the Hermann Goering Division, though he would have prized the Wooden Madonna on the altar of the side chapel to which Angela prayed daily and from whom she derived much comfort.

She liked to walk on the terrace, even though it was freezing, scanning the surrounding snow-clad mountains and wondering how Augusto could possibly survive in such conditions. But now it was too dangerous for her to go out on to the terrace because of the shells of both armies streaking over the monastery, making the massive building shake.

From Angela's Journal for Tuesday 18 January 1944:

At noon today, at the time of the Angelus, one of the shells hit the ravine behind the monastery, killing a woman and injuring several people. A girl who wasn't even two years of age was carried up to the monastery and laid on a bed in the infirmary, her brains coming out through the hole in her head made by a fragment of the shell. I knelt beside her, holding her hand until she died, and for the first time doubted my faith.

During supper on this day of death letters arrived from Rome, which the Abbot read out to the monks and which Uncle Peter told me about. The Holy Father understands the grave situation that Montecassino had been placed in, between the two armies, but nothing can be done.

'Only God can save us,' the Abbot articulated, evidently in despair.

I have not washed for days. There is a shortage of water. I have no stockings and my zupei need replacing. I tore up the blouse of a woman killed a few days ago by a shell and am using it as sanitary towels. But what are my complaints about hygiene and personal discomfort compared to the sufferings of the refugees, who have lost their homes and loved ones? The mother of the two year old who died this morning, brained by a shell fragment, lies in the cloisters like a corpse, having exhausted herself through weeping. It would take Christ Himself, walking through this monastery, to comfort the sick and bereaved. I earnestly believe that I am

receiving a matchless lesson in humility.
Why do I need stockings? Or waves in my
hair, as Mama's deft fingers fashioned
on my head as if I had grown sleek black
wings? I have an aching tooth, but there
is no dentist here. I have an aching heart
for those in distress around me. Endure,
go looking for others to help.

Official historians would point out that the Allied armies were used to fighting on flat terrain, as on the monotonous miles of the deserts of Libya, but warfare involving the ascent of mountains swept by blizzards, and the crossing of numerous rivers swollen with rain, was new to them. The advancing Allied army had reached the Garigliano River, and the next water barrier was the Rapido, which flowed alongside the eastern side of the Montecassino ridge before combining with the Garigliano. Though only about fifty feet wide, the Rapido was too deep to wade, and its banks, reaching a height of ten feet, were treacherous with mud, the flow swift and icy. The terrain on the far side, the Allies' side, was a swamp, and the Germans had impeded the movement of troops and machines and made them vulnerable targets by blowing up dams and diverting part of the current into the plain.

The Garigliano was crossed on the night of 17 January by the British 10th Corps, with a beachhead secured on the north side of the river. The success surprised and dismayed the Germans, and the following day General Senger arrived to assess the situation. The shadow of the tame raven from the monastery swept over him on the breezy hill where he consulted the officers on the scene. Reinforcements were required urgently to halt the British attack, so he telephoned Kesselring at his headquarters and ask for more troops. He was dubious that his request was granted, but 'Smiling Albert' agreed that he could have the loan of two divisions.

These additional troops were in place when the British prepared to cross the Rapido under the dubious cover of a seeping fog on the night of 20 January. Some of the boats that the Allied soldiers carried to the river had been holed by artillery fire. On the opposite bank the Germans had stripped away the vegetation to give their gunners a clear field of fire.

Ascending the mountain slope overlooking the Rapido, Benigno and his mule train were laden with more ammunition. They passed a German officer wearing earphones. He was now only a skull, with no eyes in the sockets, and no tongue in his head to reply to whoever was on the other end of the dead line. Some of the corpses had been consumed by wolves, leaving only skeletons, gun pouches round their exposed ribs.

The four mules never looked at the corpses, but kept their eyes on the track ahead. A wolf had tried to chew the wallet of a German soldier, scattering the contents around his bones. A photograph of a young woman and child standing outside a wooden house lay under his elbow stripped to the sinews.

'Have a feed, boys,' Benigno told his mules. From his

seat on a rock the battle round the Rapido was shrouded in the eerie fog mixed with the smoke from the shells. In the illumination of the explosions the muleteer watched a boat laden with men and equipment setting out to cross the river. The fog swirled across, and when it lifted again the boat was being carried away, upside down, on the current. He heard the sounds of mines going off under Allied boots, but was spared the screams as soldiers were maimed and blinded. It was too harrowing a scene to witness, so he and his mules continued their climb.

Mussolini was sitting in his office in the Villa delle Orsoline at Garnano. As he looked around the drab environment, his sumptuous office in the Palazzo Venezia in Rome with its seductive mosaics was a distant memory. How had this fall come to pass? He had always had his doubts about the King and the Generals. To think that a veteran Fascist like de Bono could desert him! He had had to condemn his son-in-law Ciano to death, but personal feelings had to be set aside for the sake of Fascism, despite the anguish of his daughter. Though his powers were reduced, he was determined to crush all opposition, a resolution that came with a fist. But his resolution faltered with the acceptance that the Germans had saved him, only to make him their servant. They had taken Bolzano and Trieste away from Italy and had interned most of his army. But he would start another with the support of the young men who had grown up under the Fascist era. He began to sing 'Giovinezza' and would not give up hope.

'Hail, people of heroes,

Hail, immortal Fatherland,

Your sons were born again

With the faith and the Ideal.

Your warriors' valour,

Your pioneers' virtue,

Alighieri's vision,

Today shines in every heart.'

Chapter Twenty Three

'This of course is a highly dangerous conversation which could put us in front of a firing squad – or worse,' General Senger cautioned.

He was speaking in Castello Massimo, his new headquarters, having found it necessary to move from the decrepit palazzo in Roccasecca. Though more secluded and peaceful, the Castello's disadvantage was that it was further away from the front, with a visit to a battalion now taking a whole day instead of an afternoon.

'We both understand that the benefits far outweigh personal risk,' Colonel Schmidt von Altenstadt, his new Chief of Staff, answered calmly.

The two of them had moved from the big officers' mess to a smaller, more private room which they shared with several other trusted officers. The General recharged their wine glasses from the cellar of the Castello. His Chief of Staff had told him that he had become a friend of Count Claus von Stauffenberg through working with him in Berlin. Colonel Schmidt had just disclosed the dangerous information that he and Stauffenberg were trying to persuade individual Commanders-in-Chief of army groups to help to overthrow Hitler.

The flames of the fire were distorted in the General's wine glass balanced on his knee. He had a gift for putting men at their ease, of having them trust him, whatever their rank.

'I can tell you, gentlemen, the exact date on which I

realized that this war was lost. It was on 11 December 1941, the day our deluded Führer declared war on America, the time that our offensive against Moscow was halted by ice and Soviet infantry. We had committed Napoleon's error in not realizing that the weather can be an even worse adversary than a well-equipped and well trained army. As you know, I was commanding 17 Panzer Division in the autumn of 1942 in Russia, so I saw the disaster at first hand. The war is lost, gentlemen, whatever new weapons are brought to the fronts. It's now a question of ending hostilities and getting rid of the regime.'

The younger men in the room spoke of their optimism that a cessation could be achieved.

'Look at it this way,' Senger went on. 'It isn't possible to prepare a detailed plan to overthrow Hitler with so few people in the know, but if the number is increased, then secrecy is breached and the plot will be compromised. And another factor: many Germans, generals, industrialists and professors in the universities are supporters of Hitler, which is why we have got into this mess.'

The intellectual General, who had been reading Kant the previous night, didn't share all his thoughts with the others in the room. He was convinced that the Russians, having put so much manpower and weaponry into the defeat of Hitler, would pillage Germany and establish a permanent sphere of influence.

The wind was rising outside, snowflakes making delicate lace-like patterns on the windows. General Senger had another private thought which he had turned into a nightly prayer: let the Allies establish a second front by a landing in Western Europe.

From Angela's Journal for Friday 21 January 1944:

Though Dom Matronola is keeping a daily diary on behalf of the monks, I feel that I also must use my Journal to make a record of what is happening, trapped as I am in the monastery between two armies, the shells from both falling on the building, causing damage and terror. With two records being kept, perhaps at least one will survive to tell the world what happened to Montecassino in the battles.

Today was a grim day. The gatekeeper's little boy died of sickness in the dawn when I was still sleeping. Then, when I woke, more tragic news. Overnight an Allied shell penetrated the basilica. I insisted on going with Uncle Peter to see the damage, because I was frantic about the safety of the statuette of the Wooden Madonna which I had prevented from being taken to the safety of Rome. The dust was choking as I groped my way to the side altar, like a blind person, and when I found it intact I went down on my knees, clutching the Wooden Madonna to my heart and giving thanks for her survival.

'Oh God, no!' one of the monks cried out, and when we went to him, we saw that the massive painting by Luca Giordano, showing the crowds gathered for the dedication of the basilica in the eleventh century had been badly damaged by a shell which came through a window and struck the painting, almost as if out of malevolence. Most of the glass from the windows were scattered round our shoes. The Abbot ordered that nothing was to be touched until salvage possibilities have been assessed, though I can't see how pulverized marbles can be restored, except by a miracle. The Abbot has forbidden anyone to enter the church. I took the statuette down to the crypt. Some of the stained glass had been blown in, but I put the Madonna on the altar.

From Angela's Journal for Monday 24 January 1944:

It would take a Dante to describe this hell we find ourselves in. The firing started around 9.30 a.m. Several shells fell on the monastery, one smashing the north-west corner of the Collegio roof. Two have fallen on the Noviate, and one of the Brothers came in to announce that a shell has just fallen on the Bramante Cloister and demolished a column. A fragment *flew into the Physics Study, and grazed Fra Giacomo's head while he was sleeping. I went to see him, to bathe the graze, and found him saying Hail Marys in gratitude for it being such a minor injury.*

Annabelle the cat has been with me wherever I went. She was at my heels when the shell fell, but when I turned she had disappeared. It was probably terror at the exploding shell. I have been calling for her for the past hour and searching for her, but the monastery is such a huge place, she could be anywhere but, pray God, not under rubble. I will cry myself to sleep because she isn't beside me to warm me and reassure me that we will survive together.

The Abbot decided that for safety the monks must move out of their cells to two narrow corridors on the lowest floor of the Collegio, the wing where the monastery school was. The Abbot argued it was the side of the building that would best protect them from the wayward artillery of the British and Americans. It was the school's natural history museum, and it contained stuffed animals from the surrounding valleys and mountains, including a wolf. These exhibits were cleared out, and the corridors divided into rooms, including a chapel.

Beatrice and Angela were sleeping on the floor in the small room next to Dom Pietro's because it was too dangerous to lie down in the cloisters. Beatrice was very thin and her cough was getting worse. There were now only seventeen people in the monastery, the few monks and the refugees who had been sick in the infirmary when the Germans removed the rest of the refugees by lorry earlier that month.

But as more and more refugees from the ruins of Cassino and surrounding villages crowded round the gate marked PAX, the Abbot refused them entry. The monastery was out of fuel for heating, though there was water. The monks' stores were well enough supplied with food and wine, but the Abbot decreed with reluctance, conscious that he was transgressing the Founder's rule of hospitality, that there wasn't sufficient food to share with the refugees. If the battle continued around the monastery, which was practically in a state of siege, the monks would use up their stores and become weak through lack of sustenance, losing control of the monastery to which they had a prime obligation.

However, about a hundred refugees had managed to gain entry and were in the *conigliera*, the rabbit warren. The rabbits had had more room than the new occupants, but at least they were protected from the artillery fire of the British and Americans, and from the snow and rain of that tragic winter.

The few monks shared out their duties, the heaviest and most sorrowful falling on Dom Eusebio, who sawed planks to make coffins and dug graves.

From Angela's Journal for Tuesday 25 January 1944:

I spend most of my time now in the infirmary, trying to comfort the injured and dying. With the image of the Wooden Madonna in mind I pray constantly as I work, holding a spoon to a patient's lips, clasping between my hands the hand of another passing away in the hope that I am transmitting peace. A young woman was brought into the infirmary this afternoon, blood pouring from her arm from shrapnel. I had torn up old bed sheets of the monks as bandages, but this woman's gaping wound required stitching. Even if the proper needle and gut was available, no one in the monastery has the skill to close the wound.

I tore a strip of linen and knotted a tourniquet round the woman's arm dangling from the bed into a bowl to catch the lifeblood gushing from her body. Was it desperation which made me place my hand on her arm, with an intense prayer that she would pass away without pain or terror?

The blood stopped flowing and began to congeal. 'Your hand is so hot, so comforting,' the woman told me weakly. My experience was repeated with the next wounded person to be carried into the infirmary, this time a child, her shin bone exposed. Dom Eusebio saw me staunching the wound by covering it with my hand. 'Has this happened before?' he asked. 'Not until today,' I told him. 'But why?' I wanted to know. He said that I pray so much to the wooden statuette of the Madonna that she has given me healing powers.

This is Burns Night. The national bard of Scotland wrote in hope that

man to man, the world o'er
shall brithers be for a' that.

How ironic that worthy sentiment is in such a situation. However, as I was trying to comfort another woman wounded by a stray shell, I sang her to sleep with Burns's wonderful song 'Flow Gently Sweet Afton Among Thy Green Braes.'

I am still sad because my beloved Annabelle hasn't been found. The monks have been calling for her and helping to search the monastery, because they too love animals. I cannot bear the thought that she is lost in this vast building, lying trembling, starving.

From Angela's Journal for Friday 28 January 1944:

The wound on the arm of the woman who was bleeding to death is healing, and *she's regaining her strength. As I passed her bed this morning she clutched at my dress and thanked me for the 'miracle.'*

Each monk celebrates a private daily Mass, on his own, usually in a different place. I accompanied Uncle Peter down to the crypt today, and we could hear the pounding of the guns as we knelt in prayer. I thanked the Wooden Madonna for the gift of healing, and hope that I can repay the faith she has vested in me.

'So far they have failed to cross the Rapido,' 'Smiling Albert' Kesselring observed to his senior officers, but didn't share with them his respect for the bravery and tenacity of the American troops who had given their lives. 'However, we must halt them in their tracks at Anzio.' He indicated the landing place on the map, over which his finger had travelled many times as he worked out a strategy. 'The Führer considers that this is an abscess that must be excised at all costs, and he has personally ordered more troops, more artillery and aircraft to burst the abscess. General von Mackensen is transferring his headquarters from Verona to the Anzio front to take charge of the counterattack. He plans to cut the beachhead in half. I can't help feeling, however, that the enemy has lost the advantage because they have only a division or so of infantry, and no infantry armour.'

When the moon rose Augusto Faccenda approached the

fortified De Santis house in which the German machine gun battery crew were sleeping. Because he was an accomplished hunter he moved among the inert men stealthily, observing their unshaven faces. He could have extracted a pistol from a holster at the waist of one of them and shot the four of them because they had invaded his country, but he decided to spare them since they looked so vulnerable, two of them no more than boys. Besides, he had too many deaths on his hands already in North Africa.

He looked up at the monastery, shell bursts lighting up its windows. He hoped that that was where Angela was likely to be, under the protection of her uncle the monk. He knew that he had to arrive at the door of the monastery before dawn, otherwise he would be a sure target for snipers. But he was brave, and he was in love.

The first service of the day had just ended, and Dom Pietro was descending the steps of the basilica when he heard hammering on the gate.

'Who's there?' he shouted through the thick timber.

'A refugee.'

'We don't have room for any more refugees.'

'I'm by myself.'

'I'm sorry.'

'Does the name Angela Boni mean anything to you?' the voice from the other side of the thick wood enquired.

'I'm her uncle, Dom Pietro.'

'Is she with you?' the voice continued.

'She is.'

'Tell her that Augusto Faccenda is at the gate.'

'I know who you are,' the monk said, opening the gate. 'Where have you been?' he asked as they embraced.

'It's a long story,' the fugitive said. 'Right now I want to see Angela.'

In his sleep the Abbot heard a distraught voice calling out the name of the monastery three times, and he took this as a prophecy of its destruction for the fourth time in its history which he would pass on to his monks.

From Angela's Journal for Monday 31 January 1944:

> *It seemed to be another dream about Augusto. This time we were on a mountain slope together. I was trying to warn him that he was in danger, but when I opened my eyes he was standing, smiling down at me. I took his hand and we went down to the crypt. I didn't need to ask this Communist to go down on his knees beside me to give thanks to the Wooden Madonna for our safety. We prayed shoulder to shoulder.*

In the first week of February German and American soldiers exchanged fire on the Montecassino ridge a few hundred metres from the monastery. Dom Matronola noted in the monks' diary his belief that before long the monastery would find itself *on the other side*. Several days later he wrote: *We are impatiently watching the gradual destruction of the monastery, with our hearts full of bitterness.* He estimated that the building had already been hit by several hundred shells.

The following morning Dom Pietro was summoned to the main gate from his devotions, to find it being pounded by the fists of ten demented women. The German guards had fled from the gate marked PAX, because the battle on the ridge was reaching its bloody conclusion, and every soldier was needed for the defence.

Dom Pietro listened to their pleas through the thick timber and went to take the Abbot's instructions.

Diamare waved a hand, as if relinquishing command of a hopeless situation: 'Let them in!'

The ten women, their knuckles bleeding from the pounding, were followed by many other refugees, driven from the mountain caves they had been hiding in by the ever-increasing artillery bombardment and the violent thunderstorms, the lightning as dazzling as the massive guns below.

Soon 800 men, women and children were rushing through the monastery, their way stopped by Dom Pietro and Dom Eusebio guarding their refuge.

'Respect this house of God!' Dom Pietro warned them, raising his voice to a shout for the first time since he had come to the monastery as a youth.

They were hungry, but they stopped and turned away

from the refuge. Dom Pietro hurried after them, not to offer them a share of the monks' food, but to warn them that the cloisters were a dangerous place to linger in because of exposure to artillery, a warning borne out by the killing of a man drawing water from the cistern. Most of the refugees had foraged for food which they had wrapped in their bundles, all that remained of their worldly goods. When a shell killed one of the monastery's animals its butchery was completed by knives produced by refugees, its meat shared out. One man who had persuaded the monks to hand over a quantity of maize was selling it by the kilo to starving families. The cloisters became a kitchen, with fires burning on the flagstones for cooking and warmth, with curtained corners as latrines. A sheltered place where, for centuries, monks had walked in contemplation, became a site of degradation, sickness and death.

'There's no point in me making any more coffins because we can no longer bury the refugees,' Dom Eusebio told the Abbot.

A boy, playing in the cloister, was badly injured, and Augusto carried him to the infirmary where Dom Pietro prayed over him while Angela placed her hand on his life-threatening wounds. Dom Eusebio had taken on the responsibility of looking after the sick. Helped by Angela, Augusto and Beatrice, the selfless monk laboured day and night, trying to halt an illness whose name they didn't even know, but which was caused by the non-existent sanitary conditions, with the cloisters running with urine, and heaps of excrement in the corners, waiting to be shovelled over the parapet.

Dom Pietro counted over one hundred shells which hit the building on a single day, each one seeming to penetrate his heart. On 10 February, the feast day of St Scholastica, Dom Matronola, fearless of shells because he was confident of a life to come, was the sole celebrant at Scholastica's tomb. In the gloom of the stairs leading down to the crypt he discerned a young couple lying together. But he hadn't surprised them in the act of making love. He closed the eyes of the dead man and picked up the woman's wrist, but the pulse was fading. Kneeling, the monk gave them absolution.

From Angela's Journal for Thursday 10 February 1944:

I am exhausted, and go down to pray to the Wooden Madonna, now removed from the crypt to the small chapel in the monks' refuge. 'Holy Mother, I believe firmly that you can see and hear me, and I ask that you and the Lord my God bring this terrible war to an end, even if there is no victor. I am tired, but I will continue to try to help the wounded with the powers you have placed in my hands.'

Chapter Twenty Four

From Angela's Journal for Friday 11 February 1944:

I am expecting this ink to run with my tears any second because my beloved Aunt Beatrice has passed away on this, the Feast Day of Our Lady of Lourdes. Aunt's brother Peter administered the Last Rites and asked Our Lady to accompany her soul to the Heaven she deserves. She wore herself out through her labours in the kitchen, feeding the refugees, and had lost the will to live because she had come to believe that her beloved husband Benigno was dead. They have both been so generous, so loving towards me since the day - in another life, it seems - I arrived in Italy. Then she was evicted from her home and had to endure harsh conditions here in the monastery, getting no sleep in the cloisters because of the cold and the explosions of shells in the surrounding countryside.

'Will you build a coffin for Beatrice?' Uncle Peter asked Dom Eusebio. 'But where are we to bury your dear sister?' he enquired. 'In the monks' cemetery. The Abbot has given his permission. He thinks that it will be the first female interment - apart from St Scholastica, that is - in

the whole history of Montecassino.' Uncle Peter added that the Abbot agrees that if the monastery survives the war, Beatrice's remains can be removed to the cemetery outside where our family are buried.

Augusto helped Dom Eusebio to make Aunt's coffin. He dug the grave and helped to carry the coffin to the cemetery. I went with Uncle Peter, but couldn't hear his prayer because of the noise of the bombardment. It felt as if at any moment a shell would land in the grave, giving her no peace, even in death.

Tonight Augusto asked: 'Will you marry me?' When I had recovered from the shock of his proposal I said: 'Why do you ask me at such a time?' His reply was: 'Because I love you and we can give each other strength.' But I told him that we could get strength through prayer. 'I pray each morning that we'll both be spared,' he revealed. 'I've gone back to Catholicism, after being a fool and deserting it. Please marry me - now.' I told him: 'I can't, Augusto, not because I don't love you, but because it isn't the right time or place. I want to be married by my uncle in this monastery with my family in Scotland present when the war is over, whenever that will be.' 'But we might not survive,' *he pointed out. I asked: 'Is that a good reason for marrying? We're together here, helping where we can. Isn't that sufficient for you? And if we're killed, we'll find each other after we've passed over, and will be together for eternity.'*

The nib wavered on the page of the monks' diary as Dom Matronola wrote the date 13 February and recorded through his tears: *Alle 3:45, pie obit in Domino d. Eusebius Grossetti, monachus et sacerdos Montis Casini R.I.P.*

The deathbed scene was a subject worthy of the palette of Pietro Annigoni. Eusebio was in much pain, perhaps from a fever he had contacted while tending to the refugees. Dom Matronola was gentle and loving as he prepared his Brother to receive the Last Sacrament. The Abbot administered it, imparting to Eusebio the apostolic absolution in *articulo mortis* above the din of the ordnance of the opposing armies, and reciting the prayer of the dying while the monks stood round the bed. At Vespers the prayers in hope of eternal life were for the departed.

The monks dressed their Brother in his habit and laid him in one of the corridors, lighting candles and taking turns to pray over his mortal remains. It was Dom Pietro's turn in the dawn, and Angela kept her uncle company.

'This is what it has come to,' the weary monk told his niece as they kept vigil in the freezing corridor. 'The most saintly has been taken from us. Dom Eusebio was a man who never spared himself, sustaining us with his faith and burying us, a man who always had a comforting word and a morsel of bread, especially if it was his own, for a refugee.'

Both armies were now using thousands of mules because of the impossibility of vehicles making progress in the all-pervading mud. The animals moved in trains through the clogged valleys and up and down the shattered mountains, carrying deadly loads of ammunition and dismantled guns. Benigno's quartet of mules was transporting a 75mm mountain gun that weighed 1,700lbs and had a maximum range of five and a half miles. They had been stripped down into ten loads for transportation by mules, with six other mules behind carrying the remainder of the terrifying weapon.

Benigno was leading his four animals down the treacherous track. The moon was full, above the mountains, and by its benevolent light in pre-war days the muleteer would sometimes bring provisions in panniers on the mules up from Cassino for his neighbours. But tonight the way in which it illuminated the valleys and the mountain slopes was treacherous, allowing gunners on both sides to select targets. Shells burst against the mountain, and splinters of rock that could kill as well as lacerate men and animals whizzed around. An endless supply of ammunition was required for the insatiable artillery, the blasts scattering roosting birds from the trees that hadn't already been uprooted. There were ample pickings for ravens and wolves.

Benigno had thought of deserting, leading his animals over the mountain he knew so well, but if he were captured he would probably be executed, the mules used by the Germans until they were broken, then left to die in agony. It was better to stay with them, to look after them, in this endless climbing and descending, and even to die with them.

'I'm sorry boys for this hard labour,' he spoke to them.

The rest of his endearments were obliterated by the sound of an approaching shell. As Benigno turned he saw Samuele, the last mule in the line of four, airborne, as if he was using his large ears to fly to the moon, the section of gun still strapped to his saddle, like an illustration in a child's story book. Then the animal began to fall head-first to the valley. His three companions were showered with rocks, but managed to maintain their footing.

'No! No!' Benigno was shouting, tears streaming down his face. He put his arms round the neck of Paolo, whose rump was bleeding, telling the terrified animal: 'We've both lost a brother.' He raised his fists to the sky and cursed both armies. 'Kill each other if you must, but leave the innocent creatures of this earth alone!'

On 14 February, the day after Dom Eusebio's death, Angela walked among the refugees who had fallen asleep, clutching their rosaries. American guns fired shells at the monastery, but instead of explosives they contained leaflets which drifted down. One of them was brought to the Abbot, who read it out to his monks.

ATTENZIONE!

Italian Friends,

BEWARE!

We have until now been especially careful to avoid shelling the Montecassino monastery. The Germans have known how to benefit from this. But now the fighting has swept closer and closer to its sacred precincts. The time has come when we must train our guns on the monastery itself.

We give you warning so that you may save yourselves. We warn you urgently: Leave the monastery. Leave it at once. Respect this warning. It is for your benefit.

THE FIFTH ARMY

'We could hang as many white sheets as we can collect over the east wall of the monastery - the one that faces the British and American positions,' one of the young men sheltering in the building who had gathered up the airborne leaflets suggested. 'Then we could go out in the hope that there'll be a ceasefire which will allow us to escape.'

It was pointed out that the Germans would shoot as soon as anyone stepped out of the monastery, because they had done that before.

'I'd like to try it,' a university student from Cassino

volunteered. He and two friends left the monastery by the rear, where the Germans were. They were carrying a white flag, but a machine gun pointing at them warned them to go back into the monastery.

'Everyone must do what he or she thinks fit,' the Abbot sent a doleful message to the hundred or so refugees in the *conigliera*, the rabbit warren. The old man was in tears, bewildered, frightened, not for himself but for the safety of his monks, the refugees and the monastery. Were the advancing army's guns, loaded with shells, already elevated to St Benedict's foundation on the mountain? In silence and fear the monks ate what might be their last supper in what was their home. Their scant possessions were already in suitcases in their cells.

The monks' refugee was above the *conigliera*. Dom Matronola was on his knees, praying, when shouting made him hurry to the window. The young Italian refugee who had suggested hanging out white sheets in a plea for a cease-fire so that the threatened building could be evacuated was standing, screaming in German in the passageway where caged rabbits had been fattened for the refectory.

'In the name of God, will someone come and tell us to leave this place!'

The other refugees huddled against each other, in fear of his hysteria as well as the arrival of targeted shells.

Another of the young refugees came in to say that he had at last succeeded in speaking with two German soldiers at one of the monastery's outlying buildings. They told him that a German officer would come into the monastery at five o' clock the following morning to talk to the monks about leaving the monastery.

'He made a condition,' the youth cautioned. 'He said that Dom Matronola was to come, since he's a German speaker, but if anyone else came with him, the officer said they would shoot.'

From Angela's Journal for Monday 14 February 1944:

> *Augusto handed me a Valentine's card he made himself from a scrap of card, with a drawing of me kneeling in front of the Wooden Madonna. 'I hid where you couldn't see me do it,' he confessed. 'You've certainly got artistic talent,' I complimented him. 'I'll treasure this,' I told him, hugging it to my heart. When I turned it over there was a drawing of two hearts intertwined.*
>
> *Is there hope for me?' he asked plaintively. I smiled and pressed his hand.*

For years Dom Matronola had risen in the pre-dawn to attend the first devotions of the day, a reassuring ritual which never varied. But it was too dangerous to enter the damaged basilica, so he said Mass in the monks' refugee, adding a special prayer that his mission to the German officer might be successful before going to escort him to the Abbot.

'I'm authorized to speak for our Abbot,' he told the officer, Lieutenant Deiber, the commander of two tanks stationed near the monastery.

The Abbot sat slumped in silence as his secretary put his request to the impassive officer.

'We ask that we be allowed to leave the monastery and cross the lines to the opposing army,' Dom Matronola began.

'We?' Deiber requested clarification.

'The monks and only the monks.'

'What about the people sheltering here?' the officer asked.

'I'm coming to that,' Dom Matronola asked for patience. He was a careful man, laying out his requests like the holy accoutrements on a Mass altar. 'We were told by your Command that we could remain here and await the coming of the opposing army, but that has become too dangerous because of this message.' He passed the 5th Army's leaflet which had been delivered by a shell.

'Translate it for me, please,' Deiber ordered.

The monk read out the warning that the opposing army's guns were being trained on the monastery.

'It's propaganda, designed to frighten you,' the German officer responded contemptuously, tossing aside the leaflet.

'Which it does,' Dom Matronola confessed. 'So you're saying that we're to stay here and may be shelled?'

The Abbot continued to sit in silence, as if he had given up all hope.

'I asked you already about the people sheltering with you. How do they figure in your plan?' Deiber wanted to know.

'Will you allow the refugees to go to the rear of your lines?' Dom Matronola requested.

'We can't permit anyone to cross our lines. If the refugees venture out, some of them are bound to be killed by gunfire on the road.'

'Intentionally?' the monk challenged him.

Lieutenant Deiber avoided giving an answer to his aggressive interrogator.

'So the monks and the refugees are doomed,' Dom Matronola summed up the hopelessness of the situation.

The Abbot's lower lip was trembling, as if he were about to suffer a seizure.

'Listen to me,' Deiber ordered, leaning forward. 'We're not the barbarians you seem to imply we are. I've discussed your situation with my commanding officer. There's a mule path that leads down from the mountain, into the Liri Valley, away from the fighting. We'll open it to the monks and your refugees from midnight tonight until five tomorrow morning.'

At these words the Abbot became revitalized, rousing himself and making the sign of the cross as he muttered a prayer to Mary. He knew that he had to take the decision to vacate his beloved monastery, otherwise his remaining monks and the refugees would probably be killed.

'But there's a condition,' the German officer cautioned. 'You must stay on the mule path at all times. Anyone foolish enough to attempt to go down the main road through our defences to Cassino will find themselves under fire.'

'But midnight might be too late,' Dom Matronola protested. 'The opposing army's shells could arrive this afternoon.'

'The arrangement cannot be changed,' Deiber said, standing up. 'Now I have a request.' He turned to the Abbot. 'May I visit the basilica?'

'By all means, Lieutenant. We're most grateful for your help. But the state of the basilica will shock you. Take care that you aren't injured.'

It was still dark when Deiber pushed open one of the massive bronze doors. As the beam of his torch swept the masonry brought down by stray shells, it hovered on a fallen angel from the frieze, wings broken. He shook his head and snapped off the beam.

From Angela's Journal for Tuesday 15 February 1944:

> *Is it any wonder that some of the refugees, who have eaten hardly anything for a fortnight, are weak and irritable? In their hunger and terror they miscall the monks, accusing them of having arranged for the leaflets to be dropped, because, they say, the monks want the refugees out of the monastery. I tried to tell them that this wasn't true, but they wouldn't listen, and one woman threatened me if I didn't shut my mouth. When Dom Matronola*

explained that everyone had to leave as the building was likely to be attacked, it looked as if there was going to be a riot. I left the refugees and went to join the monks at prayer in the small room in their refuge which they have set up as a chapel. We were on our knees reciting: 'Ave, Regina Caelorum,' and had come to the phrase 'Et pro nobis Christum exora' when there was a huge explosion above. I was reminded of how Virgil advises Dante to accept fate in Canto VIII of Inferno as they approach the city of Dis, lower Hell:

Non temer, ché il nostro passo
non ci può torre alcun: da tal n'è dato.

(Fear not, for our passage none can take from us: by Such has it been given to us.)

Major General Francis Tuker had received the new wonder drug penicillin for what was thought to be rheumatoid arthritis, but felt so debilitated by the large dose that he had reluctantly handed over command of his 4th Indian Division, which, it had been decided, would storm the monastery of Montecassino, clear the surrounding high ground, then enter the Liri Valley several miles north of the Rapido River. In their rear 5th Brigade would occupy the monastery after its capture.

But what was the nature of the structure of the building

his Division was detailed to attack? Tuker dispatched an Adjutant to Naples, who returned with a book, published in 1879, which gave details of the construction of the monastery. Though he had relinquished his command to his deputy, Brigadier Dimoline, Tuker was still the dedicated General, and wrote from his sickbed to Lieutenant General Sir Bernard Freyberg, commander of the New Zealand Corps:

> The Main Gate has massive timber branches in a low archway consisting of large stone blocks 9 to 10 metres long. This gate is the only means of entrance to the Monastery. The walls are about 150 feet high, are of solid masonry and at least 10 feet thick at the base…Monte Cassino is therefore a modern fortress and must be dealt with by modern means…It can only be directly dealt with by applying blockbuster bombs from the air.

Freyberg visited Tuker at his headquarters. Tuker knew that the Allies had been negotiating through the Vatican about the protection of religious buildings, Montecassino included. He had seen a communication from the Germans, stating that there was no sizeable body of their troops in the immediate vicinity. But Tuker didn't trust the Nazis, and urged Freyberg to recommend that the monastery be bombed. Brigadier Dimoline agreed, and asked Freyberg for this to be done.

Freyberg concurred. He had seen too many attacks on

impregnable positions in the last war. As far as he could, he had always tried to spare the lives of his New Zealand troops. He owed the same duty of care to Tuker's Indians, and passed the request for the bombing up the chain of command.

Lieutenant General Mark Clark, in charge of the United States Fifth Army, brooded on this request, involving morality as well as munitions, since he was a Roman Catholic. He would have refused, had Freyberg been one of his American corps commanders. The decision was referred to General Sir Harold Alexander, Commander of all the Allied Forces, who put his sentiments down on paper:

> When soldiers are fighting for a just cause, and are prepared to suffer death and mutilation in the process, bricks and mortar, no matter how venerable, cannot be allowed to weigh against human lives.

This was also the instruction of General Dwight Eisenhower, the Allied Commander-in-Chief, Mediterranean:

> If we have to choose between destroying a famous building and sacrificing our own men, then our men's lives count infinitely more, and the buildings must go. But the choice is not always as clear-cut as that.

When he wasn't listening to music on the radio or on his gramophone, General Senger selected a book to read from the extensive library in his grand headquarters. One evening he discovered an Eastern Philosophy section and took a volume on Taoism through to his sitting room, studying it with the aid of a whisky. He read with fascination that the great Taoist sage Lao Tzu had written that the good general *effects his purpose and then stops.* Furthermore, *He does not glory in what he has done.*

Senger copied out a saying of Lao Tzu: *He who delights in the slaughter of men will never get what he looks for out of those who dwell under Heaven.* He put the note into his pocket book, beside the illustration of Christ. How Senger wished that, having translated this wisdom into German, he had the courage to send it to Hitler. Would the epitaph for this unnecessary war come from the wisdom of Lao Tzu: *Where armies are, thorns and brambles grow?*

Chapter Twenty Five

Usually Benigno would have presented his beloved Beatrice with a poesy of early flowers on St Valentine's Day, and then gone up to the monastery with her for Mass. The following day he was leading his three remaining mules up the mountain slope because a truce had been agreed to collect the putrefying dead. About forty mules were gathered to await their tragic burdens.

'You're not German,' a voice at the muleteer's back said accusingly in Italian as Benigno lifted a corpse on to the wooden saddle of one of his mules.

'No I'm not.'

'Then you're a traitor. You should be on our side.'

'I'm a prisoner.'

'Can't you escape?'

'Not with three animals to look after. If I was by myself I would be over the mountains, but the snow is as high as the roof of a house, and the Germans would shoot me for deserting. Then they would work my mules to death.'

The Italian soldier, who had joined the Allies, held out a packet of cigarettes to Benigno.

'I don't smoke.'

'I wish we had some wine to share,' the soldier said wistfully as he slung a body on to another mule. He drew smoke deeply into his lungs. 'What a mess they're making of our countryside. I wish it was like the old days, a girl to share the sunshine with.'

'Hurry up!' a voice shouted, and the soldier and Benigno loaded more corpses.

In the dawn of Tuesday 15 February 1944 One hundred and forty two American Flying Fortresses were being prepared to lift off from an airfield near Foggia in south eastern Italy, carrying 253 tons of high explosive and incendiary bombs. As they approached Montecassino in perfect formation Angela and Augusto were up and about, helping in the kitchen.

'Planes!' Augusto shouted, pulling her under the table as the ceiling cracked.

Every night and also in the morning, on his knees beside his sleeping bag in the tent, Captain Dr Christopher Murchison prayed for Angela's safety, now that Father O'Brien had taught him how to speak to God in a natural way. When he went outside, he could see clearly the monastery on the mountain. If only the Allies would push forward, driving the Germans back into the Liri Valley, he would desert if necessary to search for his beloved. This resolution kept him going and allowed him to concentrate on the surgery he assisted with.

That Tuesday morning in February the Captain was preparing for the first casualty of the day when he heard the deep drone of approaching planes after 9 a.m. He hurried out of the surgical tent and shielded his eyes as the huge bombers passed. When he saw the first string of bombs falling on Montecassino he clutched his head and screamed:

'No! No! For Christ's sake no!'

As the monastery's walls began to crumble a soldier threw his cap into the air.

'Hurrah! We won't have to look at that thing anymore. It's been getting on our nerves, like a huge skull watching us from the mountaintop as we lie in the mud and our own shit.'

The Captain turned and hit him on the mouth, then felt a restraining hand on his shoulder.

'That's not the way,' Father O'Brien told him gently, pushing him down, then, kneeling beside him, faced the disintegrating monastery.

Lieutenant General Mark Clark was catching up on paperwork in his trailer at Presenzano, seventeen miles from Montecassino, when he heard heavy bombers passing overhead. He knew where they were going, and couldn't bear to be among the spectators to witness the wanton destruction of the monastery he revered as a Catholic and had tried to save. His pen wavered on the paper as the Flying Fortresses passed on.

Judging by the number of eager spectators in the surrounding countryside, it seemed that the bombing of Montecassino was a well-publicised show among the Allied armies. Soldiers couldn't take their eyes off the mountaintop building glinting in the sunlight as they smoked and waited. Cameras were poised.

General Senger was in his mansion headquarters at Castello Massimo when blasts rattled the window beside which he was sitting, studying a campaign map. When one of his officers put his head round the door and asked anxiously what it was, Senger's response became a furious refrain: 'The idiots, they've done it after all! All our efforts were in vain.'

However, he called for his *kübelwagen* and was driven along the Liri Valley to watch the destruction of the monastery from the bunker that General Baade used as his headquarters five miles from Montecassino.

'It's a great sin,' Senger told his host. 'Kesselring wanted it neutralized. He respects such buildings. He's ordered that if we have to retreat, nothing must happen to the cathedrals at Veroli, Alatri and Anagni.'

'In this war anything and everything has become possible,' Baade observed.

'It would have been insane for us to have occupied the monastery as an observation post,' Senger continued angrily. 'It's so conspicuous that it would have been shelled out of action after the big battle started. The enemy must have known through the Vatican that for months we've been sparing and neutralizing the monastery. That's why the Abbot took in hundreds of refugees.'

He lowered his field glasses in despair and crossed himself.

From Angela's Journal for Tuesday 15 February 1944:

When the first bombs hit the monastery this morning after 9 a.m. I wanted to go up to make sure that Augusto was safe, but Uncle Peter warned me that it was too dangerous, and that he was responsible for my safety to Mama and Papa and to God. I joined the monks in the circle they made on their knees round their Abbot, who told us: 'Prepare yourselves to meet God.' Why did I not feel fear? Is it because I sense that my guardian angel is with me, invisible yet always vigilant? After the Abbot had given the monks and myself absolution I was handed some of the wadding they were tearing up to stuff into their ears to muffle the blasts that were making the walls tremble as if at any moment they were going to collapse inwards, turning the room into a tomb. The flash of the explosions through the narrow windows blinded me, and my throat was choked with dust. The deaf-mute servant whom everyone loves for his simplicity and faith came staggering into the room and collapsed on to his knees. His face was white with dust and terror, trying to show us by frantic sign language that something terrible had happened to the basilica above. He pulled open his shirt to show that he owed his survival to the power of the holy medal which he wore round his neck.

Shortly after 11 a.m. the explosions seemed to stop. The Abbot wanted to go up to inspect what had been done to his beloved monastery. Uncle Peter and Dom Matronola helped the frail old man up the stairs, and I went with them. When the Abbot saw that the façade of the basilica seemed intact he crossed himself, then, when he observed that the roof had gone, I saw the anguish in his face. He moved on the arm of Dom Matronola among the traumatized refugees in the cloisters, many of them injured, some of them clawing at the rubble in search of relatives. He made the sign of the cross to them and stopped to lay his hand on a bleeding head and to give his blessing. Really, he is such a kindly and caring old man, and perhaps he will be numbered among the saints in the future.

When I saw Augusto was safe I ran to him and kissed him on the mouth, the first time I have ever done that. People were dying under the heavy blocks of stone that had been hauled up the mountain by mules with strained hearts when the monastery was being rebuilt after the earthquake. Augusto and I didn't have the strength to lift the masonry, and could only bring what comfort we could to the buried. I held a hand that emerged from a heap of rubble, to let the man know that at least someone was with him as he died. A dog was whining piteously, but I could neither see it nor reach it.

Uncle Peter came clambering over the rubble. 'Please hear my confession, Father,' a disembodied voice below whimpered. 'You're absolved,' he told her tenderly, making the sign of the cross. 'But you haven't heard my sins. I committed adultery with a neighbour -' 'Forgiven,' Uncle answered promptly. 'Even if it were several times?' the weakening voice queried. 'Forgiven.' The voice, almost a whisper now, asked: 'How many Hail Marys must I do in penance, Father, before I go to God?' Uncle Peter advised the voice: ''Say them to yourself, so as not to waste your strength.'

Some tenant farmers were pleading with the Abbot to be allowed to join him and his monks down in their refuge. 'It's not safe,' he warned them. But they clutched his habit, and he relented. 'You must come with me,' Uncle Peter told me, taking my elbow. I said: 'No, I must stay with Augusto to try to help these poor souls.' Uncle replied: 'But Augusto can come with you.' 'No, Uncle, we must stay and help.'

After the Abbot and Uncle Peter had gone down to the refuge, followed by refugees, I asked Augusto as I knelt by a dying woman: 'Do you believe that I have a healing gift in my hands?' This is what he replied: 'Before this war I dismissed such claims as the ignorant superstitions of country people - including my own grandmother. I believed with the Communists that such beliefs had to be swept away, along with the churches that fostered them to keep the people in thrall. After my experiences in this war I no longer believe in the reforming doctrine of Communism, and I believe that miracles are possible, because I am with you and will never leave you.'

A further strike of eighty seven planes lifted from their bases on Sardinia off Italy's western coast and headed for Montecassino with their deadly cargoes of four 1,000 lb bombs each, appearing over the monastery around 1.30 p.m. The Abbot and his monks cowered in a corner of the room in their refuge, trying to keep out of the range of the metal and stone shrapnel streaking through the slit window as their monastery was pulverized. A massive explosion dislodged the lintel, a barrier across the door. The wall seemed to vibrate with the hysteria of the wives and children of the tenant farmers on the other side.

When the bombing ceased the Abbot raised his arms

to the fractured ceiling in gratitude, and they all crossed themselves. They knew that they had to find a way out if the room wasn't to become their sepulchre. It was going to be impossible to shift the fallen lintel, but Dom Matronola, who had been asking his Maker for assistance, saw a metal screen between the top of the wall and the ceiling. He clambered up the rubble, asking Heaven for strength as he hauled at the screen. His robe was sticking to his flesh through perspiration and the knowledge that there could be more bombers approaching, but he succeeded in wrenching out the screen. It had been said of him that he could have been a weightlifter if he hadn't taken holy orders, and so the Abbot was lifted easily up to the hole and passed through to be lowered gently into the arms of the monks on the other side.

Injured and terrified refugees were screaming in the other rooms of the refuge as the monks seized the small suitcases they had packed, and when they went up into the light they found even worse damage than in their earlier inspection after the first phase of the bombing.

From Angela's Journal, for Tuesday 15 February 1944:

> *Augusto and I clutched each other and prayed when another attack came. After the bombers had passed over we saw the new destruction. The cloisters are smashed, the stairs to the basilica a jagged heap. St Benedict's statue still stands, but his head has gone. The bodies of refugees are*

scattered among the flattened building. We looked into the basilica. The aisles are blocked by piles of rubble which must be fifteen feet high. The pipes of the ancient organ are shredded as if they were made of paper. The exquisite monks' stalls, executed by Neapolitan carvers, are now firewood. Fragments of marble inlay are scattered everywhere, like multi-coloured hailstones. More refugees have lost their lives. We were told that a distraught woman, screaming that Hell had been opened up, had thrown herself off the terrace. The few refugees who hadn't been injured or who had fled are crowding around, begging for guidance. The Abbot looks as if he's about to collapse. I am sitting on the fragment of a column to write up this Journal, because never has there been more need for me to record what is happening.

The *torretta*, the tower built over the cell St Benedict had occupied and where he had gone to God, was still intact, a miracle, the Abbot pointed out. He seemed to take this as a sign of their own survival, because he told his monks to salvage their bedding and food supplies from their refuge. Dom Matronola was dispatched to inspect the *torretta*, and found injured and traumatized refugees sprawled on the stairs, clutching the hem of his robe as if he were Christ and could heal their wounds and still their racing hearts. He gave them a blessing, but was summoned by someone screaming outside. He found a woman in agony, both her feet gone, and with the help of several of the men carried her into the *torretta*. Angela came in and, kneeling beside the woman, grasped her by the lower legs. As the bleeding was staunched one of the men pulled off his shirt and tore it into strips, handing them to Angela to bind the stumps.

The monks went into the Chapel of the Pieta where Dom Pietro shared out salvaged bread and cheese.

'Can I have some water?' the exhausted Abbot requested, slumped on a chair in the midst of his monks.

But the cistern had been destroyed in the bombing.

Chapter Twenty Six

Lieutenant Deiber came up to the monastery that evening and was given a tour by torchlight of the ruins.

'The British and Americans are barbarians,' he said angrily. 'The enemy has no appreciation of the importance of Montecassino as a spiritual place. The Führer is appalled by what they've done. The Pope has been in touch with him, and the Führer has asked the enemy for a truce so that you can be evacuated.'

'That means you think the bombers will come back,' the Abbot said.

'They'll be back,' the German answered emphatically. 'They won't be content until they've flattened the monastery. That's why we've got to get you out as soon as possible. We'll arrange for you to be taken to a place of safety behind the lines, but first you'll have to make your own way on foot down the mountainside.'

'Some of the refugees can't walk,' Dom Pietro pointed out.

'They'll have to be carried by the others,' the German officer said abruptly. 'It's too dangerous for us to supply men to help. The enemy will think it's a trick for us to get into the monastery, so that we can fortify it. Before I try to arrange a truce I need a note from you, stating that there were no German soldiers in the monastery at the time of the bombing,' the officer told the Abbot.

'I can do that,' the Abbot said, and Dom Matronola went

to fetch pen and paper.

Both the Abbot and Lieutenant Deiber signed the paper on the altar of the chapel.

'You'll need to tell the refugees what's going to happen to them,' Dom Matronola warned the Abbot.

'I don't have the strength. You'll have to do it.'

Dom Matronola went out to muster the refugees round the tower.

'The mule track is our only hope of getting out of here alive,' he told the assembly.

'It's a trick!' a man shouted from the back.

'What do you mean, a trick?' Dom Matronola challenged him.

'A trick to get us out of here,' the same man replied. 'We can still shelter here despite the damage.'

'It's not a trick,' the monk responded angrily. 'The British and American bombers will be back and we'll all be killed. We need to leave the monastery.'

The olive trees outside the monastery, which had been set alight by the morning's bombardment, were still burning like giant torches. The monks were waiting for the German officer to return to tell them that he had arranged the promised truce.

'We took vows to St Benedict to remain in his house, but these vows no longer apply since the monastery is no longer habitable,' Dom Matronola pointed out. 'If we're to serve our founder, who venerated life, we need to leave now with the refugees who are left. Thank God for one thing: we got most of the treasures out before this hellish destruction from the skies hit us.'

Dom Pietro sought out Angela, who was trying to help the wounded from the bombing.

'Lieutenant Deiber told us that arrangements have been made for us to leave the monastery between midnight tonight and five o' clock tomorrow morning via a mule track down into the Liri Valley, away from the fighting, but that was before this morning's bombing,' the monk explained to his niece.

'What about the refugees?' Angela asked.

'Most of the able-bodied have fled. We'll have to take the wounded and the orphans with us.'

Dom Pietro went into the little chapel to pray to the Wooden Madonna: '*Mother of God, teach me how I am to contain my anger and disgust at what our so-called Allies have done to us, sending a hundred planes loaded with bombs over our monastery, to destroy the building and kill and maim so many innocent people. At times like this we begin to doubt...*' But he was unable to finish his prayer.

It was midnight before all the monks had settled to sleep in the Chapel of the Pieta, but an hour later they were wakened by a massive explosion as a delayed-action bomb detonated in the *torretta*.

'Is it another attack?' the Abbot called out, his voice weakened by smoke and dust.

Screaming refugees fell on the stairs as they tried to escape the building. The Abbot lay on the mattress, agonizing over whether he was making the correct decision in deciding on evacuation. But how long could they survive in these dangerous conditions if they stayed? Another bombing raid and he and his monks would all become martyrs. But it wouldn't be perceived as the bravery and sacrifice of the saints of the Catholic Church. It would be seen as stupidity and even suicide. There was no way of asking the Vatican for guidance. The decision fell to him and him alone. But would it be taken out of his hands if the Germans couldn't arrange a truce? Sleep being impossible, he prayed more earnestly than he had ever done in his life, calling for support from Christ and His Mother, from St Benedict, from the Abbot's own guardian angel, never seen but always sensed.

Another day, another air raid, but smaller this time, forty eight planes discharging twenty four tons of ordnance. Since Lieutenant Deiber hadn't returned to confirm a truce, it looked like another night in the chapel in the *torretta*. But its ceiling was sagging, and there were no safe places left in the ruins of the monastery.

'There's no hope of a truce,' the Abbot told his monks. 'We must leave if we are to survive.'

'What about the refugees?' Dom Matronola asked.

'We must take them with us.'

From Angela's Journal for Thursday 17 February 1944:

I must keep up this Journal in the midst of such wreckage and suffering because the world must know of the Allied atrocity in bombing this monastery in which there has not been, and is not, a single German soldier. How many dead are there among the civilians from yesterday? Who knows how many were sheltering in the monastery? Between one and two thousand, Uncle Peter estimates. And who knows how many dead - and dying - lie under the rubble?

I have been up all night, trying to comfort three small children. Crazed with grief, their father abandoned them after their mother was killed in the bombing. Is he alive or dead? Will he be reunited with them? The monks mustered the refugees in the dawn, telling them that they had to leave the monastery. Dom Matronola said to me: 'I'm going to have to make the most difficult decision of my life about these three children you're looking after, Angela. Do we take them with us?' The four year old girl was in my arms, and I said to Dom Matronola: 'She'll be gone soon, poor little darling. Why cause her more agony?' Dom Matronola bent down to pick up her brother, but he began to scream, and since both his legs had gone, like his sister he was beyond hope. The third child is a little boy, his legs paralyzed by the bombing, but Dom Matronola, always so brave, so wise, so considerate of others, decided: 'We'll take him with us because there's a chance he can be helped.'

I asked Dom Matronola if he would please delay our departure because I had something I treasured to collect from the monastery. I went into the room serving as a chapel and knelt in a brief prayer to the Wooden Madonna, asking her to be with us on our descent from the monastery. I buttoned this Journal inside my blouse before I picked up the Madonna.

The procession of monks and refugees moved out of the monastery at 7.30 a.m. Abbot Diamare was at the front, staggering under the burden of the cross which he insisted on carrying for protection against the guns. Two men were using a ladder as a stretcher to convey the woman who had lost both her feet in the shelling. Uncle Peter and Augusto were with me with the refugees at the back. I held the Wooden Madonna above my head as the monks recited the rosary, with the refugees taking up the chant: 'Ave Maria, gratia plena, Dominus tecum...'

The descending trail was stony, and some of the refugees sat down to rest, but the monks urged them on, warning them that the shelling would begin again as soon as the darkness began to lift. I felt tearful as we passed the ruined station of the cable car, where I had alighted in evenings of tranquillity and perfumed flowers, a plate of polenta awaiting me on the table in Uncle and Aunt's house, and later, going out to the stable to feed the mules handfuls of hay before they slept. Ah, how hard it is to follow Christ's advice quoted in Puurgatorio!

Amate da cui male aveste

(Love those from whom you have had evil).

There was shouting at the back when the men who had been carrying the woman on the ladder laid it down.

'Find the strength to go on!' Dom Matronola called from the front of the procession, where he was steadying the Abbot from stumbling with the burden of the cross as we left the Calvary of so many, young and old, their tombs, like that of Jesus, of rock.

The men picked up the ladder again, and the procession and chanting proceeded. 'Glory be to the Father, and to the Son, and to the Holy Spirit...' About half way down a shell came whistling, exploding nearby. The people scattered, and the woman who had been carried on the ladder was left lying on the track. One of the monks, Fra Carlomanno Pellagalli, who was approaching eighty years old and who worked in the olive groves, was found to be missing. But it was too dangerous for anyone to go back and look for him, and it was assumed that he wished to die where he had worshipped and harvested the olives for so many years to anoint the monks' salads.

After nearly three hours of walking down the rough terrain we reached a stream which dried up in summer. 'This is a sacred place of our order,' Uncle Peter went forward to inform the Abbot, who rested the cross against his shoulder, its base on the ground as he listened to Uncle the historian. 'According to the chronicles of Montecassino, which are safely in Rome, St Benedict and St Scholastica, brother and sister, met here for the last time. She wanted him to stay the night with her, but he said that he had to return to the monastery before nightfall.' 'Would that we could do the same,' the weary old monk said. Uncle explained that St Scholastica's tears had flowed and formed the stream, preventing her brother from leaving until the following morning. 'There used to be a small church here, but it was demolished in the year the war began,' Uncle recalled.

Dom Matronola hurried across to a small building displaying a Red Cross sign, to see if the procession could shelter there from the shelling which announced another day and, no doubt, many more deaths. It was occupied by German soldiers. 'We have been watching out for you,' a soldier told Dom Emmanuel Munding, the German speaker. 'Field Marshal Kesselring has put out an order; the Abbot and monks from the monastery are to be searched for and helped.' The Abbot sipped a welcome cup of coffee while the soldier announced that an ambulance was due in the afternoon to evacuate the monks and the wounded civilians. Uncle Peter went searching for the two men who had been carrying the crippled woman on the ladder, to tell her that she would soon receive medical attention. 'Where is she?' he asked her two bearers. 'We left her because she was too heavy for us,' one of them admitted, hanging his head. But the shells made it impossible to go back to fetch her. In the shelter, with the Abbot, fortified by the coffee, Dom Matronola recited the divine office for the eighth day after the Feast Day of St Scholastica. One of the German soldiers was down on his knees, to the evident surprise of his comrades.

Augusto and I lifted the child with the paralyzed legs into the ambulance when it arrived in the late afternoon. 'You must come with us,' Uncle Peter told me and Augusto when all the wounded and the monks were in the ambulance. 'No, we want to stay with the refugees, to help them if we can, don't we, Augusto?' I said, and he agreed. 'Your lives could be in danger,' Uncle warned us. 'We have this to protect us,' I said, holding up the Wooden Madonna. I felt in the pocket of my skirt and produced an envelope. 'Can you please try to get this letter to my parents through the Vatican? I've left it open so that the church authorities can see that the wording is harmless.' Uncle promised that he would do what he could. He gave Augusto and me his blessing, saying: 'You're two very brave young people.' Then he made the sign of the cross before clambering into the ambulance. Will I ever see him again?

The possible bombing of Montecassino had been discussed in the newspapers in Britain, but Rosa Boni didn't believe that the Allies could do something so barbaric. When she heard the news about the destruction of the monastery as she was making a coffee for a customer in the café, she wailed, letting the coffee cup overflow, burning her leg because Montecassino was so close to her brother and sister-in-law's farm where Angela was staying. With the loss of her husband Rosa had run the café single-handed. In the strict rationing that seemed to have lasted for ages getting supplies was a daily struggle. The coffee she was now serving was brewed from acorns, but there was no alternative, since cargoes of fragrant beans were at the bottom of the ocean. The amount of ice cream she was able to make had dropped drastically, since milk was so scarce. But the bank official who hated Italians and arranged to sell the café had retired, and his successor was sympathetic, lengthening the period in which to repay the debt, including the interest that had accumulated.

She locked up the café at seven o' clock each night, having washed the floors and scoured the toilet. But tonight it was past seven and she was still sitting in the café, her face in her apron. How could she go upstairs to tell her children that their sister might have been injured or even killed in the bombing of the monastery? Somehow she got through the days in the busy café, until the letter from her daughter arrived via the Vatican, assuring her mother that she had survived the bombing of the monastery and was leaving the ruins.

From Angela's Journal for Thursday 17 February 1944:

Augusto and I have walked for miles today, in the direction of Monte Cairo. We are in dangerous territory, with the Germans mounting a ferocious fight to prevent the British and Americans from moving forward to Rome and humiliating the Führer. All human dignity has been degraded in this landscape littered with corpses on which ravens are feasting. Perhaps Nico, the monastery pet, now homeless, is among them. We knew that we had to get to the heights as soon as possible, though there were still dangers there. We passed a soldier sprawled beside his smashed machine gun, his body crawling with maggots. As I followed Augusto, the Wooden Madonna in my aching arms, I was thinking about what we might do after this war is over. I want to go back to Scotland to see my parents and my two brothers and sister, but I assume that Augusto will want to stay here, to rebuild his home. Will I be fulfilled being a smallholder's wife, helping him to work the land and tend the livestock, or will I miss the challenge and satisfaction of studying for a doctorate on Dante under Cavaliere Grillo? Will the Professor, the committed Fascist, still be teaching at

Glasgow University, or will he have been dismissed from his chair for lauding Mussolini?

We reached a cave, but it was blocked by corpses, a belt of bullets still in the machine gun. We pulled aside the bodies and went into the cave, emerging with tins of meat and a flask of schnapps in a kitbag. Then we climbed higher, towards the snowline, and found the cave which Augusto had been living in, still containing his bedding and a small supply of candles. We sat on the earthen floor, the Wooden Madonna between us, eating out of tins and sharing the flask of schnapps. I worried about Uncle Peter, the Abbot, the other monks and the refugees. Please God that they are now beyond the reach of the shells and that the little boy with the paralyzed legs is receiving treatment. I'm using the lantern which Augusto left in the cave when he was hiding here so that I can write up this Journal of a rare day of salvation.

From Angela's Journal for Friday 18 February 1944:

We slept under the same blanket in the freezing cave. Augusto went out in the dawn with his gun, and, using the audible cover of the barrage, shot a hare which I skinned and cooked over a discreet fire, the smoke absorbed in the haze of exploded shells. As we sat eating at the entrance to the cave we could see the terrible damage that has been inflicted on the landscape that we both love, but which is unrecognizable in places, ploughed and shattered by shells. The ruins of Montecassino are obscured by a curtain of smoke, as if God is hiding the shame of its destruction from those fighting below. 'What are these flashes from the ruins?' I asked, shielding my eyes as I looked across to the monastery. 'The Germans must have occupied it,' Augusto surmised. So it was bombed for nothing. I am heartbroken.

Abbot Diamare was at General Senger's headquarters at Castello Massimo, up the Liri Valley from Cassino, the rumble of the guns like occasional distant thunder. Senger wanted to record for posterity that the destruction of the monastery was the sole responsibility of the British and Americans, so he was interviewing the Abbot for German radio. The old man had a message for history, delivered in a subdued but assertive voice: 'In the monastery there was neither a German soldier, nor any German weapon, nor any military installation,' a testimony which two monastery officials would later validate with their signatures.

Senger gave the Abbot a tour of the massive castle.

'What will be of particular interest to you is that the building dates back to the tenth century, when it served as a fortified monastery belonging to the Subiaco Benedictine monks. In 1574 it was passed to the Massimo family.'

They entered the main *salone* and stood admiring one of the frescoes created by Marco Benefial in the ceiling vaults.

'These depict the nuptials of Andromeda and Perseus,' the General explained. 'It will be a tragedy if these exquisite works are damaged or destroyed in the conflict. I have a request to make, Abbot, but if you are weary, feel free to refuse it. Will you pray with me in the chapel within the castle?'

Senger lit the candles on the altar and they knelt side by side. The old monk, his voice wavering, asked St Fillipo Neri, to whom the small chapel was dedicated, to intercede with the Lord in gaining protection for the Castello, and also to make the leaders on both sides come to their senses to stop the destructive war.

Despite the splendid dinner with his host, and a voluptuous bed to lie down in, the Abbot didn't sleep that night. Perhaps there was something else he should have told his radio audience. Though the Germans hadn't occupied the monastery, a considerable number of their stray shells, and those of the other side, had fallen on it, causing significant damage. Were these the hazards of war, being caught between two opposing armies? Sitting up in bed, hands pressed together, he told his Lord and Master that he was ready to depart this life whenever he was called, unless there was a task allotted to him which he could discharge with the last of his strength. But his monastery had been destroyed, and his heart had been damaged by grief, perhaps beyond repair. He ended his prayer with the word Pax.

Chapter Twenty Seven

Benigno was on the narrow mountain track with his three mules, but this time they weren't carrying ammunition or gun parts. They were descending with the bodies of German gunners from the high batteries, one corpse per mule. Because of rigor mortis he had had to break the limbs to get the bodies on the mules. Another had been decapitated by a shell, but the German soldiers who had hoisted the corpse to the mule's back had put the head into a saddle bag, to be reunited with the owner in a grave in the valley.

Benigno had hung his rosary round his neck as he led the grim procession down. His mules had sad eyes, not because of the burdens they were carrying, but perhaps because they had lost Samuele. The two brothers had seemed to comfort Paolo the bereaved one, standing on each side as they settled in brief respite on the mountainside before being roused for yet another journey, another cargo.

The burdens were unloaded at the bottom of the mountain, the mules fed and watered before being turned round for more corpses. As they ascended, what looked like a fiery meteor crossed the mountain above them. It wasn't a sign of warning from Heaven at the wastage of battle, but a projectile from one of the Allies' 'Long Tom' guns which could hurl a ninety-nine pound shell up to fourteen miles. The echo of the explosion didn't disturb the mules on their upward ascent. They were used to the noise, and to the ground trembling under their hooves.

Augusto went out by himself to get their supper, and was retrieving the shot hare from the rocks when he heard the click behind him. When he turned a soldier was holding a gun. The prisoner was brought before the Colonel in the cave that was his headquarters.

'How many of our brave men have you disposed of?' the Colonel wanted to know.

'I've shot nobody in this area.'

'Even aiming at one is a crime, never mind pulling the trigger. You know what I would have done in a case like this? Taken a dozen local people and executed them in reprisal, but they're all in hiding.'

'You've lost the war,' the prisoner spoke.

'Don't be too sure. Reinforcements will arrive. That's not the problem; you are. What to do with you?' he mused, as though it were a difficult decision. 'A firing squad? But that's a waste of ammunition. One bullet?'

'I want to show you something while you decide,' Augusto said. He was reaching into his pocket to produce the mother-of-pearl rosary that his grandmother had given him, to tell his captors that she had never done anyone any harm in her long life, but had been killed by the war the Fascists had started.

But one of the soldiers thought he was about to produce a pistol.

From Angela's Journal for Saturday 19 February 1944:

> *All day I have been on my knees at the entrance to the cave on Monte Cairo, praying to the Wooden Madonna: My Immaculate Mother, please bring Augusto back to me safely. Now the stars are out, and the Madonna is fading, and still no sign of my beloved. Has he had an accident with his gun, or been captured? I implore you, Mother: Carry me as I have carried you.*

Senger was visiting a machine gun crew on the front line when he saw a soldier pointing a rifle at a young woman. What attracted his attention was not only her beauty despite her ragged dress and the *zupei* on her feet: she was clasping to her breasts a statuette of the Madonna.

 He crossed to the soldier covering them with his rifle.

'Who is she?' he demanded.

The Captain of the machine gun crew hurried up.

'We picked her up on the mountainside, General.'

'What do you intend to do with her?' Senger asked.

'Shoot her.'

'Why?'

'If we let her go, she'll carry information about our position to the enemy.'

'Surely you've interrogated her, Captain.'

'I tried to, but she won't speak.'

Senger was looking at the Madonna the woman was carrying as he gave instructions.

'Take her to my headquarters. I'll interrogate her myself. She may have valuable information on the enemy's strength and disposition. The battle's reaching a critical stage.'

Angela was pushed into a vehicle and driven away as the General continued his inspection. When he arrived back at his headquarters in the castle he found her under guard in an outhouse, still clutching the Wooden Madonna.

'Has she had anything to eat?' Senger asked the guard. 'Then take her to the kitchen and tell the cook that she's to be fed – and I mean fed – on my orders. Then bring her to my office.'

The General was sitting at his desk when she was brought in.

'You don't need to wait,' he instructed the surprised guard. He indicated the chair he had placed in front of his desk for the prisoner. He asked her in Italian: 'Are you still hungry? Good, then please tell me your story.'

She told him in Italian that she was from Scotland, and that she had been staying with her uncle and aunt until German soldiers requisitioned their house.

'You're from Scotland?' he spoke in English. He saw her surprise and explained that he had acquired fluency in English when he was a scholar at Oxford University. He asked her which part of Scotland she came from, and said that, regretfully, he had never travelled to Glasgow when he was at Oxford. She explained that she had come to Italy to work as an archivist for an aristocrat.

'A Fascist, no doubt,' the General said. 'Why have you been wandering about on the battlefield?'

She told him that she was searching Monte Cairo for her friend when she was captured.

'Was he fighting with the other side?' the General asked.

She corrected him, explaining that Augusto, who wasn't fighting with anybody, had left the cave they were hiding in two days before to look for food.

'I haven't seen him since. I've been praying that he's been captured.'

The General requested: 'Give me his name, and the place where the cave is, and I'll ask if he's been taken prisoner.'

She gave his name, and told him that Augusto carried in his pocket a mother-of-pearl rosary.

The General then asked her if the missing man was a close friend. She told him that they hoped to marry after the war ended.

'War causes so much misery and heartbreak,' the General observed when he finished writing down the details.

'But you Germans started it,' she responded boldly.

'Though I'm a General. I never wanted this war. I don't want to do such damage to your beautiful country, but I must do my duty as a soldier to my fatherland. Why are you carrying a statuette of the Madonna?'

She told him that she had saved it from Montecassino.

'You were in the Abbey?' he asked in astonishment.

Angela informed him that her uncle was a monk there.

'Why didn't you go to Rome with him when we evacuated the Abbot and the monks?'

Because, she said, she wanted to stay with Augusto and to help people who had lost their homes.

The General turned in his swivel chair and looked out of the windows towards the snow-capped Abruzzi Mountains. 'I'd love to return here, to walk in these mountains when this is all over,' he said wistfully. 'The higher the better, away from the problems and sins of men. The bombing of the monastery of Montecassino was a great sin. We gave our word to the Vatican that it wouldn't be occupied or touched. They must have told your side, but still they came with their bombs. I witnessed its destruction, and it's already giving me nightmares.'

Emboldened by his frankness, she told him that she had seen the flashes of guns coming from the ruins.

'That's because our paratroopers are occupying it.'

She reminded that he had just said the Germans had given a pledge to the Vatican that they wouldn't touch the monastery.

'Our pledge referred to the intact building. Now it's rubble, and if we didn't occupy it, the enemy would, so you see how stupid the British and Americans have been. If they hadn't bombed the monastery we wouldn't have had any paratroopers within it. So you saved this Madonna statuette from Montecassino: why?'

She explained that it had been due to go to Rome with the

other treasures which the Germans had evacuated, but she had persuaded her uncle the monk to keep it at Montecassino.

'I hope that war hasn't turned me into a barbarian,' the General confessed. 'It would be wonderful if I received orders today to withdraw my troops, but Hitler won't give up Italy, for psychological as well as strategic reasons. I don't say that these reasons make military sense, because some of his decisions – and particularly the one to invade Russia – was insane. I fought in Russia, and I saw the tragic wastage of men.' He added that his earnest wish was that the war would end soon and that he could go home to Germany, to his family and his horses, but he realized that life had changed there, with the heavy bombing and the shortages. He turned to her: 'As for you, I don't regard you as a security risk, and don't want to know if you've seen a massive build-up of enemy forces in your wanderings. Tell me about yourself. You say you're an archivist.'

She explained that it was only to have been for a year, and that she had been going to return to Glasgow to study for a doctorate when the war broke out and she couldn't get home.

'What was your doctorate to be on? Ah, Dante,' he smiled with pleasure. 'I never tire of reading Dante in the original. Why do you have such an interest in him?'

She told him that she regarded herself as Italian, and that Dante was such a spiritual writer.

'His description of Hell is so terrifying,' the General observed. 'When I look at the battle around the Rapido River this quotation from *Inferno* comes to mind:

'Così sen vanno su per l'onda bruna,
ed avanti che sian di là discese,
anche di qua nuova schiera s'aduna.'

(So they depart across the dusky wave,
and ere upon the other side they land,
again on this side a new troop assembles.)

'Forgive me: I haven't even asked you your name in all this talk of war and sorrow,' the General said. 'To think that one of my soldiers would have shot you if I hadn't arrived,' he said, shaking his head. 'He had no appreciation of beauty. I can't let you go, Angela, because you'll either be killed by a shell, or, most likely raped by a German soldier. You'll have to stay here. But you won't be a prisoner. You'll work in the kitchen. You can place the statuette of Our Lady in the chapel dedicated to St Filippo Neri. You're free to worship there whenever you feel the need. I'll arrange for the housekeeper to allocate you a comfortable room.'

When she had gone the General sat searching his conscience, assisted by another bonbon. Was he attracted to this young Scottish woman, or sorry for her? Certainly she was beautiful, and as a Dante scholar she appealed to his intellectual interests. But he had always been faithful to his wife Hilda. The young Scottish woman clutching the Wooden Madonna was more like a daughter to him, he decided, though he already had a daughter in Germany. To protect her, separated by the war from her future husband, who could well be dead, would be some redemption for being a soldier.

His conversation – amounting to a confession – with her had once again raised in his mind the question he was reluctant to confront: why was he fighting in this unwinnable insane war started by a megalomaniac? Before Oxford he had completed a year's compulsory military service in a Baden artillery regiment. The experience hadn't attracted him to a military career. Instead in the garden of St John's College he had read in French *Du côté de chez Swann*, the newly published first volume of Marcel Proust's monumental quest for time remembered. Senger had envisaged himself an elegant Charles Swann, charming society in select *salons* in several capital cities with his insights into the *beaux arts*. But the following year in the Great War he found himself in a waterlogged trench and not a fashionable *salon*. His beloved younger brother was a casualty of the conflict, and Senger had risked his life to find his mass grave in no-man's-land. Digging frantically with the assistance of other soldiers, he was forced to take cover among the dead because of the ferocity of British artillery fire. But at last they reached down to the third layer, to locate his brother's body. The Rhodes Scholar with a passion for Proust had grasped his brother's legs and dragged him to his car, sitting him in the passenger's seat.

Senger's participation in the counter-revolution against the Bolsheviks in Saxony had exposed him to the threat to the world of totalitarianism. But wouldn't the new democratic constitution of the Weimar Republic repulse right and left wing ambitions? A skilled equestrian, he could recite by heart *The Army Manual of Horsemanship*. He had witnessed the destruction done by the tanks at Cambrai, yet he didn't endorse the conviction, held by many military experts, that the crawling steel machine, armoured and armed, would be the decisive weapon in all aspects of warfare. His own experiences had shown him that success in battle would depend on infantrymen.

Senger knew about the increasing violence, particularly towards Jews, that had brought the Nazis to power, but he ignored it, or dared not express an opinion. He was a career officer, loyal to the party in power, and when Poland was pulverized at the outbreak of a second world war, he regretted deeply that he had been denied a part, and believed that his army career was over. But when fellow officers briefed him about the appalling atrocities perpetrated by the SS on Polish civilians, Senger confided his anger in a letter to a lady friend, writing: 'There seemed to be a refrain: "I'm ashamed to be a German." What can one do but stay silent? I do.'

He could have resigned his commission, but was prevented by a sense of duty, and perhaps also by the hope that it would be a short war, after which he could retire to devote his time to his wife and his horses. But he was frightened, because Hitler could have interpreted resignation as a mark of disrespect and distrust of National Socialism, and might have ordered his liquidation as a possible articulate critic.

At Montecassino Senger had tens of thousands of infantrymen under his command, supported by massive guns sending shells miles, and what remained of Goering's much vaunted Luftwaffe. He couldn't offer up prayers for each infantryman killed, but every evening, as tonight, he made a point of kneeling in St Filippo Neri's chapel, asking for repose for the souls of soldiers of both armies killed that day, and also asking forgiveness for being in a role he couldn't withdraw from.

He also prayed for the soul of the dearly beloved brother whose body he had rescued from the battlefield because, even after so many years, he didn't feel that his sibling was as rest. Once, being driven up to Montecassino, he had the impression that his dead brother was sitting beside him. Was this because of fraternal love, or a warning that he should get out of this accursed war?

Angela's Journal for Tuesday 21 March 1944:

> Today is the Feast Day of St Benedict. The monastery he founded is now rubble, not through a natural disaster like an earthquake, but through man's folly. I remember the joyful celebrations at Montecassino in 1939, before the war changed everything. This morning in the chapel dedicated to St Filippo Neri, General Senger and I said our prayers to St Benedict. On our knees before the Wooden Madonna, a supreme example of survival, we asked for the Saint's forgiveness on

behalf of those who began this terrible war, and those who are carrying it on.

Chapter Twenty Eight

Angela was working in the kitchen with the cook, a Bavarian. He spoke no Italian, and assumed that she didn't know German, which was why he articulated his hatred of Jews as he struck the cleaver on the board, preparing the sumptuous dinner for the officers' mess. He would have liked to tell his new assistant that the Italians had betrayed Germany by declaring war on his country. The servants whispered that the General had saved this attractive young Italian from the firing squad for his sexual pleasure. But he had been cunning, in case his action reached the Führer: instead of installing her in a bedroom and giving her the run of the railings of designer dresses belonging to the dispossessed chatelaine, he had put the young British woman into the kitchen, to make it appear that his rescue of her had been an act of humanity and not of lust. This was why the cook apparently treated her with respect, and fed her the same food as was served to the officers.

Angela decided that the best strategy was to stay silent and look contrite, to carry out whatever tasks the cook set her. There were other assistants in the kitchen, and so her duties were light. When she was finished in the early evening she went to pray to the Wooden Madonna in the Saint's chapel for the survival of Augusto.

At eight thirty on the morning of the Ides of March, 1944, Roman Festival of Mars, God of War, Benigno watched from the mountain track where he was leading his mules up with ammunition as Allied planes appeared over the white summits. General Freyberg, pulverizer of Montecassino, also witnessed the final destruction of what had been the town of Cassino from his safe headquarters in the hills. The blasts travelled through the valleys, blowing men and animals off their feet, and the smoke from the wrecked town drifted up through the mountain passes. Angela Boni heard the bombardment as she went down on her knees in front of the Wooden Madonna, having helped to prepare General Senger's breakfast in the kitchen. At the end of the massive raid deadly statistics would be computed for the history books: 775 bombers discharging nearly 1,000 tons of bombs, followed by 1,000 tons of shells from the Allied bombardment.

Senger was wakened by the cock crowing. From his window he looked beyond newborn lambs to the serrated whiteness of mountains. That year Easter fell on the second Sunday in April. On top of the cook's iced cake he placed a small porcelain figure of Christ provided by the General. An Italian priest, taken capture but under the protection of Senger, said Mass in St Filippo Neri's chapel to a congregation of a dozen, including the General and Angela, with the Wooden Madonna on the altar, surrounded by candles.

In mid April General Senger temporarily handed over command of his Panzer Corps in order to be decorated in person by the Führer. The coastal road took him to Ravenna, and in St Apollinare this man with the eye of an artist stood enchanted by the mosaic of the procession of the twenty-two Virgins of the Byzantine period, led by the Three Magi, moving from the city of Classe towards the group of the Madonna and Child surrounded by four angels. Though it was a millennium since they had been laid down, they had retained their freshness. Senger saw the women leaving the trials and tribulations of this earth, to go to a place of heavenly peace, their resolute strides creating a solemn harmony in his head.

At Hitler's lair at Obersalzberg, where the dictator almost had his head in the clouds, General Senger was decorated with the Oak Leaves of the Knight's Cross by the Führer's own hand, trembling as though he were developing palsy. There was no hint that day of the ranting voice that had terrified Europe. The Führer sounded comparatively rational, though Senger had been told confidentially that he had become addicted to narcotics in medicine prescribed for him by his roguish doctor Theodor Morrell. The Führer admitted to his small phalanx of front-line officers that the war was at a critical stage. He couldn't deny that Germany had made a number of strategic withdrawals on the Eastern Front. The possibility of an invasion in the West had to be reckoned with, but the Allies would find the fortifications on the French coast a formidable barrier. Senger noted that he barely mentioned the skilled way in which the army had been holding up the enemy in Italy. Hitler then launched into his peroration. He promised that the enemy would soon be stunned by the impact of the new secret weapons which were nearly ready to be deployed. With these, and the courage of the German soldier, and his unshakable faith in the Fatherland, the Reich would win through in the end.

What was to be done about this dangerous fanatic who had dragged down Germany to ruin, Senger speculated as he listened? He could have brought a pistol and shot the dictator dead as he was being presented with the decoration. But if not gunned down on the spot by Hitler's bodyguard, he would have been tortured to death. That was a sacrifice the decorated General could have made, but it would probably be futile, since the jackbooted gang of thugs and criminals around him would fight and murder among themselves to fill the Führer's shoes.

Senger returned to Italy in May. In his absence Angela had spent her spare time from her duties in the kitchen in the magnificent grounds which Senger saw himself as the custodian of, insisting that they be kept up, because it reminded him of his beloved wife's passion for her garden. He deployed Italian prisoners to tend the Castello's flowerbeds.

Angela had placed violets in a vase on the altar beside the Wooden Madonna in the Saint's chapel, where she and the General prayed each morning, after which they would walk to the main fountain which was surrounded by iris, wisteria and lemon trees, the combination of scents intoxicating. They were resting on a stone bench, discussing the spirituality of Dante, each supplying quotations in Italian from memory, when they heard a rumbling sound.

'Is it a thunderstorm?' Angela asked anxiously.

'These are guns – many guns.'

The Allies were launching the most devastating cannonade of the Italian Campaign, with 1,600 guns opening up along a twenty-five mile front, aimed at every plotted German position. On the morning of 18 May a Polish soldier stood on the ruins of Montecassino. Raising a bugle to his lips, he blew the *Krakow Heynal*, 'St Mary's Dawn,' regarded as a virtual national anthem of Poland. The tune was amplified by the surrounding mountains and the Liri Valley, informing the world that the German paratroopers who had been occupying the pulverized monastery had surrendered. The jubilant bugle call didn't reach General Senger in his headquarters in Castello Massimo, but the news didn't surprise him, because on the previous day he had had a directive from Kesselring, ordering a withdrawal to the Hitler Line, nine miles behind the Gustav Line.

After they had prayed side by side on their knees in the small chapel on the morning of Friday 19 May, General Senger informed Angela that Montecassino was now in Polish hands, and that he had to move his headquarters because of the advance of the British and American armies.

He told her: 'I'm going to send you up to Rome, where you can make contact with your uncle, the Montecassino monk. He'll find you safe accommodation, hopefully in a convent.'

She was adamant that she wasn't going to Rome.

'You can't come with us,' he warned her. 'It's too dangerous because we could be bombed.'

She told him that she wanted to get back to the Montecassino area.

'But why? The monastery's a ruin. You couldn't possibly climb up to it, with the amount of firepower that's about.'

She replied: 'I want to go back to try to find Augusto.'

He said that he had asked his Adjutant to send a messenger round the various German units, asking if they were holding a prisoner of the name of Augusto Faccenda, or had sent him for slave labour in Germany, but they had handled no one of that name. The General wondered if the missing man had given his captors a false name.

'Augusto would never do that,' Angela told him proudly. 'I don't believe he's dead. He's always been a survivor, and I want to go back to Monte Cairo where we were hiding to be reunited with him because we're meant to be together.'

Without any trace of sarcasm in his voice, the General asked her how she intended to get there. She said that she would go up through the mountains.

'Do you know these mountains?' he asked.

She assured him that she would find her way. He emphasized that even if he supplied her with maps and food, she would never reach Monte Cairo.

'Though we're going to withdraw, there's still a heavy rear bombardment involving the mountains,' Senger cautioned. 'I admire your loyalty to your husband-to-be. I could send a soldier with you, but he'll be shot if he's caught, and then you'd be by yourself.'

She insisted that she still wanted to go. The General was pacing the room, knowing that she wasn't going to change her mind.

He spoke eventually. 'The best I can suggest is this. You know Marco, one of the gardeners. I saved him from being sent to Germany because he's got such a beautiful singing voice. He's been singing arias from Italian opera for me after dinner, when I've been feeling dejected. I can ask him to accompany you. He's likely to know the way, since he was captured at Cassino. I'll give you two mules, and we'll put on their sides Red Cross flags, so that you'll at least have a chance when the gunners are looking for a target through their binoculars. I suggest you leave this evening. There's a moon; travelling by night's safer than by day.'

Marco the gardener was sent for. He glanced at the maps which the General produced and said that he knew the way. In the early evening Angela went down to the kitchen, to take leave of the cook, and to ask him through gestures for food for her journey. He filled a saddlebag with the finest cuts of meat, and also two truffles. Meantime two mules were brought to the headquarters, Red Cross flags secured to their girths by ropes. Before taking her leave of the General she went into the chapel and picked up the Wooden Madonna.

'Are you taking Our Lady with you?' he asked, surprised.

'She's my guide and my strength,' she told him.

'It's been wonderful to have both you and Our Lady as my guest,' the General said. 'I'm going to miss you both,' he added, clicking his heels and lifting her hand to kiss it. 'I've enjoyed our discussions on Italian literature, and if I survive this futile war I'll look out for a distinguished work of scholarship on Dante by Dr Angela Boni. I may even have the pleasure of meeting you again. Who knows? This war has shown that anything is possible.'

A motor cyclist roared up to the castle, to inform the Marchese Battagliero that the Germans were in retreat. He was fearful of his life and property, not from the Allied troops, but from Italians who hated Fascists like himself, blaming them for bringing the war to their homeland.

'Hurry up, for God's sake!' he shouted to the Marchesa.

Using one of the servants as the guide, he intended to try to reach Rome, where he had a house and where he hoped to mingle with the crowds. That was why he was dressed in old clothes given to him by a footman. But the Marchesa was standing in her dressing room as her maid sewed the best of her jewellery into the hems of a dress whose sleeves she had mutilated.

There were three corpses, and the ground was stony, but Benigno dug because the dead from the battlefield deserved a decent burial. It took him an hour per grave. The sun was warm, and he had no water to drink. That didn't concern him;

it was the comfort of his three mules standing patiently by that was always his priority, so he put them into the shade of a solitary tree that had somehow survived the bombardment.

As he dug, overturned burnt-out tanks, their tracks off, were smouldering near him, agonizing tombs for the crews. In the distance he saw guns and trucks loaded with soldiers moving northwards, and he realized that the Germans had lost the battle in that part of Italy at least. There were no soldiers around him now, shouting at him to take his mules for another load of ammunition, to be carried up to a machine gun nest on the mountain. For the first time in months he could sit on a rock and relax. He had been told about monks and civilians coming down from the bombed monastery one morning, and prayed that Beatrice and Angela were among them.

It had taken Angela and Marco two days of hard travelling, climbing northwards to avoid the Liri Valley, praying that the Red Cross flags on the sides of the mules would save them from gunners of both sides contesting the territory. Senger had given Angela a pair of German boots to save her feet in her disintegrating *zupei*. They slept in the ruins of a shelled steading before reaching Monte Cairo. They were a thousand feet above Benigno, searching the area round the cave where she had hidden with Augusto, but there was no sign of him. It was hard on the two mules, taking them off the tracks into areas of stone that hurt their hooves, so they left them grazing as they traversed the slopes. Angela feared that every corpse she approached would be Augusto's, but ravens and wolves had so disfigured some of them that she couldn't tell.

Hours after the capture of Montecassino thousands of French Moroccan, Algerian, Tunisian and Senegalese troops attached to the French Expeditionary Corps were swarming across the slopes of the surrounding hills. Some of these men had earlier brought in the ears of German troops, demanding to be paid a bounty until this barbarism was stopped. A dozen Moroccans were ascending the hill towards the castle and when they crossed the drawbridge and found the stout door locked, they scaled the walls. The Marchese saw the swarthy face at his window, but before he could draw the revolver he had armed himself with, a cord from the curtains was round his neck from the back, and it seemed to him that the *salone* was filling with water, the embalmed Cardinal's coffin a glass boat.

Boots clattered along the corridor to the room where the last of the ancestral diamonds was being sewn into the Marchesa's hem. She and her maid had their dresses ripped off and were raped together across the same bed, the Marchesa murdered first, an hour and thirty men later. The castle was looted of everything that looked valuable and portable, the jewels that had spilled from her hem scooped up and thrust into one of the violators' pockets. As they departed they wrenched a candle from its holder and threw it on a sofa, breaking the fingers of the strangled Marchese under their boots.

From Angela's Journal for Sunday 21 May 1944:

I wonder if Augusto would have gone down the mountain in search of me and seen me captured by the Germans, but doesn't know where I was taken. As Marco and I descended this morning with the two mules we heard from the direction of the Liri Valley the bell of a church being rung at the German retreat. As we stood, crossing ourselves, my heart seemed to be swinging with the jubilant peals. As we approached the pile of rubble that had been the house of Uncle and Aunt, I saw an unmanned machine gun sticking out of the window of the bedroom I had occupied. 'Here's someone coming with a mule pack,' Marco pointed out. When I recognized Uncle Benigno I ran towards him, arms outstretched, throwing them round his neck.' Have you seen Augusto?' was my first breathless question. 'No I haven't. Where's Beatrice?' I pointed up to the monastery, shaking my head, then turned away at his grief.

Moroccan troops rampaged through the villages of Ciociaria and Esperia, and every woman and girl, even those who had just become teenagers were raped repeatedly. Where their menfolk tried to protect them, they were slaughtered. Houses were set on fire after being looted.

The news of the atrocities had carried through the valleys, across the mountain ridges of the region.

'What a tragedy that they're behaving like that, after helping to defeat the Germans,' Angela said sadly.

'We're going to have to be very careful,' Benigno told his niece.

Half a dozen Moroccan troops descended on the bonfire where a goat was being roasted near the ruins of Benigno's house in celebration of the German retreat. The rampaging soldiers had guns and knives, and when the men tried to defend the twenty women, they had their throats cut or were shot. Blades ripped the clothes from the women and they were violated in the mud churned up by shells where four mules had once grazed. Angela hugged the Wooden Madonna to her breasts for protection, but her arms were forced to her side, so she couldn't cover her ears to the screams of a girl of eleven, whose lifeblood was leaking from between her legs.

'Ah, you're saving the prettiest one for me,' the leader said, and spat on his palms as he opened his trousers.

Angela was remembering how she had smeared cow dung on her inside thighs to prevent being raped by the German soldiers who came to demolish the house, but there was no Darlene now to provide such protection. The leader of the marauding Moroccans was coming from the other side of the fire to claim his prize when he stood on a mine, one of many which the Germans habitually left in the places they retreated from. The explosion destroyed his sexual organs. Angela and Benigno were shielded from the blast by the Moroccan soldiers standing in front of them. The two holding Angela staggered away. Benigno caught his niece's hand to drag her away, but she broke free to retrieve the Wooden Madonna. One of the Italians had snatched the gun off an injured Moroccan soldier and mowed him and his comrades down.

From Angela's Journal for Monday 22 May 1944:

'I want to see my dear wife's grave,' Uncle Benigno said this morning after I had been saved (by a mine) from being violated. Marco had taken the two mules to his home, and Uncle and I ascended the tortuous track to Montecassino with his beloved mules, following the white tape through the minefield, an ascent that took us three cautious hours. We clambered into the ruins, past a cracked church bell lying beside an unexploded shell. I almost trod on the decapitated head of a statue of Christ. Uncle held up a tattered Missal. We went to the monks' cemetery, but the bomb craters and broken crosses made it impossible for Uncle and I to locate Aunt Beatrice's grave. 'I'll have nowhere to bring flowers to in the future,' Uncle sobbed, and the three mules looked sad.

In July General Senger, still trying to stop the Allies taking Italy, though Rome had fallen, received a message that a bomb had gone off beside Hitler. Senger sent an orderly to the cellar to bring up the choicest bottles for a celebration. The first was being uncorked when word came through that Hitler had survived relatively unscathed.

'You must have known our beloved Führer was going to live, General, to order a celebration,' his orderly said. 'It shows the faith you have in his invincibility.'

When Senger received word that Count von Stauffenberg, primary conspirator in the failed bomb plot against Hitler, had been shot he wept before going into the chapel to pray for the soul of the bravest and most scrupulous of men.

PAX

Count Pier Luigi Bellini delle Stelle hated the Germans. His father, a Cavalry colonel, had died of maltreatment in prison the previous year. The Count's objective was to oppose Germans and Fascists, so that Italy could have peace, which was why, half a mile south of Dongo on the northwestern shore of Lake Como, he had set up a roadblock with a tree trunk, stone blocks and barbed wire. Informed that a German column was advancing on Dongo, the Count ordered that it was to be stopped at the roadblock. 'No one is to move, whatever happens.'

When the convoy was halted the German commander informed the Count that his orders were to convey his men to Merano, near the Austrian border, from where they would proceed into Germany, to continue the fight against the Allied invaders. 'We have no intention of fighting the Italians.'

The Count informed the German officer that he had orders to let nobody through the roadblock. The officer insisted that there was an agreement between his army's High Command and the Italian partisans' High Command that German troops would not attack the Partisans, in return for them not attacking the Germans.

The Count was a good actor, warning the German officer that he had large, well-armed forces deployed through the whole area, and that the mortars and machine guns covering the German convoy could riddle the vehicles. The officer countered by warning that the convoy consisted of twenty-eight trucks full of German soldiers, an armoured car, the German commander's vehicle and ten cars full of civilians. Each truck, Urbano Lazzaro, the Count's second in command warned him after an inspection, contained a heavy machine gun, machine pistols and several light anti-aircraft guns.

The Count informed the German officer that he couldn't take the responsibility of permitting the convoy to proceed, and proposed that they drive to his headquarters about two miles away so that he could receive instructions. The German officer agreed, but only if they went in a German vehicle.

At Musso, close to the roadblock, Don Mainetti, the parish priest, was accosted by a bearded man who was surrendering. He revealed that he was Nicola Bombacci, a fellow revolutionary Socialist of Mussolini's three decades before. The name meant nothing to the priest, until the fugitive added that he was one of Il Duce's closest advisers. But he had information which startled the priest.

Meantime the Count and the German officer had returned to the roadblock from the Count's headquarters, where he claimed to have received orders that only German vehicles and German soldiers could proceed, and that all the Italian and civilian vehicles were to be handed over.

The German officer seemed satisfied with this decision, and was drawing on a soothing cigarette when Don Mainetti the priest called the Count across to tell him: 'Mussolini is in that convoy over there.'

A soldier in a Wehrmacht greatcoat and askew helmet was curled up sleeping in the back of one of the vehicles.

The partisan doing the careful inspection observed the incongruity of the expensive leather boots. The soldier was taken to local headquarters and interrogated. Benito Mussolini had almost got away.

He was locked in a peasant hut with his mistress Clara Petacci, who had pleaded to join her lover, and who had also been in the convoy. There was a dispute over his destination. The Partisans holding Il Duce wanted to deliver him to the National Committee in Milan, but Communists, Socialists and others in the Committee didn't want him handed over to the Allies. Italy could administer its own justice.

Mussolini and Clara wouldn't have been able to copulate that night because they were heavily guarded. He was indignant, not afraid. Who did these Communists think they were to stand in judgement of an Italian patriot? Did they suppose that an old Bersagliere was going to beg them for mercy? He had always been ready to die for his cause, but why did they have to kill Clara?

A Garibaldi leader, on instructions from leftist Partisan officials, raced to Dongo to take custody of the dictator. He burst into the bedroom where they were being held, shouting: 'I've come to liberate you!'

A mile from Dongo he stopped the car and ordered them out, making them stand against a stone wall.

'I'm instructed to do justice for the Italian people.'

Mussolini held open his jacket.

'Shoot me in the chest!'

The following day the Partisans dumped the bodies of

the dictator and his lover in front of a garage in a piazza in Milan. The crowd laughed or shouted obscenities, and a mother produced a pistol, firing five bullets into Mussolini to avenge her five dead sons. As the mutilated corpses were being hoisted by the heels a participator preserved Il Duce's mistress's modesty by securing her skirt between her thighs.

Two years earlier the dictator had made a prophecy that his fate would be to move 'from dust to power back to dust.'

In May General Senger was involved in the surrender of German forces in Italy to his adversary Lieutenant General Mark Clark. Senger passed through several British prisoner of war camps in Italy, ending up in the generals' camp in Bridgend, Wales, where he was a prisoner for three years. As he worked in the garden, helping to grow vegetables, and also tending his own flowerbed, he was tortured by the thought: *Was I partly responsible for the destruction of Montecassino because, the day after I attended Mass there on Christmas Day 1943, I gave the order to create defences up to the Abbey walls, if necessary?* Even after his release from British captivity in May 1948, and his subsequent appointment as a housemaster at Salem, the public school near Lake Constance, he would still torment himself with his role in the destruction of Montecassino as he walked in the hills. He returned to his wife and to the company of his decorated son, who had lost an arm in the war. Frido Senger went riding on mornings of birdsong, with shining filaments of spiders' webs, like ethereal lace, draped on perfumed hedgerows. Later in the day he wrote up his war memories in which he took no responsibility for the destruction of the monastery of Montecassino.

Angela Boni was reunited with her uncle Dom Pietro when he came through to Cassino to see the ruins of the monastery. When she presented him with the Wooden Madonna he was astonished.

'Have you been carrying this with you since you left the monastery?' he asked in amazement and awe.

'It saved my life.'

She kept hoping that Augusto had been sent as forced labour to Germany, but as the months went by she accepted that he had been killed, and that his remains were among the many unidentified strewn across the landscape. She was due to sail home to Glasgow from Naples in July, but the week before she fell sick with malaria. She was taken to hospital in Naples, and in her fever she had nightmares that she was back in Montecassino, with the basilica falling on top of her. One night she distinctly saw Augusto standing smiling beside her bed.

'Are you sure you can bear this?' Dom Pietro asked the old man sitting beside him in the back of the car labouring up the winding road. 'There's no shame in turning back.'

'No, I must see what they did,' Abbot Diamare answered, looking out on the landscape still strewn with the debris of war.

The driver and Dom Pietro helped the old monk out.

'We must be careful where we place our feet,' the monk warned his superior.

'This must be heartbreaking for you,' Dom Pietro told his Abbot as his superior picked up a fragment of mosaic from the basilica.

Abbot Diamare died at Monte Cassino that same year.

On his discharge from the R.A.M.C. Dr Christopher Murchison returned to Glasgow, to extend his medical studies. On his first day in his home city he went into the Boni Café on Byres Road and, fearing the worst, asked her mother about Angela.

'She survived, by the will of God,' Rosa said, crossing herself. 'We hope that she's coming home to us next month.'

Every day, before he went to work in the Infirmary, he called at the café to ask if there was a definite date yet for Angela's return, and at last was told: 'Tomorrow. I'm dreading her walking through that door and finding out that her father's dead.'

Christopher waited for several days, until she had been reunited with her mother and siblings and learned about the loss of her father before he went into the café.

'She's upstairs,' Rosa told him. 'I'll go and get her.'

When she entered Christopher saw that even with the grief of the loss of her father on her face, she was more beautiful than his last cherished memory of her seven years before, though she was thin after the malaria.

'I'm so sorry about your father. I thought you were dead,' he told her tearfully as he hugged her.

'I never stopped praying for your safety, Christopher, though I lost the beautiful locket you gave me.'

Rosa served them both coffee at a corner table.

'You were always in my thoughts,' he told her, 'and when I landed in Italy – '

'You were in Italy?' she asked in amazement.

'I was at Montecassino. I could see the monastery from the medical unit I was working in, and assumed that you were sheltering in it with your uncle. I wished to God that the fighting would cease and that I could climb up to the monastery to tell you that I love you and want to marry you. And then, when I watched it being bombed, I thought you were dead.' He unbuttoned his collar to reveal a crucifix.

'After you left Glasgow I continued going to Mass at St Peter's because it made my memory of you stronger. Gradually I came to see the beauty of the Mass, and I absorbed the lovely Latin liturgy. I converted to Catholicism under Father O'Brien, our priest, after he introduced me to the power of prayer. He gave me this cross and I'm sure it brought me through.'

Angela leaned over and held both his hands.

'You've no idea what this means to me.'

'Are you going to do your doctorate in Italian?' he asked.

'No, I'm going to transfer to medicine, because of my experiences with the refugees in the monastery, though at twenty-eight I'm probably too old.'

'Of course you're not too old. You'll make a wonderful doctor. Will you marry me?'

Angela's brother Tony had turned eighteen in 1942 and was about to proceed to Glasgow University to study engineering. A female called Gilda Camillo was a friend of Rosa's through being a regular customer in the café. She invited young Italian males to her house and tried to persuade them to register as either Conscientious Objectors, or to refuse to register for military, or any other form of military service. Because his father had been treated as an alien, with the support of his mother Tony decided to follow Gilda's advice to refuse to register. However, in 1942 Gilda was detained by the authorities, accused of influencing these young men with regard to their military duty to Britain.

One of Tony's Italian school friends was sentenced to a year's imprisonment for having refused to submit himself for medical examination, so Tony decided not to challenge his call-up. He joined the Royal Air Force and because he was gifted at mathematics, became one of the most skilful navigators in Britain on the bombers sent to raid Germany. On a raid to Hamburg a German fighter destroyed the instrumentation of the Lancaster, but Tony managed to navigate it back to base and was awarded the DFC. After the war he decided to make the RAF his career and would become an Air Vice-Marshal.

Armando, the second child in the Boni family, was twenty in 1946, and was studying at Cambridge. He had inherited his sister Angela's love of Italian, and would become a distinguished Dante scholar. Maria, the third child, was sixteen in 1946, and would train as a nurse.

Rosa had written to the authorities, claiming compensation for her husband, a naturalized British subject who shouldn't have been on board the *Arandora Star*. The matter had been raised by her Member of Parliament in a House of Commons debate in October 1940, but it wasn't until after the war that she received a confidential settlement of £2,000 plus costs, since the Treasury didn't want to attract unwelcome publicity which would lead to new claims for compensation.

When Angela went up to the university to see Cavaliere Ernesto Grillo, the secretary informed her that he had retired in 1940. 'He had a house down the Clyde coast, but is living in Glasgow now. I'll give you his telephone number because I'm sure that he would like to hear from you. He often spoke about you.'

Angela asked Grillo if they could meet at her mother's café. He had aged drastically since she had last seen him in 1938.

'I never dreamed that there would be a war when we parted,' he confessed. 'I thought you'd be back in Scotland the following year, to start your doctorate under me. I read in the Italian newspapers how you were in Montecassino during the bombing, and how you helped the refugees through your healing gift. The new Italian Government wanted to give you an honour, but I believe you refused.' He paused. 'I was wrong in what I said.'

'I don't follow you, Professor Grillo.'

He stirred his cup of coffee, eyes downcast.

'You remember how I never lost an opportunity to praise Mussolini, hailing him as the saviour of Italy? But I was wrong. Fascism seemed to be such a powerful, creative force when Mussolini came to power. But he brought my country close to ruin, and caused the deaths of many, many innocent people. And I was wrong also about Gabriele D'Annunzio. He was a rabble-rouser and libertine.'

'I've decided not to do a doctorate in Italian, but to study medicine, after my experiences at Montecassino,' she informed him.

'I'm not surprised, after how you helped the injured and dying in Montecassino, that you wish to change to medicine. You don't need to become a Dante scholar; you lived Purgatorio. I'm sure you'll make a brilliant doctor,' the contrite Fascist predicted as he gave her a farewell peck on the cheek.

In July 1946 a former classmate of Angela's came into the café with the news that Cavaliere Ernesto Grillo had died. Angela mourned him as a superb teacher, but tragically mistaken in his political views.

Montecassino looked as if it would remain a ruin to man's folly on its mountain. But it had been rebuilt before, and years after the destruction a bus took Dom Pietro and other monks up the tortuous road. They went down on their hands and knees to search for precious fragments of the basilica mosaics to piece together the serene face of Christ in a labour of love, using historic photographs. Giordano's great canvas of the consecration of the basilica in 1071 hadn't survived, but the modern Italian master Pietro Annigoni painted a new one, featuring St Benedict surrounded by monks, bishops, and nuns who lived in holiness by following the Saint's rule. There are three Popes in the foreground.

Dom Pietro was privileged to be invited to the forge to witness two new bronze doors being cast, the access one on the right side depicting the third destruction of Montecassino caused by the earthquake in 1349, and the fourth panel the bombardment of 15 February 1944. The statue of St Benedict was restored, and a copy made of the one of St Scholastica which had been destroyed in the bombing. Dom Pietro was present throughout the years of the complex reconstruction of the monastery, remembering, advising, encouraging, though his Abbot hadn't lived to see the miracle.

On the day in 1964 when Pope Paul VI reconsecrated the restored monastery of Montecassino, Professor Angela Boni, a neurologist with an international reputation, and a healing gift which she applied in her work, was an honoured guest. Seated beside her was Professor Christopher Murchison, a distinguished trauma surgeon from his experiences in the war. They had married, and she had retained her maiden name out of love and gratitude for her parents.

When Christopher had told his mother that he had converted to Catholicism and that he intended marrying a Catholic, she responded: 'It doesn't matter to me what beliefs the woman in your life has, as it mattered to your bigoted father. I'm only so grateful that you survived the war. Now when are you bringing her to meet me?'

The Murchisons had two children, twins. Gina was planning to study Italian at Glasgow University, and her brother Joseph intended to train for the priesthood. During the celebratory Mass for the reconsecration of Montecassino in which her uncle Dom Pietro participated, Angela sat between her husband and her uncle Benigno. As the reconsecration proceeded she wondered if the bones of the refugees who had lost their lives in the bombings had been recovered from the rubble and given a proper burial.

After the ceremony Angela was introduced to the Holy Father and given a blessing for her work among the wounded and dying at Montecassino. Before the Murchison family left Montecassino they walked down the slope to the De Santis's former smallholding which held such treasured memories for Angela. But where the house in which much love and wine had been dispensed had stood were the graves of the Poles who had taken the monastery. Benigno, looked after by nuns in rebuilt Cassino, had buried his three adored mules among the trees near his former home. Beatrice's remains were left undisturbed where they had been buried.

Former General Frido von Senger und Etterlin had died the year before the reconsecration of the monastery. He had always intended to get in touch with Angela, to learn if she had been reunited with her missing husband to be, but writing such a letter would have brought back painful memories of Montecassino.

St Thomas Aquinas had been born on a hill above Senger's headquarters at Roccasecca, and the German General, in absolving himself of responsibility for his role in the war, cited the Saint's belief that *no man can be blamed for the crimes of others in so far as he has no influence over them*. Hitler, and the German people who had elected him and supported his ruthless dictatorship, were the culprits, not officers carrying out commands.

Field Marshal Harold Alexander, Earl Alexander of Tunis, acknowledged in his memoirs that the destruction of the monastery was 'necessary more for the effect that it would have on the morale of the attackers than for purely material reasons.'

Lieutenant General Mark Clark, accused of mishandling the Italian campaign through wanting to be the first into Rome with his American troops, confessed later:

> I say that the bombing of the Abbey…was a mistake, and I say it with full knowledge of the controversy that has raged round this episode…Not only was the bombing an unnecessary psychological mistake in the field of propaganda, but it was a tactical military mistake of the first magnitude. It only made our job more difficult, more costly in terms of men, machines and time.

The treasures of Montecassino were brought back from Rome and put on display in a specially built museum, including the Wooden Madonna denied to Reich Marshal Goering, which, Angela Murchison earnestly believed, had protected her. She bequeathed her Journal to Glasgow University in memory of her misguided teacher, Ernesto Grillo.

To the ends of their days Dr Maximilian Becker and Lieutenant Colonel Julius Schlegel would dispute as to which of them was the inspired saviour of the bombed monastery's treasures and the Old Masters of the Museo Nazionale, Naples.

Lightning Source UK Ltd.
Milton Keynes UK
UKOW04f2126290116

267417UK00001B/7/P